Amma MEIGA
Sorcery's Silent INFLUENCE

Ad Dalhotra

BLUEROSE PUBLISHERS
India | U.K.

Copyright © Ad Dalhotra 2024

All rights reserved by author. No part of this publication may be reproduced, stored in a retrieval system or transmitted in any form or by any means, electronic, mechanical, photocopying, recording or otherwise, without the prior permission of the author. Although every precaution has been taken to verify the accuracy of the information contained herein, the publisher assumes no responsibility for any errors or omissions. No liability is assumed for damages that may result from the use of information contained within.

BlueRose Publishers takes no responsibility for any damages, losses, or liabilities that may arise from the use or misuse of the information, products, or services provided in this publication.

For permissions requests or inquiries regarding this publication, please contact:

BLUEROSE PUBLISHERS
www.BlueRoseONE.com
info@bluerosepublishers.com
+91 8882 898 898
+4407342408967

ISBN: 978-93-5819-702-0

Cover Design: Muskan Sachdeva
Typesetting: Pooja Sharma

First Edition: September 2024

For my parents,

Mr. Shiv Charan and Mrs. Ram Rani,

whose unwavering support has always

been my strength.

Soorej and Vipul,

thank you for being my lantern

in the tunnel of darkness.

"Imagination is the organ that sees beyond the present moment into the possibilities of the future."

- C.S. Lewis

Explanatory

In this book, you will encounter some elements deeply rooted in Indian culture, with references to Sanskrit woven throughout. While the Indian theme is prominent, the narrative also embraces a fusion of diverse cultures, mythological allusions, and surreal historical references. The story delves into intense and unsettling themes, including strong content and gore, reflecting the brutal realities of survival. Survival, by its very nature, is often bloody and gruesome, and this tale does not shy away from portraying that harsh verity.

-The Author

Contents

CHAPTER-1: HOME SWEET HOME 1

CHAPTER-2: REENA'S SECRET 11

CHAPTER-3: BEHIND THE PINK DOOR 18

CHAPTER-4: THE WHISPERS 24

CHAPTER-5: THE GUIDING SHADOW 31

CHAPTER-6: AN UNTOLD TALE 38

CHAPTER-7: DEVOTION OR CREDENCE 42

CHAPTER-8: THE GOOD, OLD FICUS 46

CHAPTER-9: A SHARD OF MIRROR 53

CHAPTER-10: DECISIONS AT THE DAGGER'S EDGE 62

CHAPTER-11: ECHOES OF DISCORD 67

CHAPTER-12: PEACEFUL SLUMBER 72

CHAPTER-13: ALL EYES ON CAKE 77

CHAPTER-14: THE CONFLICTED HEART 86

CHAPTER-15: THE LAMB AND THE GODMAN 90

CHAPTER-16: GULIVER'S TRAVELS 95

CHAPTER-17: LURKING IN THE SHADOWS 110

CHAPTER-18: WORSE THAN DEATH 116

CHAPTER-19: THE BLAZING HOPE 122

CHAPTER-20: EVERYTHING IN ITS RIGHT PLACE 132

CHAPTER-21: UNEXPECTED ARRIVAL 140

CHAPTER-22: VALIANT COWBOY 144

CHAPTER-23:	THE DELIVERER	153
CHAPTER-24:	THE SPARKLING ORB	160
CHAPTER-25:	THE TENT AND THE BROOM	163
CHAPTER-26:	BEHEMOTH	176
CHAPTER-27:	BEWITCHED	193
CHAPTER-28:	SOFT WINDS OF CHANGE	203
CHAPTER-29:	SHIMMERING SHANTIES	209
CHAPTER-30:	HUNTER	214
CHAPTER-31:	WOLVES	226
CHAPTER-32:	WARRIORS	231
CHAPTER-33:	GUNNY NEEDLE	237
CHAPTER-34:	THE STONE DWELLING	243
CHAPTER-35:	HOME SWEET HOME	255
ACKNOWLEDGMENTS		266

CHAPTER-1

Home Sweet Home

On a tranquil morning, as Amma busied herself in the kitchen, the air filled with the heartwarming aroma of seasonings, Reena and Lily languished at the dining table, their expressions a portrait of ennui. Reena, the eldest, and Lily, the youngest, were sisters, with their brother Bhushan nestled between them. Growing weary of the protracted wait, Lily commenced her playful engagement with her beloved doll. She was a sprightly five-year-old, her dark tresses perpetually fashioned into charming double buns. Her cheeks were a delightful shade of piggy-pink, complemented by large, beetle-black eyes that imparted a soft, huggable allure. Her plump figure rendered her akin to an enchanting stuffed doll, and she darted through the house with an exuberance that belied her cherubic appearance. Renowned for her unwavering sincerity and compliance, Lily adorned herself in pastel-hued frocks each day at the behest of her cherished Amma. Amma often proclaimed her to be the finest child in existence. Yet, her incessant pleas for playtime, unperturbed by Reena's fluctuating moods, became a source of considerable fatigue for her.

Yet, even more vexing to Reena than frolicking in the open field was Lily's peculiar, dark doll, which bore a disconcerting grin and a pointed hat, adorned with a crimson mark upon its forehead. This doll was Lily's most treasured possession, having been the sole toy she had ever possessed, a gift bestowed by Amma when she was merely three years old.

Still, Reena harboured a deep disdain for the doll. Seated sulkily on a chair with her arms crossed, her face flushed crimson and then a shade of purple as time wore on, she found it intolerable to endure her younger sister's delight in what she considered the most grotesque object imaginable.

However, it wasn't Lily who was causing Reena's frustration; it was the food they were about to consume. The dish, known as "Mugas," was a source of annoyance for all the siblings—a green, gooey, jelly-like substance they were expected to eat twice a day. However, Sick in the dome, Reena was adept at masking her emotions and maintaining her composure.

Reena, a twelve-year-old who affectionately referred to herself as a "big lassie" harboured dreams of emulating Amma in her adulthood. She eagerly anticipated the moment when she would match her mother's height. With a complexion of wheat, dark hair elegantly braided into a single plait, and enchanting peacock-brown eyes, she possessed an added charm with a delightful mole nestled beneath her left eye. Adorning her oval face were handcrafted earrings and a headband crafted from delicately stitched flowers, each piece enhancing her natural beauty. She frequently gathered blossoms of vibrant hues from around the majestic Ficus tree that stood sentinel outside their home. Fashioning headbands and earrings beneath the tree's comforting shade became her cherished pastime, a solitary pursuit that brought her immense joy. The tree towered majestically, its broad trunk able to conceal five people behind its sprawling form. On occasions when Lily grew weary, she would rest her head on Reena's lap, allowing her sister to weave a crown of blossoms into her hair. Lily delighted in the floral adornments, but nothing compared to the sheer joy of playing beneath the vast canopy of the great Ficus tree, where her imagination could roam freely.

As they sat in anticipation of their meal, a distinct sound of something being dragged across the floor reached Reena's ears. She recognized the sound all too well. Turning her gaze toward the corridor that seamlessly flowed into the dining room, she caught sight of a pair of languid feet shuffling across the vintage checkered floor of cream and Oxford blue. Upon reaching the dining table, Bhushan slumped into his seat with a surly demeanour, resting his hands behind his head while propping his feet up on the table. His gaze drifted lazily toward the grand chandelier that hung elegantly from the ceiling, its crystals glinting in the soft light.

Reena regarded his behaviour with increasing annoyance. They were moments away from dining at the table where Bhushan had carelessly rested his legs. Rather than confronting him directly, Reena opted for a clever strategy. She called out Bhushan's name, subtly gesturing towards the clock adorning the lilac wall behind them.

"You're late again, lazy bum," Reena taunted, a mischievous grin spreading across her face as she knew precisely how to get under his skin. Sunlight streamed through the three oriel windows behind her, illuminating her figure while casting shadows over her face, enhancing her wicked demeanour. Bhushan's eyes flicked to the clock; it was nearly 9 AM. Enraged, he hastily dropped his legs from the table and pounded his fists down, the sound reverberating through the room.

"Don't you dare heckle me," Bhushan retorted sharply. "Those blasted nightmares stole away my chance for a good night's sleep."

"Yeah, yeah, the nightmares of a colossal one-eyed monster, devouring you alive. Isn't he tired of feasting on a simpleton like you?" Reena taunted.

Bhushan retorted, "He wasn't merely devouring me; he was feasting on all of you too! He had your served head clutched in his bloody jaws, and I failed to rescue you... If I hadn't misplaced my hat, perhaps I could've savoured a decent night's sleep."

"Oh, your lucky cowboy hat! What kind of hat can save you from nightmares? I can only imagine if you had lucky shoes instead of a hat. Would you have been willing to sleep with your shoes on?" Reena sneered.

"That's none of your concern," Bhushan shot back.

He rose from his seat and shifted beside Lily, attempting to evade Reena, whose relentless teasing had only deepened his irritation. A lively nine-year-old boy with mud-brown skin and a square jaw, Bhushan possessed strikingly bright blue eyes and fashionable short hair. His head was typically crowned with a brown cowboy hat, which had mysteriously vanished a few days prior.

The hat, a cherished gift from Amma, was his shield against the world as he drifted into slumber. Whenever the terrifying nightmares of the one-eyed monster plagued his sleep, he believed that donning the hat granted him the courage to confront the creature in his dreams. To Reena, however, this idea was as ludicrous as it was entertaining, a clear reflection of Bhushan's fondness for the fanciful and absurd. Despite being shorter than Reena, Bhushan perpetually asserted that he was taller, engaging in a relentless rivalry with her. One of his pockets was perpetually stuffed with stones, and his right hand was usually wrapped around a wooden slingshot—a contraption he proudly claimed as his own invention, though it was a tool introduced by Amma. Hitting targets with remarkable accuracy was a skill in which he took great pride, showcasing his natural talent for precision.

As time flowed on, they lingered at the table, each enveloped in their own palette of mood. Moments later, the sound of footsteps echoed, mingling with the faint scent of the food they all abhorred. From the subtly hidden kitchen, Amma emerged, making her way toward them. Upon catching sight of her mother, Reena's frustration and irritation began to fade, replaced by a warmth that only Amma's presence could evoke.

With her raven tresses cascading in the air and her hourglass silhouette elegantly adorned in a green saree, Amma radiated beauty. Reena found herself entranced by her mother's allure; however, the sight of the purple, steaming pot cradled in Amma's hands swiftly rekindled her earlier discontent. As Amma approached the table and set the pot down, her emerald green eyes surveyed her children, shifting from Reena to Lily. The diamond-shaped bindi adorning her forehead sparkled in the light. Her luscious, full lips parted in a warm smile as she inquired, "Who's ready for a delightful breakfast?"

"Is it still mugas?"

"Yes!"

The mood palette turns green. "Gross," they all replied in harmony.

With her vine-like fingers, Amma elegantly lifted the lid from the steaming pot, allowing a fragrant cloud to escape as she ladled the green mugas into the matching purple bowls that adorned the table. "It's not as dreadful as you all make it out to be, my little kittens. In truth, it's rather delightful; I've tasted it myself... we all require nourishment to thrive... it's simply unfortunate that we lack any alternatives," Amma reassured them, her smile radiating warmth, her teeth sparkling like the gold jewellery adorning her ears and neck.

"Ugh, it feels like an eternity; we've been trapped in this endless cycle of the same monotonous meal," Reena lamented, her tone laced with exasperation.

With her tender emerald eyes, Amma gaped at Reena, sensing the turmoil brewing within her regarding both the meal and her own feelings. A gentle smile graced her lips as she affectionately stroked Reena's cheek. "I understand how difficult it is to consume the same dish repeatedly, but do we truly have any other option, my precious kitten? The Ordinarium world, the world beyond these walls lies in ruins, and Mugas is our sole means of survival. Must I sketch it anew each day for you?"

The silence took over the house.

Amma paused, her gaze lingering on Reena as if sensing the depth of her frustration. She gently took Reena's hand, her touch warm and reassuring, and spoke softly, "I am sorry, honey. I... I wish I could provide better food for all my children, sometimes it feels like I've failed you. I'm sorry for being a poor mother. It's unfortunate that you were born into such a troubled era... But... if you ask me, I remain grateful to have such wonderful kittens, bound by eternal love... Aren't we a family?"

Reena replied, "Yes, we are a family," her arms still crossed over her chest, her voice softer yet resolute.

Amma wrapped Reena in a warm embrace, her touch soothing as she encouraged all her children to finish their meal, reminding them of the energy needed for their outdoor play. Despite their shared distaste for the food, the children reluctantly began to eat, each spoonful taken with the promise of playtime lingering in their minds. Amma abodes for a moment, watching them with a tender smile, before quietly returning to her chores and leaving the room.

Reena forced down the green mugas with visible reluctance. Shifting her gaze to Bhushan, she asked, "Bhushan, do you truly believe there's nothing out there but bloodthirsty monsters?"

Bhushan, his mouth still full and his fiery temperament ignited, retorted bitterly to Reena's comment, "Yes, I believe in Amma, If they haunt my dreams, they must exist in reality."

Reena, though irritated, attempted to dismiss his aggravating tone with a sigh of patience, "I don't know, Bhushan. Sometimes I can't shake the feeling that Amma... she's hiding something from us, a secret, maybe... Don't get me wrong, I love her and always aspire to be like her. I don't even want to entertain doubts about her, but this nagging sense of being kept in the dark keeps resurfacing in my mind."

Still irritated by Reena's earlier teasing, Bhushan swiftly finished his bowl of Mugas, chased it down with a glass of water, and slammed the empty vessel onto the table. "You've brought this up before, Reena," he snapped. "We've looked into it and found nothing. Amma's never even scolded us; she's always been forgiving and devoted. Why can't you just trust her?"

Reena hesitated for a moment, then casually took another bite of food and conceded, "Yeah, maybe I'm just overthinking it."

After finishing their meal, they eagerly rushed toward the main door, brimming with excitement for outdoor play. But as they flung the door open, they were met with an unexpected onslaught of rain, thunder, and a biting wind that chilled them to the bone. The trio spent the rest of the day huddled by the window, their wide eyes filled with melancholy as they watched the storm rage outside, their hopes for playtime shattered.

With a heavy heart, Reena glanced at her siblings and softly suggested, "Let's head to the room, fellas." She took the lead, her shoulders slightly slumped, while Lily and Bhushan followed quietly, their earlier excitement dampened by the storm outside.

As they made their way to their room, Reena paused before a singular pink door, her peacock-hued eyes glinting with intrigue. It was the only door of its kind in the entire house, apart from Violet's. Bhushan, attuned to Reena's unspoken thoughts, interjected with a tone of warning, "I can sense your curiosity... don't even think about it. That room is strictly off-limits, by Amma."

Reena whipped around to face Bhushan, her eyes ablaze with indignation. "I'm not thinking anything of the sort! Besides, how could I possibly get inside a locked door?"

After listening to her, Bhushan strode purposefully toward their room, with Lily trailing closely behind. Reena lingered a moment longer, her gaze fixed on the pink door, before finally turning away and following them to her own room.

The following day, the sky was painted in golden hues, and the children brimmed with delight, immersed in a game of hide-and-seek. Reena tiptoed softly across the cream and blue checkered floor, her heart racing with excitement as she searched for her hidden siblings within the cosy confines of their home. Twisting the doorknob of one of the violet doors, Reena stepped inside and scanned the room, her eyes narrowing as she spotted two dark buns poking out from behind a small cupboard. The telltale sign of her sister's presence hinted at a hidden secret, igniting her playful determination to uncover Lily's hiding place.

"SHOW YOURSELF, LILY!" Reena exclaimed, pointing at the two exposed buns.

Lily emerged from her hiding spot, her eyes meeting Reena's with a playful glint. "Oh no! The firsth one to be foundh," she sighed, her tone a blend of mock defeat and cheerful camaraderie.

Reena chuckled, grasping Lily's hand as they pressed on in their quest to find Bhushan. After scouring every nook and cranny inside the house without success, they finally decided to venture outdoors. As they neared the tree, a flash of red caught Reena's eye, nestled beneath the leaves. A smirk spread across her face as she pointed triumphantly and shouted, "SHOW YOURSELF, BHUSHAN!"

Bhushan heard Reena's voice but chose not to reveal his hiding spot just yet. Reena, growing impatient, called out again, "I CAN SEE YOUR RED SHIRT, BHUSHAN! NOW COME DOWN!" Bhushan finally jumped from the tree branch, landing deftly on his two feet. In his enthusiasm, he inadvertently crushed a few delicate flowers beneath his boots, their vibrant colours blending into the lush green grass, leaving a trail of scattered petals in his wake.

"Hey! Be careful with the flowers, I want them for my headband," Reena yapped. Bhushan ignored her, feeling regretful for choosing a red floral shirt.

However, spotting Lily alongside Reena, he felt a wave of relief wash over him, grateful that it wasn't his turn to seek them in the next round.

"Lily, it's your turn to seek us now," Bhushan declared, revelling in his victory.

"Othay," Lily replied.

Lily started counting, "One, two, three..." Her voice rang with the glee of anticipation. Bhushan slipped inside the house, darting through the door to discover a new hiding spot, confident in his mastery of excellent hiding places. Meanwhile, Reena quickly manoeuvred behind a nearby tree, its thick trunk providing the perfect cover. As Lily reached the end of her count, she shouted, "Readhy or noth, here I comeh!" With a determined glint in her eye, she set off toward the house, her footsteps echoing with excitement as she began her search for her elusive siblings.

Reena was initially at ease, as Lily had headed towards the castle. However, her attention was suddenly drawn to a curious sight on the ground. A delicate hint of pink emerged from beneath the leaves, slightly damp from the dew. With a gentle hand, she brushed aside the foliage, revealing a book nestled at her feet. She lifted it carefully, brushing off the dust that mingled shades of brown and green with the pink cover, remnants of grass and mud clinging to its surface. As she read the title, *"Family Comic's Company: Home Sweet Home,"* a sense of intrigue washed over her. It was a peculiar book, one she had never encountered before, not even in her wildest dreams.

CHAPTER-2

Reena's Secret

The clock neared the stroke of 11 p.m. as the children clustered around Amma Meiga, their eyes fixed on the green hardcover book titled "Spooky Fables." Reading a story from chapter seven, her voice gentle and laced with suspense as she began to weave the tale—"*So... the three wayward kittens, both defiant and inquisitive, disregarded their mother's stern warnings and dared to cross the threshold of their home, venturing into the shadowy, foreboding forest beyond. As they wandered through the eerie woods, a menacing wolf caught their scent and savoured their tender flesh. Rawrrr...*" Amma growled theatrically at the end, casting a glance at her children. The room was thick with fear, as Bhushan and Lily sat petrified, though Reena, unamused, found the tale irksome and wearisome. Amma's eyes lingered on Bhushan and Lily, their expressions a mix of terror and fascination.

"Now, who among you shall enlighten me with the moral of this tale?"

"Always heed your mother's words," Bhushan replied nervously, his anxiety heightened by the chilling story.

"Precisely, my kitten," she said, casting a sidelong glance at Reena.

"I am utterly weary of these tedious tales," Reena complained, her face flushed a deep crimson.

Amma gazed at Reena, her hand softly patting her head. "Is something troubling you, my dear?"

"Amma, why do we have to listen to these monotonous tales every night? They all preach the same lesson: *obey your parents and stay within the walls.* We've endured these stories for years. It seems like you want to exert your authority over us," Reena retorted.

Amma gazed at Reena, her smile tranquil, and spoke, "I understand your feelings, Reena. I went through the same when I was your age. The phase you're in is quite complex. But trust me, the stories I share are meant to shield my kittens from the world... A world that was once beautiful until monsters, bombs, and war marred its splendour. The realm beyond is filled with terror. My tales may echo my own insecurities, but my paramount concern is the fear of losing my cherished kittens."

"...I cannot bear the thought of my kittens becoming the next meal for the wicked wolves lurking beyond the wall," Amma lamented, her eyes glistening with unshed tears.

Reena observed Amma's silent tears, the glimmer of concern in her peacock eyes softening from crimson to a warm wheatish hue. Leaning forward, she summoned the courage to voice her thoughts, her heart aching at the sight of her mother's distres.

"You lippy dimwit, Amma is crying because of you!" Bhushan barked, his voice cutting through the tension like a sharp knife.

"But... I"

"It's not her fault, Bhushan; it's a twist of fate. I—I genuinely feel sorry for all of you, born in such a dreadful era. But one must live... sometimes I get tired of her questions. I know she has every right to ask, but I wish I could answer all of them. Many things were lost with your father, and there are many truths I can't reveal to you yet, until you grow up," Amma explained with a deep sigh, her voice laden with the weight of unspoken truths and unhealed wounds.

"Amma, I don't mean to..."

"Don't say it, Reena... I'm alright. Sometimes, it feels heavy to carry such a burden," Amma replied, her smile tender yet fragile, as her eyes shimmered with unshed tears, revealing the depths of her hidden sorrow.

The silence lingered for a few moments, enveloping the room in a heavy stillness until it was gently interrupted by a sweet, cherubic voice.

"Whath are bombsh, Amma?" Lily inquired with curiosity.

"Such dreadful things, my dear, can snatch away those you hold dear. And that is all you truly need to know," She said softly, brushing away her tears with a delicate touch.

Amma cast her gaze upon her beloved children, who all beamed back at her, save for Reena, whose mood was a tempest, intent on pricking her mother's heart. With tender affection, Amma pressed a kiss to each forehead and declared, "Tomorrow, we shall revel in play together, and oh, what joy awaits us!"

"Yaayyyh!" Lily burst with happiness.

Amma rose from the bed, her movements fluid and graceful as she glided toward the door that stood against the pale lilac floor. Pausing at the threshold, she turned to face her children, her emerald eyes shimmering with warmth and affection.

"Reena," she said, her finger gently pointing in her direction. "I need you to prioritize your health, my sweet kitten. You're becoming as thin as a withered branch, and I long to see you as plump and vibrant as Lily." A warm smile graced Amma's lips, a comforting assurance that she bore no resentment toward her daughter.

"Good night, Amma," Reena replied, her voice light and cheerful, as if a weight had been lifted from her heart.

"Good night, Amma," Lily and Bhushan chimed in unison, their voices filled with cheer as they marched off to their beds, the earlier tension fading into the warmth of their familial bonds.

After almost an hour, Reena woke up. The room was filled with the rhythmic sound of her siblings' gentle snores, Bhushan's deep rumble blending with Lily's soft whimpers, creating a comforting symphony in the quiet room. With a cautious grace, she retrieved a lantern from beneath her bed, its soft glow casting flickering shadows on the corner. From under her snug mattress, she carefully extracted the comic she had stumbled upon near the ficus tree, its vibrant cover beckoning her curiosity. Her curiosity urged her to read it during the morning, yet the last thing she desired was to be caught by her siblings or Amma. After all, Reena's candid remarks unintentionally hurt her mother's feelings countless times. She settled the comic in her lap, ready to delve into its pages while ensuring her movements remained silent as a whisper.

She glanced at the title, *Home Sweet Home.* The cover featured whimsical cartoon characters—a family of four: a mother, a father, and two-spirited young girls. As she turned the page, her gaze fell upon a delightful pink door, strikingly reminiscent of the one near the stairs of her own house. The door seemed to beckon her, its vibrant hue igniting a sense of nostalgia and curiosity. Flipping further, she encountered enchanting illustrations of two young girls bustling about in a rectangular-shaped contraption referred to as an oven in the dialogue bubbles, piquing her interest. Engaging with the playful text, she murmured, "Wow, is this a kitchen? It's so beautiful, unlike ours. We only have an old rusty cauldron, a collection of peculiar jars, and a handful of basic food ingredients."

The aesthetic allure of the book heightened her curiosity, and as she delved deeper into the comic book, a wave of joy began to uplift her spirits. She continued to leaf through the pages with an eager heart, captivated by the sisters' journey of baking a birthday cake. Each turn of the page revealed the myriad challenges the sisters faced as they grappled with the intricacies of their task, from measuring ingredients to overcoming unexpected mishaps, all in their quest to create the perfect cake for their father's birthday. Despite nearly giving up, the sisters discovered the strength to persevere, determined to try again after failing three times. Reena turned the pages with delight, savouring each panel of the comic, her imagination ignited by the colourful illustrations and charming dialogue. She felt a sense of kinship with the characters as they navigated their culinary misadventures. Finally, she reached the last page—a joyous scene where the girls triumphantly presented a beautifully baked cake, adorned with sprinkles and candles, alongside an array of delectable dishes that were utterly unfamiliar to Reena. Simultaneously, a wave of memories surged through her—a fleeting glimpse of her father, a man she had never met, lost beyond the wall. This topic, laden with sorrow, was rarely discussed in their household, for Amma preferred to avoid the painful narrative that accompanied it. Reena felt a bittersweet ache in her heart as she pondered the stories of a man who had vanished into the shadows of her family's history, leaving behind only whispers and unanswered questions.

Turning to another page of the comic, she was greeted by a vibrant cover illustration that captured the family celebrating their father's birthday with unrestrained joy. The scene was alive with laughter and warmth, a stark contrast to her own muted existence. At the bottom of the cover, enticing labels described the diverse array of foods adorning the table, each dish a tantalizing promise of flavors and experiences unknown to her.

She began to read the names at the bottom, her eyes dancing over the delightful offerings: chicken curry, gulab jamuns, jalebi, kadai paneer, and rotis. Each name evoked a sense of wonder and intrigue, but it was the pink strawberry cake that captivated her imagination the most. Its soft, pastel hue seemed to whisper sweet promises of delight, painting vivid images in her mind of the fluffy layers and the luscious frosting that might adorn its surface.

Gazing at the picture ignited a symphony of flavours in her mind, tantalizing her taste buds with the imagined flavours and richness of the feast. As she observed the family on the comic book cover page, their laughter and joy radiating as they indulged in the delectable spread, Reena felt an ember of longing kindling within her. The vibrant colours of the dishes stood in stark contrast to her monotonous meals of mugas, deepening her fascination with the culinary delights she had only dreamed of.

She flipped back a page, scrutinizing an illustration that revealed the intricate details of the pink strawberry cake. This three-tiered masterpiece, lavishly adorned with plump strawberries and a delicate cascade of glistening strawberry syrup, captivated her attention. As she immersed herself in the dialogue bubbles that detailed the cake's ingredients, Reena found herself transported into a world of imagination. She envisioned the delightful experience of savouring the cake, picturing its velvety texture melting in her mouth and the burst of sweet strawberry flavour dancing on her tongue. In her mind, she was surrounded by laughter and joy, sharing this scrumptious delight with her imaginary family in the fantastical realm of the comic.

"Wow, is this food? It looks incredibly delicious. Should I share it with Amma and ask her to cook it for us...? Ahhh, but she's not keen on us reading books, and she doesn't even know I can read. If she finds out, she'll be curious about where I learned. Amma, Bhushan, and Lily are clueless about it; I'll have to keep it a secret, or she might get mad at me."

As she leafed through the pages, she scrutinized each illustration with rapt attention. Upon turning the book, the iconic pink door reemerged. An overwhelming surge of curiosity enveloped her, igniting musings about the secrets concealed behind the pink door in her household.

"Perhaps some delectable delicacies lie hidden behind it, secreted away by Amma," she murmured, enchanted by the tantalizing mystery that awaited behind the door.

CHAPTER-3

Behind the Pink Door

In the gentle light of morning, after breakfast had been cleared away, Amma and the children gathered for a game of Seven Stones. Today, Lily was Amma's partner. The makeshift ball, a humble creation born of old, threadbare socks sewn together, rested in Lily's small, pudgy hands. With a determined gleam in her eye, she positioned herself, bending slightly to perfect her aim. In one fluid motion, she released the ball, and it sailed through the air, striking the pile of stones with precise force, sending them scattering.

"Bravo, Lily!" Amma exclaimed, her voice ringing with pride.

Lily and Amma swiftly gathered the scattered stones, working together to rebuild the pile. Meanwhile, Bhushan and Reena darted after the wayward ball, which had bounced mischievously away from the stones. With the speed of a gusting wind, Bhushan closed the distance, snatched up the ball, and with a mischievous grin, hurled it, striking Amma squarely in the back.

Lily let the stones slip from her fingers. "Oh noh! We've losth, Amma," she lisped, her voice tinged with dismay.

"It's all right, Lily. It's merely a game," Amma replied, a warm smile gracing her lips.

Perched beside the half-assembled stone pile, Amma and Lily were soon joined by Bhushan, who stood panting from his recent sprint. Amma turned her attention toward him, her gaze curious and inviting.

"Excellent shot, Bhushan," she remarked. Bhushan's chest swelled with pride, and his heart soared as he revelled in the triumph of making the shot from an impressive distance. Hitting the target from such a range had appeared daunting, yet he achieved it with remarkable ease.

They all spotted Reena sprinting toward them across the sprawling field surrounding their castle, a vast expanse adorned with lush green grass stretching as far as the eye could see. A solitary tree stood sentinel in the open space before the purple castle, its vibrant hues contrasting against the serene landscape. The children had never experienced a close-up view of the boundary wall, which loomed in the distance, visible from the castle but appearing hazy and indistinct. Their curiosity often compelled them to race toward it, yet after hours of fervent running, all they acquired were cramps and exhaustion, while the wall remained tantalizingly elusive.

Reena joined them, her eyes sparkling as she noticed Bhushan's chest swelling with pride. To further elevate his spirits, she offered another compliment. "Amma, Bhushan has become remarkably skilled with slingshots."

"He certainly is! My talented little kitten," Amma affirmed, bestowing Bhushan with a warm smile.

"Amma, would you care to vouch for my slingshot skills in action?" Bhushan boasted, a confident grin spreading across his face.

"Honey, I must take my leave for now. Perhaps later, if that's alright?"

"Alright, Amma."

Before departing, Amma pressed a tender farewell kiss upon them. They watched her for a while as she made her way toward the house, her figure gradually fading from view.

"Let'sh play somethingh else," Lily said.

"Slingshot targets?" Bhushan proffered.

"Yayy! Swingshotsh!" Lily jumped with excitement

"Haha, it's slingshots, Lily."

"Swingshots!"

"Never mind," Bhushan gave up.

"Well, you two enjoy your game; I'm going to rest for a while," Reena declared, turning to make her way toward the castle.

As Reena entered the castle, she stealthily positioned herself behind one of the lilac walls. Her intention was to watch Amma leave the house, granting her a chance to sneak a peek inside the forbidden Pink Door room—a venture best undertaken in her mother's absence. Patiently, she awaited her mother's departure, watching as Amma faded from sight through one of the oriel windows. Once she was certain her mother was gone, Reena slipped into her Amma's room, her mind racing with questions about where Amma went each day, especially if the world beyond the wall was so treacherous. Having assisted her mother in tidying the room countless times, Reena quickly spotted the pink, old-fashioned key among the others, the key to the pink door room. Grasping it eagerly, she dashed toward the terminus.

With a rush of excitement, she swung the door open. The once-dominant thoughts of Amma's mysterious journeys beyond the wall faded, replaced by visions of the delectable cake she had seen in the comic. As she stepped into the room, the door shut with a resounding bang, but Reena paid it no mind, utterly absorbed in her quest for the tantalizing treat hidden behind the pink door.

The room, expansive and cloaked in darkness, descended into pitch blackness as the door shut behind her. Her widened irises adjusted, gradually revealing the surroundings in varying shades of grey and black. As she moved forward, a faint odour wafted toward her, a peculiar blend of mugas and decay. The delightful mood of Reena, buoyed by the prospect of culinary treasures, was quickly soured by the unpleasant scent. As she surveyed the dimly lit space, its eerie dark grey walls closing in around her, her unease deepened, prompting her to reconsider and retreat.

As Reena turned to leave the room, her eyes were drawn to a pitch-black silhouette etched against the grey wall. Driven by curiosity, she approached it, and with each step, the shadow became clearer—a figure seated upon some unseen object. She halted, her steps faltering as apprehension washed over her.

"Perhaps it's some sort of statue," She thought.

As she drew closer to inspect the statue, two brilliant white dots suddenly emerged on its surface, revealing two eerie eyes that seemed to glow, void of any eyeballs, upon the dreadful head of the silhouette. Reena's legs turned to ice, and her heart pounded fiercely against her ribs. Though a part of her screamed to flee the room, she found herself paralyzed, trapped in the chilling moment.

The white, luminous dots began to shift in her direction, and the eerie head of the silhouette seemed to fixate directly on her. Squinting for a closer look, she realized the figure was seated on something square. Beside it stood a lantern that flickered to life, casting a soft glow in front of the dark figure and unveiling a glimpse of the scene— Reena noticed a lantern resting on the table beside a stack of grimy, overweight books, one of which lay open as if someone had been reading it recently. Adjacent to it sat a plate with half-eaten, decaying mugas, their once vibrant colours now faded and sickening.

In this unfolding scene, a pair of ragged blue jeans caught her attention behind the table. A figure was seated on the sofa, his bare waist exposed as he leaned toward the table, the top of his head emerging into the lantern's light as if absorbed in reading. In a loud, eerie voice, he recited, *"And the brave kitten who wishes to live must break the chains of lies and illusions, and fly away with the wind."* Pausing, he turned his head toward Reena. His thin, pale face emerged into the light, revealing purple, droopy eyes locked onto her and streaks of light red staining his nose and lips. As he smiled gloomily, blood dribbled from his mouth, sending shivers down Reena's spine and conjuring vivid images of zombies from the tales Amma had shared with her. This was precisely how she had envisioned zombies.

The zombie-like boy rose from the sofa and swiftly advanced toward Reena. At the same time, the lantern on the table levitated into the air, illuminating his face with an eerie glow. Despite closing the distance between them, a chain around his neck held him back, tethered to something obscured in the shadows of the dark room. Reena observed him intently, her eyes absorbing the unsettling details. As his arm reached out toward her within the lantern's glow, she realized that his arms were missing, sending a chilling shock coursing through her veins. An unsettling question formed in her mind: What was this hideous creature doing in their house? His arms were gruesomely chopped more than halfway, suggesting a deliberate and malevolent act. He extended his mutilated arm toward Reena, his intentions unclear.

"Hello there," the zombie-like boy said in a surprisingly normal voice. "Did you come here seeking the truth?"

Reena remained silent, her mind wrestling with the notion that zombies were not supposed to speak. How was this one able to communicate?

As she contemplated, a growling sound reached her ears, emanating from the zombie boy's stomach, diverting her attention. The ravenous boy moved his mutilated arm toward his mouth, grasping it with his yellowed teeth, which gleamed in the soft light of the lantern. Managing to seize a sizable chunk of his own flesh, he tore it from his arm, blood oozing, and began chewing it as Reena would chew on mugas. Blood smeared his lips, and Reena's eyes widened in terror as she finally understood the source of the light red stains on his face. The boy had been feasting on his own flesh.

The scene filled Reena with a creeping dread, an overwhelming urge to flee the room surging within her. Yet, her frozen legs compelled her to remain where she was.

"Don't you know how to speak?" the zombie boy inquired, the sound of his rigid chewing echoing in the air. He then extended his blood-dripping arm toward Reena, offering her a piece from his previous bite. "Have a taste," he smiled. "The flavour of blood is far richer than the mugas you consume every day."

Petrified, Reena screamed at the top of her lungs and fled the room, her feet moved with the speed of the wind.

For the remainder of the day, she remained silent, concealing what she had witnessed behind the pink door—a blatant act of disobedience to Amma's orders. As everyone else slept at night, Reena lay awake in her bed, unable to shake the haunting images of what she had encountered behind that door. She couldn't erase the unsettling sight from her mind and was consumed by questions—why was he in their house? Did Amma know about him? Why was he feasting on his own flesh? How was the lantern floating in mid-air? Had he consumed his own arms? With the countless queries swirling in her thoughts, she resolved to speak to Amma in the morning.

CHAPTER-4

The Whispers

In the morning, Reena awoke late, weariness etched across her face. The questions about the zombie boy had haunted her throughout the night, robbing her of sleep. With her mind swirling with inquiries, she made her way to the lavatory, murmuring the questions she longed to ask Amma. She went through her morning routine, lost in thought, unable to erase the image of the talking, terrifying boy in the room behind the pink door.

She dressed in a blue suit paired with a white pajami and chunni. As she prepared, she walked toward the dining room, still murmuring questions in her mind—Who was the zombie in the pink room? Why did he consume his own flesh? How was the lantern on his table floating in mid-air?

A sudden clatter disrupted her reverie, a chair crashing to the floor. Reena glanced around, recognizing that she was in the dining room. She hadn't observed anything amiss until the sound of the chair's fall snapped her back to reality, the result of her own inadvertent brush against it.

"Be careful!" Bhushan exclaimed in an exasperated tone. Reena glanced at Bhushan and Lily, who were seated at the dining table, before bending down to retrieve the fallen chair.

"Who's the lazy bum today?" Bhushan remarked, a mischievous smile playing on his lips as he crossed his arms.

Reena glanced at Bhushan once more while arranging her chair but opted not to respond.

"I've waited ages for someone to be late for breakfast just so I could call them a lazy bum," Bhushan said, raising his right eyebrow, his smile growing even more mischievous.

"Seal your mouth!" Reena exclaimed as she took her seat beside Lily.

As she waited for Amma, she quietly contemplated her questions, bracing herself for her mother's potential anger after disobeying a firm directive. A clamorous voice echoed in her mind: "I have to ask her! This is essential... It was utterly disgusting... Who offers someone their own flesh to consume? Aren't zombies supposed to devour the flesh of others? So, gross, so gross, so gross, so gross!"

"Breakfaaast is ready, my beloved kitteeens," Amma sang cheerfully. Reena looked at her mother, who stood beside the table, holding a pot of steaming mugas and wearing a warm smile. She glanced at her siblings, who sat at the table with their faces turning a shade of green.

Today, no one complained. Amma served the mugas into their bowls and then departed. Reena contemplated revealing what she had discovered behind the pink door but decided to wait until her siblings had left the house.

The kids eagerly began devouring their food, hastily finishing their meals to maximize their playtime outside. Reena also consumed her meal quickly, her mind fixated on the impending conversation with Amma. Lily and Bhushan dashed outside, with Bhushan pausing momentarily at the main door.

"Are you coming, Reena?"

"In a minute," Reena replied, then exited the corridor and stood at Amma's door.

As the door creaked open, Amma stepped out, moving briskly. Reena followed closely behind.

"Amma."

"Oh, hi, honey. Aren't you playing with your siblings today?" Amma glanced at Reena with a sidelong look as she walked briskly toward the stairs.

"Amma... I need to discuss something," Reena said, disregarding her mother's question.

Amma started climbing the stairs.

"Give me a minute, honey. I'll be right back," she replied without meeting Reena's gaze.

As she waited for Amma, Reena stood near the stairs. The confidence that had once swelled in her chest to speak was now supplanted by uncertainty. She began muttering to herself, trying to regain her resolve as she paced in a circle near the stairway. As she walked, her eyes lingered on the pink door, and her legs felt as though they had turned into lifeless vines. She couldn't help but fixate on the door. Suddenly, the doorknob turned, and with a long, hollow creek, the door swung open. The pitch-black silhouette with gleaming white voids reemerged, staring intently into Reena's eyes. An eerie whisper brushed past her ears: *"Love is a chain, Love is forged, Fathom the truth, Enter the door."*

The whispers, though shrill, were unnervingly clear, causing the hair on her neck to stand on end. Her feet seemed to move of their own accord, irresistibly drawn toward the silhouette, toward whatever lurked inside the pink room.

"Reena," a voice called to her from upstairs. She turned her gaze to see Amma descending the stairs, a wooden basket in her hands, its lid covered by a red and white checkered cloth. Reena glanced back at the pink door, only to find it securely latched.

"Did I imagine that?" Reena murmured to herself.

Amma reached the bottom of the stairs and stood before her.

Sorry, honey, my old basket broke, so I had to go fetch a new one."

"It's alright, Amma," Reena replied, her gaze lingering on the pink door.

"You wanted to discuss something important?" Amma inquired.

"Amma... I... I"

Speak up, honey, what is it?," Amma encouraged with a warm smile.

"Pink lehenga, Amma, I-I want a new pink lehenga. You know the old one is torn," Reena said.

"That's all?"

"Yes."

"Of course, my dear, you shall have it," Amma assured her, her voice soothing and melodic. "When something holds great significance for you, never hesitate to express your wishes." Their conversation faded into the gentle embrace, as they both stepped out of the house.

Several hours had slipped by since Amma departed, and Bhushan and Lily were blissfully absorbed in their game beneath the tree. An imaginative idea ignited in Lily's mind as she sprinted through the verdant field, clutching a doll aloft. Meanwhile, Bhushan, racing alongside her, attempted to strike the doll with his slingshot. It was no easy feat, but as they laughed and ran over the lush grass, the game became an endless wellspring of delight for the siblings.

Meanwhile, Reena sat beneath the shade of the ancient ficus tree, needle in hand, carefully crafting a headband by threading together delicate, flimsy flowers. As she became absorbed in the intricate task, her thoughts drifted back to the unsettling words that had recently echoed in her mind. Although the precise verse slipped from her memory, Reena couldn't dispel the lingering sensation that the enigmatic presence behind the pink door was calling to her, enticing her into a dialogue. A torrent of questions surged within her mind— Should she dare to approach him? Could it possibly be safe to engage in conversation? What might he wish to divulge? And what if the voices that echoed in her thoughts were nothing more than the phantoms of her own imagination?

"Ouch!" A sharp cry tore from her throat as a sudden, searing pain surged through her. Her gaze darted to her thumb, where she saw the needle had pierced an inch deep into the flesh. The intensity of the pain was overwhelming, almost coaxing tears to her eyes.

With painstaking care, she withdrew the needle, now stained with blood. Her thumb revealed a sharp puncture, blood welling from it like a hot geyser. Instinctively, she brought her thumb to her mouth, and the metallic taste of blood met her tongue. Strangely, she found the flavour more satisfying than the Mugas she was accustomed to. This caravan of thought drew her back to the figure behind the pink door— the zombie-like boy gnawing at his own flesh continues to haunt Reena, souring her mood each time the image crosses her mind. The unsettling experience behind the pink door seems to have left a lingering shadow over her thoughts.

Removing her thumb from her mouth, she spat beside the tree several times until the metallic taste of blood had completely dissipated. Gathering the delicate flowers, she carefully covered her wounded thumb with their soft petals, then bound it with the shimmering silver thread she had been using to stitch the blossoms onto the headband.

Once she had secured her thumb with the petals and thread, Reena reclined amidst the lush grass and vibrant blooms, finding solace in the shade of the tree. She gazed up at the leaves swaying gently above her, lost in a labyrinth of puzzling thoughts. Watching Bhushan and Lily play in the distance infused her with a sense of calm, their laughter echoing softly in the air. Taking a brief respite from her swirling thoughts, Reena closed her eyes and surrendered to the tranquillity beneath the ficus tree. Yet, the calm was abruptly shattered by an eerie whisper that slithered into her consciousness: *"Love is a chain, Love is forged, Fathom the truth, Enter the door."* The chilling words sent a shiver coursing down her spine. Startled awake, she found herself mumbling, *"Fathom the truth, Enter the door."* A powerful yearning to engage in a dialogue with the enigmatic presence behind the pink door surged within her, pulling at her curiosity and dread alike. Rising to her feet, Reena dashed toward the castle, her heart racing with determination. She seized a knife from the kitchen counter, its cool metal providing a semblance of courage amidst her trepidation. Standing before the pink door, a whirlwind of bravery and fear enveloped her senses, creating a tumultuous storm within. As her heart thundered in her chest, she approached with unsteady legs and a trembling hand, finally inserting the key and turning the handle, she stepped into the pink room. She lifted her twitching hands, the knife glinting in the darkness as she called out, "Hello... I-I came here to talk." Silence enveloped her, stretching the moments into an uncomfortable void. "Are you there?" she cried out, her voice quivering like a fragile leaf in the wind. "I need to know about you... Who are you? What is your purpose here? I-I have questions." Her heart raced as the stillness deepened, an unsettling tension hanging in the air, urging her to press on despite the fear gnawing at her resolve.

For a fleeting moment, silence enveloped the space, thick and oppressive. Then, a voice resonated from the shadows, smooth yet chilling, "Hello, girl... I knew you would come. I have a story... A tale that will upend your world." As the words echoed, a lantern flickered to life, suspended in mid-air, casting a ghostly glow that revealed the lad's haunting purple eyes and a blood-stained smile.

"Welcome," he said. "Welcome to my cavern."

CHAPTER-5

The Guiding Shadow

As Reena stood enveloped in the suffocating darkness of the room, confronted by the enigmatic zombie-like boy, a cold shiver coursed through her, rendering her nerves nearly translucent with fear. Yet, amidst the encroaching dread that threatened to consume her, she summoned her inner strength, striving to uphold an illusion of bravado against the shadows that loomed around her. The boy approached her with deliberate strides, each movement drawing him nearer, as the ghostly glow from the lantern hovering over his shoulder illuminated the haunting contours of his face. Yet, he came to a sudden stop, held back by the chains that bound his neck, creating an invisible barrier between them.

"You summoned me here?" Reena asked, her voice steady despite the chill that crept into her bones.

"Maybe," he replied with a smile.

"I was drawn here by the eerie whispers that beckoned me," Reena declared, her eyes locked onto his ominous face, partially illuminated by the dim light.

"Must have been wind. The wind tends to speak when answers we seek," he said, his blood-stained smile glistening in the lantern's light.

Reena's fear escalated as she was gawking perpetually into his eerie face illuminated by the soft glow of the floating lantern.

"It spoke of the truth I seek; those words compelled me to come here," Reena stammered.

"Hmm... an intriguing subject indeed," mused the zombie boy. He pivoted and began to retreat toward his sitting place, the lantern trailing behind him. Once he reached a distance, the lantern settled back onto the table, extinguishing itself, and the room was flooded with light, revealing every shadowy corner. Reena turned her eyes upward and beheld the exquisite chandeliers that now illuminated the room with a warm glow. The previously dim atmosphere transformed into a vivid display of detail, allowing her to discern the features of the armless zombie boy as he stood before the latte-hued wall.

She drew nearer, and with each step, the nuances of his appearance sharpened into focus. He was a tall, gaunt figure, his pallor accentuated by the shadows that danced around him. Short, buzz hair framed his face, while his wolf-like purple eyes bore into her, filled with an unsettling intensity. As Reena approached, the smile on his diamond-shaped face stretched wider, an eerie expression that sent a shiver down her spine. Reena reached him and positioned herself beside the table, her heart racing. The boy lowered himself onto the checkered floor of honey and scarlet, settling next to the ragged olive-green sofa.

"Take a seat," he commanded Reena, his tone brooking no argument. Yet, she lingered in uncertainty, her thoughts swirling with lingering doubts. The boy's gaze pierced through her, and he caught sight of the kitchen knife clutched tightly in her hand. "Ah, I see you've come well equipped," he remarked, his voice laced with a biting edge.

"It-It's for my protection," Reena replied, her voice trembling as she concealed the knife behind her back, a wave of vulnerability washing over her.

"Do you truly believe a kitchen knife could bring me down?" he inquired, a mocking tone lacing his words. Reena, disregarding his taunt, shot back, "I am here seeking the truth. Speak it, and allow me to escape this wretched space at once."

"Of course, but first, kindly take a seat," the boy said, gesturing toward the floor with his wolf-like gaze. Reena scanned her surroundings; aside from the grimy stains of blood and mugas near the sofa, the floor appeared relatively clean. Reluctantly, she lowered herself to the surface in front of the enigmatic stranger.

"Speak," Reena grunted.

"Why the frosty demeanour, madam? If you judge me by appearances and believe I'm some sort of monster, then you are gravely mistaken," the boy shot back, his tone sharp and defiant.

"I witnessed you guzzling your own flesh with my own eyes, a grisly spectacle indeed. Doesn't that alter you as a monster... a zombie?"

"You have yet to comprehend who the true monster is," the boy retorted, a flicker of irritation flashing in his eyes at Reena's remarks.

"What do you mean? Who is the true monster?" Reena inquired, her curiosity piqued as she searched his unsettling gaze for answers.

"If you seek the truth, it awaits you, but I will reveal it only after you respond to my inquiries. Should you agree, you may remain; if not, the door is open for your exit at any moment."

Reena heard the boy's words. Though a sense of alarm coursed through her, she whispered in a voice barely audible, "I consent."

"Very well," the boy replied, a glimmer of intrigue flickering in his purple eyes. "I'm curious about what lured you into this forbidden realm. It's off-limits for you, isn't it?"

Reena's jaw dropped. "How did you know that the area is off-limits?"

"I happen to know things you don't," the boy replied with an unsettling calmness. "Was it Amma who sent you here?"

Curiosity surged through Reena, prompting a flood of questions, but she settled on one: "How do you know Amma?"

"Another rule, Reena. Only I shall pose the questions," he stated, his voice firm yet eerily calm.

The boy's words left Reena Dumbfounded. "How do you know my name? I haven't even mentioned it yet."

"Correct, but your mother did. Your name slipped from her lips once," he added, his voice steady yet chilling. "Now, answer my question first, and then I shall entertain your queries. Why did you come here?"

"I came here for the food, zombie boy," Reena retorted, her fierce gaze clashing with his enigmatic purple eyes.

"Call me Nindhi," he added.

"Nindhi... I came here for the food. I thought there might be something delicious to eat in this room," Reena clarified, her voice tinged with defiance.

"What led you to believe that there would be food behind the pink door?" Nindhi inquired, a chuckle escaping his lips, as if amused by her naive assumption.

"Near the tree, I stumbled upon a book, labelled as a comic book on its cover. It was a strange book. As I leafed through its pages, I was captivated by vivid illustrations of delectable dishes crafted behind a pink door. The pink door depicted in the comic bore an uncanny resemblance to the door of this room, which led me to wonder—

perhaps Amma had concealed a treasure trove of food within these confines. It was my insatiable curiosity that ultimately lured me here," Reena explained.

Nindhi's wolf-like eyes gleamed with intrigue. "And where is this book now?" he inquired, leaning forward with an intensity that seemed to pierce through the dimly lit room.

"In my room," she said.

"Show me, please," Nindhi implored, his voice laced with an eagerness that was hard to ignore.

Reena gazed at Nindhi for a moment, her heart racing, before rising from the floor. She exited the room, returning moments later with the comic book clutched in her hands. With a swift motion, she tossed it onto the floor before him. As he read the title, the book began to levitate, hovering in mid-air, its pages fluttering gently as if caught in an unseen breeze. Reena watched in wonder, captivated by the spectacle of the comic book gliding effortlessly before Nindhi, the air whispering through its pages as he absorbed the illustrations within.

"How is this possible? Is witchcraft real?" she murmured, her peacock-brown eyes widening in disbelief as they remained fixated on the levitating book.

Nindhi glanced at Reena, his expression a mix of curiosity and surprise. "You can read?" he asked.

"Yes," replied Reena.

"Who bestowed the gift of reading upon you?" Nindhi inquired, his curiosity piqued.

"Amma," answered Reena.

"If you dare to hoodwink me, I shall have no inclination to reveal the truth to you any further," Nindhi cautioned, his tone sharp and resolute.

"It's a secret I cannot divulge," Reena replied, a hint of defiance in her voice.

"Your secret will be kept safe with me, I assure you," he said, offering a reassuring smile that softened the tension in the air.

"What if I choose not to tell?"

"The door remains ajar for your exit," Nindhi replied, his gaze fixed on the comic's pages as he continued to skim through them.

Reena hesitated, caught in the crossfire between her desire to guard the secret of her education and an insatiable curiosity to unearth the truth. With a heavy heart, she sank back down onto the floor, wrestling with her conflicting emotions.

"The one-eyed master—he was the one who taught me how to read," Reena admitted, her voice barely a whisper as she averted her gaze to the floor, the weight of her revelation heavy upon her shoulders.

"Who is this one-eyed master?" Nindhi inquired, his interest ignited by the mention of the enigmatic figure.

"He used to visit my dreams," Reena elaborated. "At first, he appeared terrifying—one enormous eye set in the centre of his forehead, sharp teeth glistening like daggers, and braids that resembled writhing tentacles, always styled into a peculiar comb-over. He asserted that he was my mentor. Though I was skeptical of his claims, he insisted he would prepare me for the challenges that awaited me in future. He urged me to keep this secret from my family in exchange for the knowledge he promised to impart."

"What future challenges does he wish to prepare you for?" Nindhi inquired, his intrigue evident in his tone.

"I don't know; he said I would eventually find out," Reena admitted. "He always carried a dark suitcase filled with books. He taught me various subjects—English, science, maths, and more. However, there was one particular subject he insisted I master completely."

"Which subject?" queried Nindhi.

"The witchcraft," replied Reena.

Nindhi's wolfish eyes widened to their fullest at the mention of witchcraft. "Have you ever perused a book before?" he inquired, his curiosity palpable.

"Not in reality; aside from my dreams, this comic was the first I ever read. Amma doesn't truly want me delving into books," Reena divulged.

"And the book has set you on a quest in pursuit of the food illustrated within its pages?" Nindhi inquired, a mocking tone lacing his words.

"Yes, and all I found was a freak instead of the food," Reena retorted, her disappointment evident.

"A 'freak,' you say?" Nindhi chuckled darkly. "You have yet to grasp the essence of what a true freak is. Just wait until you uncover the real tale of Amma Meiga."

CHAPTER-6

An Untold Tale

"AMMA MEIGA?? What about her?" asked Reena.

"Well, let me begin, Reena. But before that, I need to clarify something. The tale I am about to unfold may be deeply unsettling for you. You might question its veracity, but I assure you, it's not a lie. You deserve to know every facet of the harsh reality about your mother... her darkest secret," Nindhi stated.

Paralyzed with fear, Reena hesitated, but a deep-seated suspicion had always lingered in her heart about the quaint ongoings in the house. She turned her gaze toward Nindhi, who was glaring at her with the gaze of a wolf, without a blink. Despite the unnerving intensity, Reena took a deep breath and, in a shaky voice she uttered, "I want to know the truth."

"Okay, let the story begin... "

Ages ago, Amma brought me to this castle from someplace, unknown. She was a sweet, loving lady with a warm smile always adorning her face. As I grew up, she took care of me as any mother would. Toys, movies, and books were a constant part of our lives – we played together, read together, and enjoyed movies together. She often said that those were the best days of her life, cherishing every moment spent with me. I felt the same way, finding solace in our time together. At around the age of three, I was adopted by Amma. She always said she saved me from extinction and transformed my life into something beautiful, far beyond what it could have been if I had somehow survived. Everything seemed perfect and alluring after I heard the story that nothing remained of the world beyond; everything had been decimated in a great war including foodstuffs, and now the realm was ruled by monstrous beings. I always considered myself lucky to have survived the great war, unlike so many others, but there was a constraint – I wasn't allowed to eat anything other than Mugas. One day, Amma found me eating flowers in the field, and that very day, the flowers were uprooted. My cravings for other foods grew stronger—those I saw in movies or picture books were nearly impossible to resist. Yet, I always cherished my beloved mother's wishes and adhered to her guidance. Years passed, and my perspective on life evolved. I began to watch movies and read books with a different perspective. Curiosity about the world beyond the wall and a desire to create items were kindled within me. I conducted experiments with wood and metals, and crafted models and toys. The joy of creating something was truly amazing and in no time I was enveloped by the blanket called Art.

Reena mumbled, "Hmm," as she, too, loved crafting headbands out of flowers.

When I matured enough to take care of myself, Amma stopped spending time with me. She became engrossed in her business outside the wall, and in return, she inundated me with more books and movies. The intention behind providing me with books and movies was clear – to anchor me within the castle. She realised that I was ripening, she knew that confining me within these walls required a delicate touch—making it so engaging that I would never perceive it as a prison. She aimed to bind me to entertainment, ensuring I would never desire to leave the castle. But there was one thing in which she failed, to cure my loneliness. Imagine having an array of incredible toys with no one to share the joy, possessing a vast collection of films without a companion to watch with, reading a multitude of books with no one to discuss. It felt like having almost everything the cosmos could offer,

...yet finding no true happiness in the midst of it. In some way, it tainted my mind. Even indulging in art and crafting felt futile, as there was no one to appreciate my work. I felt intense loneliness as I immersed myself in romance novels, a yearning to meet someone special—someone who would devote their time to me—began to bloom within my heart.

Amma continued to instil a fear of war and deadly creatures beyond the wall within me, but at some point, she ignited the rebel in me. Questions began to stir within me: What if I ventured out, fought these monsters, and made the world a better place? I could no longer bear the loneliness; perhaps out there, I might find someone special. The only risk was taking the leap beyond the safety of the walls, which I think was worth it. Years of seclusion had disturbed me, and I could no longer bear this way of life. Taking a step towards my goal, I decided to craft a crossbow. It was the first functional weapon I had ever created, aside from toys and models, and I succeeded in making it work.

That pivotal day arrived when I confronted Amma about my dream. I told her I wanted to venture outside and fight the monstrous beings, to make the world a better place for both of us, so we could live in peace and freedom. She broke my crossbow and called me foolish for thinking I could fight the monsters beyond. She said I was naive to believe I could make a difference. Her response marked a turning point in her behaviour – she became increasingly angered and stripped me of my books and movies. The subjects she had once tutored me were abandoned. As her oppressive actions intensified, I felt trapped in a cage. Determined to escape the castle for both our sakes, I slinked into her room and retrieved the books she had taken from me. Among them, I discovered volumes on witchcraft. I was astonished to discover that magic existed and even more surprised to learn that I was a wizard by birth. It was all settled—the monsters beyond could be vanquished with the help of magic. Engrossed in learning different spells and crafting magical objects, I embarked on creating a magical tent described in the book named The Craftworks of Gnows. Gnows was a wizard credited with introducing gadgets in the society of witchcraft and had conceptualized the magical tent. The means of escaping my confinement. For the sake of my mother's and my own freedom, I had to do it. I had to fight those monsters and make this world a better place. Though I worked diligently for years, the challenge of creating the tent alone persisted. My research and experiments remained a secret from Amma. Driven by passion, I neared success, and the dream of leaving the castle was on the verge of becoming reality.

However, one fateful morning, Amma Meiga seized me by my hair and ruthlessly dragged me into this room. Instead of serving me a bowl of Mugas for breakfast, she shackled me with a chain around my neck.

"Amma did this?" Reena's voice trembled.

"Yes," Nindhi continued, "...she brought her cleaver knife and severed my arms. My arms were roasted in front of me, and then consumed, and washed down with a glass of blood. After indulging in my flesh, she declared that I was raised to be her endless source of meat for a lifetime.

"No way," Reena protested. "Amma can't possibly do that. Why would she commit such a monstrous act?"

"I know, you'll find it hard to believe," Nindhi Peered into Reena's eyes and declared, "She did it because... Amma is a cannibal witch."

CHAPTER-7

Devotion or Credence

"Cannibal Witch?? What are you insinuating with these absurd claims??" Reena cried, standing back on her feet.

"Yes, a cannibal, for she feasts upon human flesh, and a witch, due to her profound mastery of dark sorcery. We are all mere ingredients in her grotesque recipe. Our sole purpose is to replenish her supply, ensuring she has a perpetual stock of meat to savour throughout her lifetime," replied Nindhi.

"Could you please treat this matter with the gravity it deserves?" Reena implored. "She can't be a witch. She has raised us for years... just look at me. I am twelve years old, soon to be thirteen, and I am unscathed. She has never even laid a hand on me all these years. I vividly remember every jiffy with Amma. She showered us with boundless care and affection, attending to our every need. And now you're suggesting that she has been raising us merely to devour our flesh? Are you out of your mind?"

Nindhi scrutinised Reena for a moment and then asked, "Have you ever wondered why she only ever fed you Mugas, and nothing else?"

"Yes, because it's the only source of nourishment left, and there's no other food available in this world," Reena replied with unwavering conviction, her voice firm in defence of Amma's actions.

Nindhi continued to gaze at Reena and said, "Do you realize, Reena, that our mother's cunning and malevolence surpass even the darkest villains ever described in literature? After imprisoning me in this room, the grim truth about Mugas once slipped her lips. It is concocted from rare insects and lizards, mixed with green raisins and magical potions. When fed to a child over the years, it grants the ability to regenerate their organs once they turn thirteen. But there's a catch: the person must consume nothing but mugas, with water as the sole exception."

"LIAR!" Reena cried out.

"I am not fabricating this. I speak only the truth. Even as Amma has consumed my organs for years, my body persistently regenerates," He calmly asserted.

Reena beheld his arms, now an inch longer than during their initial encounter, sending a shiver down her spine. *"Is he right about Amma? No... he can't be. I must be imagining things; his arms are the same as before."* her mind echoed shrilly. " Can you grow your organs back?" she asked.

"It's a sinister form of sketchy immortality. My legs and arms have regrown countless times," said Nindhi. "Whereas I am not certain about my head. Amma never attempted to sever it. However, there was a moment when I provoked her so profoundly that she warned me she would kill me by decapitating me. But when I said I preferred death over this hideous life, an outlandish reticence appeared on her face.

Reena chuckled acidly. "So, a green, gooey Mugas that grants the power of regeneration," she said "and a zombie-like chap imprisoned in the house with the ability to levitate things in the air, ...and a mother who wants to dine on her own children? I think I've had enough... enough of this absurdity... Please someone wake me up from this nightmare!!"

""This is no dream, my friend," Nindhi said. "If you dismiss the truth, you will face the same fate, and eventually, you will find yourself alongside me."."

"That will never come to pass," Reena grunted.

"Reena, you don't have to take my word for it. You can uncover the truth yourself. With my assistance."

"Oh, and how can an armless lad shackled in chains possibly assist me?" Reena retorted sharply.

"By keeping a watch on your mother... I can guide you on how to uncover the truth yourself."

"You want me to spy on my mother?" Reena exclaimed. "How dare you suggest such a thing?" Her peacock eyes turned into something like the flaring sun in the summer.

"Either you choose my way or endure the relentless brutality of your mother for the rest of your life. The choice is yours," Nindhi said, his voice as calm as the sky outside.

"You are unbelievable," Reena spat. She turned around and began to walk towards the door. Apprehension surged in Nindhi's heart, and the facade of his tough demeanour began to crack. Rising from the floor, he said, "If you change your mind... all you need is a shard of a mirror to discover the tru..." The door slammed shut with a resounding bang, leaving Nindhi once again shrouded in darkness, companionless.

The rest of the day was spent in uneasy contemplation. Reena's quest for answers only raised more questions in her mind. She glanced at her mother thrice with doubt, harbouring the suspicion that she might be a witch. Overwhelmed by guilt, she slapped her own face violently, chastising herself for such thoughts. The answers she discovered behind the pink door filched her sleep. Frightening thoughts about her mother kept her awake all night. Cannibalism was a topic once discussed by the one-eyed master, in her dream, and it turned out to be the worst nightmare she ever experienced.

The next morning, she woke up late, the fearful thoughts of the night keeping her awake for most of it. Lost in contemplation, she went through her morning routine. Walking into the dining room, she found Bhushan boasting about waking up before her, again. Exasperated, she silently devoured her bowl of mugas with water.

The rest of the day was spent outside, sitting under the shade of a ficus tree, watching Bhushan and Lily play with Amma. Despite being called to join them, Reena remained seated, diligently working on her unfinished headband, all the while observing the scene in contemplative silence. The more Reena observed Amma's interactions with her siblings, the more she sensed the depth of her affection for them. Amma's tender and loving behaviour toward the siblings brought a wistful chuckle to Reena's lips. After playing for a while, Amma prepared to leave. She showered Lily and Bhushan with affectionate kisses before approaching Reena, where she placed a tender kiss on her cheek as well, before heading off to attend to her usual duties.

Suddenly, Nindhi's words erupted in her mind like a hurricane. "How can he make such vile accusations about my mother?" she muttered, her voice laced with anger and disbelief. Rising from the ground, she dashed toward the castle. With footsteps, ablaze with fury, Reena entered the room behind the pink door, where Nindhi was engrossed in his book, illuminated by the gentle light of the lantern. As he beheld Reena, she said, "Give me the shard of the mirror."

CHAPTER-8

The Good, Old Ficus

Nindhi's pale face, once again adorned with a wide smile. The lantern extinguished, and the chandeliers illuminated. Rising from his seat, he approached Reena.

"So, you've come to believe me now ?" he inquired.

"I do not," Reena retorted sharply. "I came here to prove you wrong about Amma."

They exchanged a glance, and Reena's eyes wandered to Nindhi's arms, noting with unease that they had grown an additional inch since the previous day.

"Your arms... they've regenerated?" Reena asked, a shiver of disbelief running down her spine.

"Told ya, didn't I?" He replied.

Reena's unwavering trust in her mother began to waver. Doubts gnawed at her: Could Nindhi be telling the truth about Amma? Was she merely overthinking, or had his arms truly grown an inch?

"You're familiar with witchcraft too, aren't you?" She asked, probing the matter further.

Nindhi directed his gaze towards the books on the table. They began to levitate, floating gracefully toward Reena and began to dance around her shoulders. "I believe this will address your query," he said softly.

Reena's thoughts were consumed by the pressing question, causing her to barely notice the floating books dancing around her. Driven by urgency, she prepared to voice the burning query on her mind. "If Amma is indeed a witch," Reena demanded, her eyes fixed on Nindhi, "then why did she keep you exposed behind the door for everyone to see? She could have easily hidden you with her magic or concealed the pink door from us altogether."

"Have you ever considered why she chose to keep me alive, confined in this room, while remaining hidden from all of you?" Nindhi chuckled, leaving Reena speechless and without a response.

"Allow me to share something with you: witchcraft comes with its own set of hindrances," Nindhi explained. "Each spellcraft has its own set of drawbacks; powerful magics might shorten one's lifespan, and others could bring about mysterious ailments. For instance, an invisibility charm, when maintained over extended periods, begins to exhibit flaws."

Nindhi shifted his gaze to the books that had been swirling around Reena. They gracefully descended and settled on the table. As the commotion subsided, one book floated upwards—*the family comic, Home Sweet Home*, which Reena had discovered near the Ficus tree.

"My book, I forgot it here yesterday," said Reena.

"Correct," said Nindhi. "The book belongs to me."

"No, it's mine. I found it near the tree," Reena asserted with a gruff tone.

"That is correct, but the book slipped out of my workshop inside the Ficus tree. The mishap was due to a flaw in the invisibility spell I cast on the tree, to conceal it from Amma. I anticipated this might happen, so I positioned the door of my workshop against the castle, hidden from its view. It's difficult to detect magical hitches from the castle, and I've been fortunate that Amma never noticed. If Amma had used an invisibility hex on this door, the hitches might have manifested in her absence too, especially with you around the house," Nindhi remarked steadily. "It would have compromised her plan."

Reena heard Nindhi's words but remained steadfast in her love for her mother. "You're quite the storyteller, aren't you?" she retorted, her tone laced with skepticism.

"If you think I'm spinning tales, then why did you come here with so many questions?" Nindhi growled, frustration evident in his voice. "Give it some time, and you might find yourself confined in this very room with me."

Silence enveloped Reena, her heart still seething with fury. Reluctantly, she sat with Nindhi as he began to explain everything to unravel the truth.

As the sun dipped below the horizon, casting hues of purple and red across the darkening sky, the evening unfolded with Bhushan and Lily's joyful playtime echoing through their bedroom. Meanwhile, in the kitchen, Amma was engrossed in preparing dinner. Reena approached the kitchen and said, "I am going for a walk, Amma."

"Alright, honey. I'll call you when dinner is ready," Amma replied warmly.

Reena confidently strode out of the main door, her determined steps carrying her towards the open expanse around the tree. Casting a cautious glance back at the house, she ensured no one was following her. Convinced of her safety, she stealthily approached the tree and concealed herself behind its sturdy trunk. With a piece of paper in hand, she carefully recited the mantra Nindhi had shared, transcribed with strokes onto the paper in her less-than-perfect handwriting.

Dvaram Udghateya Vidrohi Agatan!!

A luminous, silvery-white door-shaped glow materialized on the surface of the tree. Reena stood there, her jaw slightly agape, as she took in the unexpected sight before her. "A portal...," she murmured, her voice tinged with a mix of shock and realization.

Reena abided before the portal, her resolve wavering as a fierce internal struggle played out. The decision to step through or turn back weighed heavily on her mind. She considered retreating to the castle, driven by the urge to confront her mother about the unsettling revelations from the armless stranger behind the pink door. However, an unshakable feeling in her heart urged her to embark on a journey of self-discovery, compelling her to uncover the truth for herself. Ultimately, curiosity triumphed over hesitation. With a deep breath and a resolute heart, Reena extended her hand towards the silver glow. Her fingers, trembling yet determined, made contact with the portal, and in an instant, she was drawn into its otherworldly embrace.

As her eyes fluttered open, Reena found herself lying on a dusty floor that mirrored the colour of the tree's bark. The room she stood in was expansive and unlike anything in her house. It was constructed entirely of polished wood, with towering walls and a magnificent chandelier that hung gracefully from the ceiling. Books were scattered all over the floor, on arch-shaped desks, and in a giant arc-shaped book rack that was embedded into the circular walls.

Reena picked up one of the books from the floor, its cover emblazoned with the title "Gulliver's Travels." After analysing it for a moment, she casually tossed the book onto the pile of fallen volumes beside the rack. As Reena moved through the room, her attention was caught by a triangular object hidden beneath a dusty cloth. Despite her urgency, curiosity compelled her to lift the cloth, revealing the triangle and releasing a cloud of dust that made her cough. Clearing her eyes from the dust, Reena found herself face-to-face with a colossal, triangle-shaped object. Upon closer inspection, she realized it had a wooden base structure adorned with cloth, resembling a large, makeshift hut. The yellow cloth of the structure was patched with pieces of blue and crimson fabric, covering various torn sections. At the top, bizarre, bat-like wings were attached, one of which had fallen to the floor. Reena found herself captivated by this remarkable, art-like object, reminiscent of her own handcrafted headbands.

While fixating on the triangle-shaped object, Reena's gaze shifted to a nearby chair. Approaching it, she discovered a thick book resting on the seat. Picking up the hefty volume, She announced its title, "*Craftworks of Gnows.*" As Reena opened the book to page 365, a folded paper slipped out. Unfurling it, she found a drawing of the yellow triangle-shaped object that stood before her, meticulously detailed. Amidst the scribbles, one bold phrase stood out: "*The Flying Tent.*" Her eyes widened with realization. "So this was what Nindhi mentioned," she murmured, captivated by the revelation.

Relishing the novelty of a revolving chair, Reena took a seat and let it spin. Though the chair, fashioned from rough-hewn wood and marred by protruding splinters, was far from perfect, it marked Reena's first encounter with such a piece of furniture. She closed the book, allowing it to fall onto the floor, and immersed herself in the joy of spinning on the chair. Her amusement, however, was short-lived as the chair abruptly broke, sending Reena crashing to the floor with a resounding thud.

Straightening herself, she brushed off the dust from her clothes and a faint call of her name echoed through the room. "Devil's eye... Amma is calling." She panicked and sprinted toward the arc-shaped desk, her feet crunching over scattered books as she fumbled to yank open the drawer. Another louder call echoed through the space as Amma's voice, now tinged with worry. The urgency in her mother's tone sent Reena's heart racing, the fear of being discovered heightening her anxiety.

Frantically rifling through the contents of the drawer, Reena's fingers were scrambling to locate the object Nindhi had described. The calls from Amma grew increasingly insistent. With time slipping away, Reena's heart raced as she finally unearthed a wrapped cloth buried in one of the drawers, after several frantic attempts. Hastily unwrapping the cloth, she discovered a shard of mirror. As she glimpsed her reflection, she noted its contrast to the grand, gold-framed mirror from her dream—this one was smaller and less ornate. Quickly, she rewrapped the mirror and secured it behind the elastic of her pajami, ensuring it was hidden and protected.

"Where were you?" asked Amma, worrying tinged in her voice.

"Sorry, Amma... I got lost in my thoughts for a while," said Reena, glancing at Amma, sitting serenely under the shade of the tree. "I've come up with a fresh concept for a headband." She rose and made her way back to the castle, with Amma trailing closely behind her.

Seated around the dinner table, they shared a meal of Mugas. As Amma hurried toward the kitchen, Reena's thoughts lingered on Amma, troubled by the unsettling truths Nindhi had revealed—truths that seemed to carry a disturbing weight of validity. The question dawdled in her mind: What if Nindhi was right about her mother?

Recollections of Nindhi's words echoed in Reena's mind as she contemplated the authenticity of his claims. She couldn't shake the doubt that gnawed at her. His workshop was exactly where he said it would be, which only raised more questions. Did his arms truly regenerate as he had asserted? A sudden realization struck her: "If Nindhi possesses the ability to regenerate or heal, then so do I."

Raising her left hand, which bore a wound inflicted by a needle, Reena unwrapped the silver thread, revealing the slightly brown and rough flower petals concealing her injury. She expunged the petals and gape at her finger, the wound was still unhealed and marginally painful. "He was lying about Mother," she murmured, emotions swirling between satisfaction and anger. "I am going to prove him wrong, and then I will tell Amma."

The bowl of Mugas became increasingly challenging to consume after Nindhi's revelation about its unconventional ingredients: a concoction of lizards, insects, and magical potions. Doubt crept in as she considered the possibility that Nindhi might have lied about the food, just as he had claimed Amma was a witch. Yet, despite the unsettling revelations, Reena pressed on, determined to uncover the truth hidden beneath the layers of deception.

After finishing their dinner and receiving tender kisses from Amma, they retired for the night, lulled into sleep by the soothing cadence of a bedtime story.

In the quiet of the night, Reena's eyes flickered open. Determination ignited within her as she awoke from her slumber, ready to undertake whatever was necessary to disprove Nindhi's claims. Silently, she retrieved a shard of mirror, wrapped in cloth, from beneath her mattress.

With resolve, Reena stood up, preparing to navigate the shadowy, dimly lit house. The only sound accompanying her was the rhythmic beat of her heart, creating a haunting melody in the stillness of the night. The mirror clutched in her hand seemed to hold secrets she was determined to unveil. She embarked on a journey poised to unravel the truths and lies intricately woven into the fabric of her reality.

CHAPTER-9

A Shard of Mirror

In the corridor of the castle, ominous and haunting like a ghostly spectre, Reena made her way towards Amma's room. The air was thick with a steep, unsettling aroma that added to the pervasive eeriness of the night. The murky, melancholic shadows of the dimly lit walls seemed to whisper words of mercy in her ear: *"Retreat."* Warning her to go back to the bed and sleep. The cloister, shrouded in darkness, found solace only in the feeble glow of moonlight seeping through the oriel windows, casting eerie rectangles on the checkered floor. Fear gripped Reena—not only the fear of disobeying Amma but also the looming dread of encountering another ominous horror concealed within the depths of her reality. The grim thoughts of her mother being a cannibal witch ran rampant in her head.

Fueled by both ego and love, Reena was flared to prove Nindhi awry. *But what if Nindhi is right? What if Amma is truly a cannibal witch? If that's the case, what are they to do?* The questions pounded in her mind, escalating into a throbbing headache. As she was marching, her feet came to an abrupt halt. Her visage was bathed in a brilliant glimmer from the moon as she turned towards the window. Gazing outside, she witnessed that the ground was glowing with the ethereal brilliance of a full moon. The grass below seemed to sway in a graceful dance with the breeze as if celebrating Reena's sinister quest into a realm from which retreat might be impossible. Even the inky night, overwhelmed by the gleaming moon, felt unsettling and threatening to her.

"What a terrifyingly beautiful view," she murmured, the size of her heart seeming to expand with each fleeting moment. Yet, she pressed forward. Tiptoeing across the floor, Reena approached Amma's door. It loomed large and foreboding, exuding an unsettling aura as if death itself were lying in wait on the other side. With her delicate, rose-stem-like fingers trembling uncontrollably, she grasped the doorknob and turned it, slowly.

Click... Click!!

"Devil's eye, the door is locked from the inside," she whispered. Leaning her back against the wall beside the door, Reena pondered whether to retreat or continue the task. However, her gaze was irresistibly drawn to the main door.

"What if I could sneak inside through the window at the back of the house?" She mumbled to herself, her voice barely a whisper in the still night. Approaching the main door, she softly unclicked the latch and left it ajar as she paused to take in the mesmerizingly ravishing landscape before her. She conscientiously closed the door behind her, making sure not a whisper of sound escaped. With deliberate steps, she headed toward the back of the house, her heart, still battering against her strut.

The alluring landscape, dancing under the gleaming moonlight, appears to morph into something even haunting. As the thought of a lurking monster crossed her mind, her heart raced even faster. What if a creature, something akin to a werewolf, awaited her beneath the moonlight? Her feet quickened, driven by escalating fear, and she rapidly marched toward the rear.

Reena stood at the back of the house, her eyes wide with angst. She leered at one of the opened windows, allowing the fresh breeze to pass through. A tornado of mixed thoughts was whirling rapidly in her dome, unlocking a new fear – the fear of getting caught. Harrowing images of Amma with sharp teeth piercing through her belly, and feasting upon her flesh were playing vividly in her mind, fueled by the wild imagination taking hold.

Yet, Reena swiftly reassured herself that these were mere figments of her imagination. She had known her mother for years. Amma was a kind, caring, and virtuous human being—the role model she aspired to impersonate. Today, she was determined to prove Nindhi wrong. Once she succeeded, a life of happiness and peace with her mother, free from doubt and fear, would resume. And she would never doubt Amma again. Ever.

Lifting her arms, Reena gripped the window ledge tightly. With a controlled pull, she hoisted herself up, settling onto the ledge while balancing her weight with careful precision. She peeked into the room, her eyes adjusting to the dim light, and observed Amma peacefully sleeping on her bed, the room filled with the soft, rhythmic sounds of her gentle snores.

A sudden thought crossed her mind, she resolved to catch a glimpse of Amma's reflection in the mirror from the window ledge. With deliberate care, she retrieved the mirror from the folds of her pajami, extending her arm with utmost effort and leaning forward into the room, straining to capture Amma's image. However, angling the mirror to capture the reflection proved challenging. Reena drew back, wrapping the mirror in her hands, and paused to contemplate her next move. Removing her slippers, she tossed them onto the dazzling grass behind her. Bathed in the moon's silvery light, which cast a rectangular glow from the window onto the floor, she stepped into the dimly lit, medium-sized room barefoot. Despite the darkness, Reena moved effortlessly through the familiar space. Her intimate knowledge of every nook and cranny stemmed from years of meticulous cleaning and care. As she stepped onto the floor, a chill crept from her feet up to her spine. On all fours, she moved stealthily with the horrifying music of her beating heart, clutching the mirror wrapped in cloth between her teeth. As she neared her mother's bed, she leaned gently against it, shifting her hips, she adjusted her position toward the head of the standard bed without storage, flanked by a narrow, one-foot-wide table positioned next to the headboard. On the table's surface rested a glass, a jug, a flower vase, and three books.

Taking her position, Reena leaned against the table with her shoulder brushing its edge. Despite her trembling hands, she unwrapped the mirror. She held it aloft, angling it carefully to catch the reflection of her mother. Adjusting her hand to the moonlight streaming through the window, she glimpsed her mother's face, and her breath snagged in her throat. The sight before her compelled her to press her left hand firmly against her flimsy lips, stifling the scream that threatened to escape.

Tears streamed down her face like a relentless waterfall, and it was an immense struggle to contain the overwhelming surge of emotions. What lay in the reflection was beyond terrifying—it was ugly, gruesome, frightening, scallywag, hideous, and menacing. Her heart swelled, and a lump formed in her throat, making it nearly impossible to breathe. The one-eyed master of her dreams, once a source of dread, seemed pale in comparison to the ghastly entity reflected in the mirror.

What she saw was a pale, white face marred by a twisted honeycomb pattern of distorted holes in the skin. A gruesome, slimy tongue, the same as octopus tentacles, dangled from her mouth, while thick hair, like snake tails, writhed as if alive.

What Reena saw exceeded her wildest nightmares. She had set out to prove Nindhi wrong, but the reflection in the mirror painted starkly a different tale. She kept her eyes fixed on Amma through the mirror, adjusting her view from various angles with tear-streaked eyes. It was almost impossible to accept that her mother possessed such a horrifying visage. Driven by desperation, Reena raised her trembling hand even higher, trying to view her mother from a different angle, hoping the reflection might change. However, the mirror revealed something even more terrifying. An array of countless glowing eyes, each varying in colour, size, and structure, stared back at her from the mirror. Swiftly, she pulled her hand back, her eyes widening in terror.

A yawn echoed through the room, and Reena's heart began to beat like the trumpet. At this point, she knew that her mother had woken up. Settled onto the bed, Amma was caught between wakefulness and slumber. Reena blanketed with fear, pressed her back against the bed, desperately wanting to move but finding herself unable to do so in that moment. Amma remained seated and reached for the jug of water and glass on the table. The sound of the water pouring and gulping, similar to the gargles of some sinister creature, was rumbling through the air, while Amma was drinking. Then, she placed the jug and glass back on the table and yawned once more. A glimmer of hope flickered within Reena as she dared to think, *Maybe Mother is going back to sleep.*

"It's too cold in here; I must close the windows," Amma mumbled. Reena's heart sank at the words, her fear of being discovered by her mother coming to vivid reality. As Amma began to stir and attempt to get out of bed, Reena caught a glimpse from the corner of her eye, of her mother's legs dangling over the edge—a clear indication of her intention to rise. Slipping into her slippers, Amma rose from the bed, stretching her arms with another yawn. She turned towards the table, walked over, and adjusted the flower vase. Meandering around the bed, she eventually reached the window. With a swift motion, she drew the window shut, sealing out the biting chill of the night. Meanwhile, from her concealed refuge beneath the bed, Reena watched her mother's every move, relieved that she had managed to remain hidden just in time.

Through the sliver of space created by the bed sheet cascading from the mattress, she watched her mother's feet traverse the room. The thunderous bang of the windows slamming shut deepened the grimness of her situation. Her heart pounded relentlessly, each beat amplifying her fear, as she worried that Amma might hear the frantic rhythm of her thudding heart. After securing the two windows on the opposite side, Amma turned her attention to the one Reena had used to enter. With a decisive, resonant bang, she shut and latched it firmly. The click of a latch heightened her terror. Now, two beings occupied the locked room: one was an ordinary human, and the other, a fearsome cannibal witch.

Reena was horror-stricken, her mind racing with anguished thoughts of how to escape the room now that the windows were securely locked.

Amma moved toward the bed, but instead of climbing onto it, she stood beside it, her feet pointing toward the nearby table. From her hiding spot, Reena watched intently. The familiar sounds of water being poured and swallowed reached her ears—Amma was drinking water again. A thud resonated as the glass was placed back onto the table.

Amma's feet then pivoted towards the bed, and a drawn-out yawn signalled her readiness to return to rest. Reena felt a wave of relief; Amma was going back to sleep, finally. However, The feet turned toward the table once more, leaving Reena to wonder, 'Why did she turn towards the table again?' Soon, Amma's knees touched the floor, and Reena, thunderstruck, realized that Amma might be trying to peek under the bed. Panic surged through her. A threatening hand suddenly reached in, gripping the bedsheet and yanking it upward. Amma's dread-filled face appeared beneath the bed, her cold emerald eyes scanning meticulously but all she discovered was an old cardboard box, untouched and forgotten for ages. "I'm imagining things again;

there's no one under the bed," Amma mumbled, before climbing back onto the bed.

Hidden behind the old cardboard box, in time, Reena almost folded herself like a ball, she strained to decipher Amma's actions through the sounds she made. It was a close call, she thought. The audible cues of Amma settling down on the bed reached her ears. For the moment, Reena had been spared, but the challenge of escaping the room now seemed insurmountable.

Her mind raced for an escape plan, and she felt a glimmer of luck at having the cardboard box as a cover. Reflecting on past moments, Reena remembered advising Amma against keeping the box under the bed during cleaning sessions. However, she was relieved that Amma had dismissed her advice and allowed the box to remain.

Reena cautiously dragged herself, attempting to reach the end of the bed for a getaway, but the palpable awareness that Amma was still awake loomed heavily over her.

The room suddenly brightened as the light flicked on, plunging Reena into fresh dismay. What if Amma decided to inspect under the bed now that the light was on? Anxiously, she scanned every angle for a glimpse of Amma's feet, but none appeared. Amma hadn't left the bed. Reena strained to listen and heard the soft rustle of book pages, punctuated by faint, playful giggles. Confused, Reena wondered if Amma was reading a book, perhaps "The Comedy of Errors," which she had once mentioned was amusing. Lying on the cold floor beneath the bed, she waited.

As she listened to the laughter, a whirlwind of thoughts swirled in Reena's mind. Is Amma truly a witch? What if Nindhi was lying? Could he have jinxed the mirror, distorting her perception of Amma? What if Amma is just a normal human, fiercely protective of her children? The questions multiplied, churning into a tumultuous storm within Reena's mind. A fleeting sense of relief washed over her as she remembered witnessing Nindhi perform magic in the pink door room, where objects had floated in midair.

Overwhelmed by the recent thoughts, Reena decided to confront Nindhi about the accusations and prove him wrong. How could an evil witch laugh so heartily when alone? Wasn't she supposed to be plotting to devour her children, as the stories claimed? This laughter convinced Reena that Nindhi was a deceiver, trying to manipulate her into turning against her beloved Amma.

Lost in thoughts, a sudden thud snapped her attention. Investigating the sound, she discovered a book that had fallen to the floor. Drawing back the bedsheet for a clearer view, she recognized the book as Amma's—*The Comedy of Errors*. As she stared at it in disbelief, the book floated in mid-air, reminiscent of the magic she had seen in Nindhi's room. Stretching her head out from under the bed, she saw the floating book gently settle into Amma's hand, settled above the bed.

Reena pulled back under the bed, grateful once again that Amma hadn't noticed her. Her thoughts, however, scattered. The defences she had prepared to shield Amma against Nindhi's accusations evaporated. The once comforting sounds of her mother's giggles, turning pages, and warm laughter now seemed hideous and tears began to stream down her face.

In the midst of Amma's laughter and the sound of her reading, Reena silently accepted the disheartening truth: her mother was indeed a cannibal witch. As Amma chuckled over her book, Reena wept silently beneath the bed, her hands pressed tightly against her lips. Her heart, once racing with fear, seemed to surrender to the grim reality, as it had already accepted its demise.

After nearly an hour, Amma began to grow drowsy. She placed the book back on the table and turned off the light. Reena waited patiently in the darkness. As the room was filled with snores, she emerged from beneath the bed. Making her way to the door, she unlocked the latch. With silent tears streaming down her face, Reena slipped out of the room, leaving behind the chilling truth she had uncovered.

CHAPTER-10

Decisions at the Dagger's Edge

Extending her arms in a full stretch and releasing a languid yawn, in the morning, Amma woke up. Rising from bed and slipping into her slippers, she made her way to the lavatory, adhering to her daily morning routine. Afterwards, she donned a cyan saree, adorned her forehead with a diamond-shaped bindi, and then proceeded towards the door. To her surprise, the latch was already unfastened. *"Who opened the latch on my door?"* she wondered, briefly considering the possibility that she might have forgotten to secure it the night before. Shrugging it off, she proceeded to the kitchen to prepare breakfast for her children.

The trio of children sat at the table, with Lily and Bhushan engrossed in an epic battle involving a slingshot and a doll perched atop the table. Laughter and playful banter filled the aura as the two siblings revelled in their morning game. However, Reena sat in silence, her eyes swollen from a night spent crying. The dreadful reflection she had seen in the mirror haunted her introspections. No longer contemplating defending her mother, Reena had witnessed Amma's abilities firsthand, including levitating the book in mid-air. Every word spoken by Nindhi seemed to materialize before her eyes. Terrified and tormented, she grappled with the grim reality of Amma's darkest secret. The prospect of continuing to live with her mother after learning the truth left her feeling anxious—an unfamiliar and unbearable sensation for Reena, who had never experienced it before.

"Who wants to eat a delicious-delicious breakfast?" a singing voice reached Reena's ears. Turning her head toward the source, she saw

Amma approaching with a steaming pot, her wide morning smile as radiant as ever. Reena's face turned pale, her fear overwhelming her to the point where she dropped her bowl onto the floor in a sudden, involuntary reaction.

"Devil's eye... careful, my kitten," Amma said, noticing the dropped bowl. She retrieved it and placed it back on the table. Reena remained silent, struggling to hide her fear from Amma. Revealing her fear was the last thing she wanted, as it would inevitably lead Amma to ask a multitude of questions—an outcome she was most eager to avoid.

After serving everyone, Amma turned to leave. Walking back toward her room, she paused and called out to Reena, "Join me after breakfast, honey. There's something I need to discuss." The words hung in the air, and Reena heard them with a jolt of alarm. Her mind raced with troubling thoughts—was Amma aware of her presence in the room last night? Had Amma somehow figured it out, perhaps through the unlocked latch, or had she used some form of magic to detect that I was there? Uncertainty loomed over her as she pondered the impending conversation with Amma.

Reena's pace of eating mugas slowed down, as the prospect of meeting Amma brewed ahead. She hesitated, secretly hoping her siblings would invite her to play, providing an excuse to postpone the meeting. However, that day, none of them extended an invitation. As her siblings finished their meals and gleefully ran outside, Reena was left alone at the table.

Eventually, slim to no morsel remained in Reena's bowl, and she knew it was time to face the impending conversation with her mother. As she reluctantly approached Amma's room, her heart raced. In her imagination, she pictured a nightmarish scenario of being brutally torn limb from limb by Amma. The fear weighed heavily on her, causing her pace to falter as the urge to turn back and hide from Amma grew stronger. Despite her hesitation, she pressed on. Reaching Amma's door, she timidly knocked.

"Come in, Reena, the door's open," Amma called out.

Reena pushed the door open with a hollow creak and stepped into the room. Amma, seated on the bed, was absorbed in folding clothes.

"Do you know why I called you here?" Amma asked, her attention still on the clothes.

"No," replied Reena.

"Do you know what happened yesterday?"

"W-What happened yesterday?" She asked nervously.

"Are you certain you don't know anything?" Amma continued folding clothes, avoiding eye contact with Reena.

"No, I don't. Did Bhushan tell you something? You know how he is—he might have spun a tale from a dream and passed it off as reality. He's quite the imaginative storyteller," Reena replied, feigning confidence.

Amma fixed a terrifying gaze on Reena, with her eyes multiplying eerily and an octopus tongue dangling from her lips. Startled, Reena instinctively stepped backwards, colliding with the door behind her.

"My devilness! Are you alright?" Amma asked, her voice tinged with genuine concern.

Reena, still shaken, glanced at Amma again. The unsettling features had disappeared, and before her stood Amma with a perfectly human, beautiful face. Reena took a deep breath and regained her composure.

"Amma, I-I'm not feeling well," she stammered.

Amma, with a mischievous glint in her eyes, unfolded a stunning pink lehenga from the pile of clothes.

"I was just messing with you, my kitten, but I think I chose a bad day," Amma giggled.

She handed the lehenga to Reena and instructed her to return to her room and rest.

Reena exited the room, using her excuse of not feeling well helped her to make a quick escape. As she walked back to her own room, intense fear and anxiety gripped her, leaving her apprehensive about what the future might hold. She couldn't shake the unsettling thought that, like Nindhi had warned, Amma might one day confine her to a room and feast on her limbs to satisfy her insatiable hunger. The fear weighed heavily upon her, leaving her not only frightened but also heartbroken. Her bond with her mother ran deep; she had always seen Amma as the most understanding person in her life. Amma was not just her mother; she was her inspiration, someone Reena aspired to become. Her love for Amma was wholehearted, and she never fathomed that her mother could be one of the monsters from the tales she had heard. The revelation shattered the image of Amma she had cherished in her heart. Almost a year ago, she had an odd inkling that Amma might be hiding something from her, but the notion of her being a cannibal witch was beyond her wildest imagination. Despite lingering doubts and suspicions, her love for her mother remained genuine. Now, in the face of revelation, she was overwhelmed by heartbreak and dread. The internal turmoil she had always experienced reached new depths, tangled in an intricate web of conflicting emotions. It was as if an army of tornadoes raged within her, making it agonizingly challenging to navigate through her feelings.

She carefully placed the lehenga in the cupboard and reclined on her bed, her gaze fixed on the ceiling. After a while, an intense headache gripped her, as if countless sharp needles were piercing through her skull. The chaotic thoughts swirling in her mind seemed to be driving her to the brink of madness. Clasping her hands to her temples, she pressed firmly, seeking relief as the pain gradually subsided. Amidst this turmoil, the sudden sound of the main door slamming echoed through the house. Curious, she went to investigate and saw Amma walking away, from one of the oriel windows, heading beyond the wall as usual. Reena returned to her room and lay on the bed, feeling a profound sense of lifelessness. After a few minutes of contemplation, she resolved to visit Nindhi.

She entered the pink door room. It was as dim as ever, but this time, the moment she stepped in, light began to flood the room, casting a warm glow across the space.

"So, you discovered the truth?" Nindhi inquired, seated comfortably on his sofa.

"Yes," Reena responded.

"Good. Look, we don't have much time left. You are turning thirteen soon, and..."

"Yes, I know, and that's what I came here to talk about."

CHAPTER-11

Echoes of Discord

"That's exactly what I'm saying... Now, you know the truth, we need to work together to get out of this," Nindhi said, his words coming out in a rush.

"No," Reena replied, her eyes fixed on the floor.

Something hits Nindhi like the lightning, his eyes widening in disbelief at Reena's unexpected response.

"No? Don't want to get out of this terrifying place?"

No," Reena replied, her eyes still fixed on the floor. When she finally lifted her gaze to answer Nindhi, she was met with a horrifying sight: his head was missing from his neck, as if brutally severed, exposing raw bone and nerves. Soon, Like writhing maggots spilling from a wound, numerous eyes began to emerge from the hole in his severed neck—eyes of various colours, reminiscent of the reflection she had seen in the mirror. The eyes floated into the air like balloons, inflating to the size almost of heads, with nerve threads trailing from the gaping neck.

The eyes stared at Reena with an eerie, lifeless gaze. Some of them burst into unsettling laughter, while others wept tears of scarlet. Still, some burned with a fierce anger, clearly directed at her. Blood sprayed from the neck like a raging hot geyser, and the eyes emitted a high-pitched, vexatious screech that gave Reena a pounding headache. "KEEYTENN..." A raspy voice echoed through. She turned to see Amma standing at the door. Fear paralyzed her. Amma's face was twisted with rage, and Reena's heart pounded violently against her ribs. With a furious intensity, Amma began to sail toward her. Bracing herself for the impending harm, Reena squeezed her eyes shut.

Reena... Reena... Reena.

Reena opened her eyes to find Nindhi standing before her.

"ARE YOU EVEN LISTENING TO ME?" Nindhi hollered, shaking his arms, which had now grown up to the wrists but were still handless.

"Don't you want to escape with me?" Nindhi asked, worry etched clearly on his face.

"No, I don't," she replied.

"Have you lost your mind? Haven't you seen the true nature of your mother?" he demanded, shaking his arms more vigorously.

"I think this is our destiny. We're meant to be slaughtered by Amma."

Nindhi's jaw dropped. "What on earth are you talking about, Reena? Just cut the baloney and help me and your siblings escape."

"Escape... I don't want to escape!! And even if I did, where would we go?"

"Any place would be better than this," Nindhi replied.

"Have you ever been outside, Nindhi? Have you ever witnessed what lies in the world outside?" Reena demanded, her body rigid and her fists clenched with frustration.

"No, I didn't."

"Then I don't understand what makes you think about escaping this place!"

"Are you serious, you dimwitted fool? Just look at me—I am held as a prisoner by your mother. I AM BEING TORTURED BY

HER TO SATISFY HER HUNGER! SHE CHOPS OFF MY LEGS AND ARMS. SHE COOKS THEM RIGHT IN FRONT OF ME AND EATS THEM WHILE LOOKING DEAD INTO MY EYES... Sometimes she even criticizes my flesh, remarking how its flavour deteriorates with each passing day. AND YOU QUESTION WHY I DESIRE TO FLEE? DO YOU EVEN COMPREHEND WHAT IT FEELS LIKE!?

"Hmm," a nonchalant hum slipped her lips as she fixed her gaze on the floor once more. The indifferent sound suggested she was not particularly interested in Nindhi's story, but he persisted nonetheless. His words reverberated through the room, laden with frustration and anger. "Do you know how excruciating it is when your mother serves my limbs? She slices them as slowly as possible and relishes my gut-wrenching screams. She is a psychopath, she is a homicidal maniac; she knows growing back limbs is the most agonizing part, but she laughs at it. SHE FINDS AMUSEMENT IN MY SUFFERING. My anguish is nothing more than a jest to her. SO YES, ANYTHING BEYOND THIS NIGHTMARISH EXISTENCE WOULD BE PREFERABLE!"

"But escaping is not feasible, Nindhi. Lily is far too young, and even if we were to flee, protecting her would be nearly impossible. Bhushan would never believe me, even if I tried to explain, and you—you're chained up. How exactly do you intend to help us?" Reena asked.

"You just need to follow my instructions. I have a plan, and if we stick to it, we'll make it out," Nindhi replied with unwavering confidence.

"I can't bring myself to do it, Nindhi," Reena said, her voice trembling. "Do you understand the depth of this anguish? I adored Amma and always looked up to her. It's excruciating to realize that we were merely raised to be livestock. The pain is unbearable; I-I wish I had never been born. I'm experiencing something I've never felt before. Should I hate her or continue to love her as I always have? It's tormenting... I don't know what to do; to me, death seems like the only visible escape." Her hands shook with anxiety, and tears streamed down her cheeks.

Nindhi responded urgently, "Don't be naive, Reena. She's a malevolent, manipulative witch who only wants to consume you. After seeing her true nature, don't even consider loving her."

Reena collapsed to her knees, her tears cascading like a torrent. Her cries, raw and anguished, echoed with a profound sense of despair.

"Stop crying, Reena," Nindhi urged, trying to soothe her. "Listen to me. I need you to go to the workshop inside the tree and start working on the flying tent you saw there. I'll guide you through it. We'll escape this dreadful place together."

Reena remained silent, her body trembling as she knelt on the floor, tears streaming uncontrollably.

Reena...Reena...Reena

"REENA, ENOUGH OF THIS ENDLESS CRYING. YOU NEED TO TAKE ACTION. BEING A HOPELESS WIMP WON'T HELP YOU GET OUT OF HERE," Nindhi snapped, his voice sharp with frustration. The words reverberated through the room.

"WHY SHOULD I TAKE ORDERS FROM YOU? WHY SHOULD I TRUST YOU? YOU'RE JUST A STRANGE LAD WHO DEVOURS HIS OWN FLESH. WHAT IF THIS MIRROR IS SIMPLY A DEVICE YOU'RE USING TO INCRIMINATE MY MOTHER!?" Reena barked, rising from the floor. Her teeth clenched, and tears continued to stream down her face.

"Just look at me, Reena. Look at my hands," said Nindhi, his voice trembling, lifting his arm-less limbs for her to see. You saw them regenerating... You know I'm not lying. Amma Meiga will come again and cut off my limbs when her hunger strikes, I am suffering... I need your help, please, I beg you."

"Not my Pooka to ride!!" answered Reena, cold enough to freeze the room.

"Are you... Are you serious, Reena!?" Nindhi asked, his heart almost turned to ice and was cleaved in two.

"You are the only hope I've seen in years. This should concern you as well. Today, I am the one suffering, but soon, you might find yourself in my place. The only way to escape this nightmare is by following my lead. Together, we can break free from this hellish existence."

"Nindhi, you're delusional. Your outlandish claims are preposterous, and there must be some absurd explanation for this mirror nonsense. Amma is the one who truly understands me. She is the only one who has always grasped my feelings," Reena scoffed.

"That's because, beside her, you've never met anyone else. It's you who's deluding yourself," Nindhi retorted.

Reena's mouth was sealed like it had been sewn shut with a needle; she was left speechless. Without uttering a word, she turned and began to walk briskly towards the door.

"Are you leaving?" asked Nindhi, a wave of panic surging through him. "Reena, I'm the only way... I can save you and your siblin..."

Bang! With a deafening sound, the door slammed shut as Reena strode back towards her room.

CHAPTER-12

Peaceful Slumber

Days turned into a blur as Reena, despite her inner turmoil, maintained a facade of normalcy for her family's sake. Juggling her behaviour became her mundane routine. Night after night, restful sleep eluded her, replaced by relentless panic attacks. Although the nightmares had ceased, tranquillity remained out of reach. Occasionally, when she managed to fall asleep, clangorous and horrifying screams jolted her awake. The corridors echoed with phantom conversations, vanishing into emptiness, whenever she investigates. The shadows of her unsettling dreams blurred with reality, leaving her in a perpetual state of unease.

Reena was in hysteria. The disquieting details of her mother's behaviour were revealed. Bizarre observations about Amma, once overlooked, now haunted her thoughts. There was a peculiar desire in Amma's eyes whenever she looked at the children, a lust that sent shudders down Reena's crest. The way Amma kissed her siblings was followed by an odd, hound-like sniffing, reminiscent of eerie tales her mother used to read about wolves sniffing lambs before devouring. She also observed that Amma persistently encouraged them to eat more mugas, seemingly intent on fattening them up to enhance their fleshiness and richness, presumably for her own consumption.

Maintaining the pretence of normalcy was becoming increasingly challenging for Reena; while outwardly she feigned composure, internally she was fractured. Feigning cheerfulness while playing with her siblings and putting on a smile for her mother grew increasingly burdensome, as her emotions remained suppressed. During the daytime, she sought out secluded places to cry, but the tears offered no relief from her anguish. She yearned for someone to confide in, to share her heavy heart, to offer a comforting embrace, and to assure her that everything would eventually be okay. Unfortunately, this longing remained just wishful thinking, leaving Reena feeling profoundly isolated in her turmoil.

One day, after breakfast, while playing the game of seven stones outside. Suddenly, Reena snapped. Abandoning the game and leaving her siblings behind, she began picking up the stones scattered on the ground, which had been struck by Bhushan.

"Hey! Why are you disrupting the game, Reena? The turn is mine, not yours," Bhushan barked, his confusion and frustration evident in his tone.

No reply was given by Reena.

"Reena... I'm talking to you," Bhushan said, his voice quivering with a tinge of fear.

Reena gathered all the stones and left her bewildered siblings by the ficus tree. She carried them to the back of the castle and set them down beside a large boulder, roughly the size of Bhushan's hat. After observing the stones for a moment, she went back inside the house. When she returned a few minutes later, she began stacking the stones, mimicking the arrangement from the game of seven stones. Once the stack was assembled, she drew a smiley face on it using the blood from her punctured finger, which she had pressed between her teeth to draw out. The small wound healed almost immediately as she sketched two dots for eyes and an arc for a smile. Reena sat back on a large stone, her gaze fixed on her creation, lost in contemplation.

"Hello, my Stoney friend," she began, addressing the stone with a gentle voice. "I'm Reena. I'm talking to you because I don't have anyone else to confide in. What do you think of the name Stoney, huh?"

"I live here with my family—my younger brother, my sister, and… Amma. We used to be one happy family. Amma, especially, used to love us so much," Reena said with a wistful smile. "But everything changed when I came face to face with the monster behind the pink door." she sighed.

"Do you know what it's like to have a family? Not a perfect one, but a family where everyone loves you? There's a caring mother, an annoying yet loving brother, and a little sister who's adorable in every way," she confided to the stone.

"But then, your path crosses with a stranger who claims that your mother plans to devour you when you grow up. Initially, you dismiss it, unable to fathom such a horrifying notion. Yet, as you delve into the truth, the unsettling reality becomes undeniable," she confessed, her head bowed, tears streaming down her cheeks.

"I honestly couldn't accept his words at first, but…" Reena gestured toward the stone, her voice heavy with resignation. "Just look at my finger… It's completely healed. Every revelation Nindhi made about my mother is coming to pass before my very eyes. It's more horrifying than any nightmare I've ever endured." Reena pressed her hands over her eyes, trying to stifle the cascade of tears.

"Do you know what it's like when your own mother harbours a monstrous desire to devour you, to inflict pain and suffering upon you? Is Lily… s-she's just a child, destined to be her victim as well?" She questioned, pulling her hands away from her tear-streaked face and gazing mournfully at the stone's painted smile. Observing the stone's cheerful expression, her voice tinged with bitterness. "Look at you, grinning so happily while I suffer. You're just like my mother."

A heavy silence lingered, broken only by the soft rustling of leaves in the breeze. Then, she spoke again, "I want to die." Retrieving a knife from the fold of her trousers she had taken from the kitchen, she displayed it to the smiling pile of stones. "But I can't bring myself to end it all, no matter how much I want to. The only way out seems to be killing Amma, but that's an impossible feat. Failure would mean being her prisoner before time, condemned to a lifetime of torment. All we yearn for is a semblance of peace in the days we have left." The knife slipped from her grasp, and she wrapped her arms around her shoulders, a palpable sense of despair enveloping her.

"I don't know why I'm pouring my heart out to you. You're no more than a pile of stones. I long to confide in Bhushan, but what if he dismisses the reality as my delusions? What if he betrays me and informs Amma? Our fate would be sealed," Reena's voice trembled with palpable distress, her anxiety nearly suffocating.

""Well, I suppose by sharing my secrets with you, we've become friends, haven't we? I remember reading something like that in a comic book," Reena said, dabbing at her tears. Suddenly, a burst of laughter escaped her, and she added, "There's one more secret I'm eager to share." She moved closer to the stone as if it had human ears, and whispered, "I will end my life in your arms, dear Stoney." Her laughter grew louder, tinged with a touch of madness. She seized the knife from the ground and thrust it into her abdomen. The blade cut through flesh, blood flowing from the deep, gaping slit. Breathless and wracked with intense pain, Reena remained silent, refusing to scream. She pulled the knife out, its blade slick with blood, and within moments, the wound closed up completely, leaving no scar behind. The searing pain was soon replaced by a strange, unsettling pleasure. This perverse cycle pushed Reena further toward the edge of sanity.

Once again, gripping the knife, Reena shoves it into her gut—again, and again, and again. "Die, you pathetic weakling!" she shrieked, her words punctuated by frenzied, hollow laughter. The relentless sound of the knife's blade slicing through flesh reverberated in the air, mingling with the haunting screech of metal and Reena's manic laughter, creating a disturbing symphony of anguish and madness. "HA...HA...HA... DIE!, DIE!, DIE!" Her tears consorted with the harrowing laughter. The once-green grass was now soaked in a crimson juice, and a splatter of blood marred Stoney's face with a macabre red stain.

Even after relentlessly stabbing herself, the bloodied slits healed almost instantaneously, as if defying the laws of nature. Eventually, overwhelmed by sheer exhaustion, she stopped, her energy was spent. A final, manic laugh escaped her lips before she crumpled to the ground. Though the wounds healed seamlessly, her dress remained soaked in a dark, chilling crimson. She lay on the ground with the red grass beneath and floating into something, making her eyes shut. It was a troubled yet oddly serene shuteye as if her mind had found respite from the turmoil that had consumed her. Enveloped in her own blood, She drifted into the most serene sleep she had experienced in a long time.

CHAPTER-13

All Eyes on Cake

A span of hours slipped away. When Reena awoke, she found herself sitting on the ground, her clothes stained with deep red and smeared with patches of mud blended with crimson. The earth beneath her had also taken on a matching shade of red, clinging to her from head to toe. Strands of her hair were matted together, encrusted with congealed blood. With a rapid survey of her surroundings, she ensured no prying eyes lingered nearby. Fortunately, the area was empty, allowing her a brief respite of privacy.

She glanced at the stack of stones she had arranged, noting with disquiet a disturbing bloodstain marring the grin she had meticulously crafted. The crimson splotch, a grim reminder of her recent frenzy, had likely resulted from the stabbing. Tenderly, she ran her hands over her body and lifted the hem of her kurta, inspecting her once-stabbed belly. To her astonishment, there were no scars or residual pain. Despite the relentless skewering, her body was completely healed.

She used her hands to scoop out a hole in the ground, carefully burying the blood-stained stones and the red grass. Once done, she covered the crimson soil with fresh earth, restoring the ground to its natural colour. Rising to her feet, she hurried to the rear window of her room and climbed out with swift determination. Amma would be back soon. Taking a moment to clean herself up, she changed into fresh clothes. The blood-stained garments were discreetly packed into a cardboard box and hidden away in the cupboard, out of sight.

Following dinner, the siblings headed back to their room. Reena settled onto her bed when Bhushan called out, "Hey Reena." Turning her head in his direction, she responded, "Yes?"

Bhushan gracefully traversed the room and settled onto Reena's bed beside her.

"Are you alright?" he inquired with genuine concern, a faint shadow of sadness lingering in his eyes.

"Yes, I am," Reena replied, forcing a seemingly genuine smile.

Bhushan fell into a momentary silence, his eyes darting nervously around the room.

"You know... when you gathered those stones and walked away, I trailed after you."

Fear gripped Reena as she realised if Bhushan had witnessed her self-inflicted wounds, he might reveal the truth to Amma.

"I noticed you talking to the stones. I was going to inquire, but I hesitated... I-I figured you might need some alone time, just as I do sometimes. There are times when I just need to be alone and not talk to anyone. I-I thought I'd give you some space and catch up with you later."

She felt a sense of relief and shared, "I was just observing them. I have this idea of creating something out of stone, like a sculpture."

"Wow, that sounds fascinating. What exactly are sculptures?" he asked, curiosity shining in his eyes.

"I'll show you when it's finished," Reena replied with a smile.

"Reena," Bhushan called her name once again.

She turned her head, ready to respond.

"If you ever want to talk about something, you can always come to me. It'll stay between us," Bhushan offered, his cheeks flushing slightly. He appeared nervous, but his concern for Reena was palpable, a side of him that had rarely surfaced before.

Reena gazed at him, a soft smile gracing her lips. Bhushan's face reddened further as he turned away, adding, "You can talk to me now if you want to."

"I will if I need to, Bhushan," Reena said calmly.

"Okay then, good night," Bhushan replied as he started walking towards his bed.

Reena observed as Bhushan made himself comfortable on his bed, a tender smile lighting up her features. With a deliberate motion, he reached beneath the bed, retrieved his cowboy hat, and settled it atop his head with an air of satisfaction.

"You found your hat?" asked Reena.

"Yes, I found it by the tree. Perhaps Amma put it there for me," Bhushan replied, adjusting the hat to shield his face.

Finding the situation somewhat unusual, Reena lay back on her bed as well. Today, she felt slightly better. It was the first time Bhushan had openly expressed his emotions towards her. The realization that someone cared for her brought a flicker of happiness. Clinging to this comforting thought, she drifted into a peaceful slumber once more.

(Arrrrrrr....... I beg you don't do it.... don't don't don't)

Overwhelmed by panic and dread, Reena jolted awake to the sound of faint whispers. Gasping for breath, she sat up in bed, her heart pounding wildly. She turned her head to check on her siblings, only to find their beds empty. Peering out of the window, she witnessed the night cloaked in darkness, illuminated only by an unusually large moon.

"Where have they gone?" she murmured, her gaze landing on a solitary hat resting on Bhushan's mattress.

Reena climbed out of bed, slipped into her slippers, and padded softly toward the lobby, her footsteps barely making a sound on the floor. Despite the slippers, the cold floor seemed to penetrate through them, sending shivers up Reena's spine. With every step she took, the whispers intensified, morphing into a cacophony of screams, echoing through the eerie silence of the night.

(No no no....... I beg you don't do it.... don't don't don't... please don't)

Fear gnawed at her heart, with the piercing screams amplifying her terror and making her steps falter. Yet, undeterred by the unease, curiosity propelled Reena forward, urging her to unravel the mystery of these harrowing hollers.

Upon entering the foyer, Reena was met with an unsettling change. The familiar setup was absent, replaced by a pristine, pastel green floor that gleamed with unnerving cleanliness—no dust, no imperfections, just an immaculate surface stretching out before her. The room was awash in bright light, unveiling a startling transformation. Elegant cupboards in soft pastel hues adorned the space, while the walls were cloaked in a soothing shade of pink, creating an atmosphere both serene and disorienting. The sudden and unexpected change left Reena in a state of awe as she surveyed her surroundings, the setting was reminiscent of the fantastical environments depicted in the comic.

"Devil's eye... look who's here," a voice slithered into Reena's ears. Turning her head, her jaw slackened and her eyes widened in shock as she beheld her mother perched on a pastel green kitchen counter, her presence more vibrant than anything in the room. Amma was meticulously scrubbing away blood splatters from the white countertop with a damp cloth. The surreal scene left Reena in stunned silence. Sharp squeaks were echoing ominously through the room as Amma was scrubbing, her eyes locked onto Reena's with chilling intensity. A bloodstain smeared across Amma's face, eerily mirroring the mark Reena had crafted on the stone earlier.

"R-Reena..." a faint voice reached her ears once more. She shifted her gaze slightly to the right and saw her brother, now fibbing on the kitchen counter. His arms and legs were severed, exposing the layers of bone and flesh, drenched in blood. The ghastly sight struck her with horror.

"A-Amama..ij-makkinuss-caakaake" He cried. His eyes were teary and red, his voice shaky and huffing like a helpless pup. Stammering, his words were unclear and laden with distress. The profound anguish in his demeanour only intensified the unsettling atmosphere. Reena shifted her gaze back to Amma and was met with the chilling sight of a severed leg. It bled slightly, its surface marred by wet, bloody fingerprints. Amma was meticulously wiping it clean with the same damp cloth. Soon, the chopping of the leg began with a pastel pink knife that levitated towards Amma from behind, humming a song all the while. The surreal and macabre scene unfolded, leaving Reena in a state of shock and horror.

She gaped at Reena while chopping the leg and said, "Honey, guess what...? I'm making your favourite cake, just like the one you saw in your comic book."

Reena was thunderstruck. How could Amma possibly know about her comic book?

"Well, you can see it's the same as in the comic, even the colour is pink," Amma replied.

Reena's eyes fell upon the cake resting on the counter. It was pinkish-red, but square peels emerged from its surface. The unsettling truth dawned upon her—the cake was crafted from the delicate layers of the raw flesh, the flesh of her siblings. Even the cherries and strawberries, mimicking the comic book cake, were fashioned from fresh eyeballs gouged from their sockets. The eyeballs, adorned with a scrap of gooey raw flesh, with a pinch of blood spots on each and corneas swivelling in different directions, seemed disturbingly alive. An eerie sensation enveloped Reena as if the cake itself were staring dead at her. The numerous eyes on the cake, yet one was conspicuously absent. As she fixated on Bhushan's eye, she watched in horror as it underwent a regeneration, gradually reassembling itself into completeness.

"Oops, the toppings aren't quite finished yet," Amma giggled. She coolly retrieved a fork from the heart-shaped compartment. Grasping Bhushan by his hair, she jabbed the fork into one of his eyes, eliciting a piercing, horrified scream from him.

"It's alright, honey, the new one will regenerate soon," Amma reassured him soothingly. As she dug out the fork, the eyeball came with it, its optic nerve still attached and trailing behind. Scissors floated towards Amma, and with a deft snip, the optic nerve was served, allowing it to dangle from the empty eye socket. She then affixed the gory topping to the cake with a flourish. "Tada, it's ready," Amma announced with a gleeful grin.

Reena remained rooted in place, her heart hammering wildly in her chest. A scream clawed at her throat, desperate to break free, but sheer terror rendered her mute. Her body trembled violently, paralyzed by the atrocity unfolding before her.

"Ummm, something is still missing," Amma mused, a twisted curiosity in her eyes. "I think… a head on top would perfect its beauty. So, whose head shall it be?" She looked between Reena and Bhushan, her finger playfully pointing at each of them in turn.

"Why are you doing this, Amma?" Reena cried.

"My dear Reena, I'm doing this for you... all of it is for you. You wanted to taste the cake, didn't you? Here, have it," Amma replied, her smile contorting into something sinister. "You tried to hide it from me, so I decided to give you a little surprise."

Reena remained silent, the gravity of the situation weighing down on her like a suffocating shroud. An awkward silence settled once more, lingering in the aftermath of the unsettling events.

"I think I'll go for a small head, the most perfect for the caaake, right?" Amma mused, her tone eerily playful.

Suddenly, something fell from the ceiling. It was Lily, her lips stitched shut with thread, her body bound with ropes, hanging like a morbid pendulum beside Amma. Picking up the largest knife in the kitchen, with a menacing smile, Amma turned towards Lily.

"NOOOOOO!!" Reena cried.

Desperation flickered in Reena's eyes as she drew a knife from the folds of her pajama and held it out toward Amma. Her voice trembled with fear and urgency as she pleaded, "Don't... don't do it, Please, I beg you!!"

Amma regarded Reena silently for a moment before replying, "Alright, I won't chop her head off, but I do need something to decorate my cake." Her smile turned sinister as she fixed Reena with a chilling gaze and added, "I want half of your head, and in return, your siblings will be spared." The surreal and horrifying proposition lingered in the air, leaving Reena trapped in the midst of an unthinkable choice.

The demand was unmistakably clear. Overwhelmed by misery, Reena seized the large knife from Amma's grasp. Without hesitation, she brought the blade down and sliced through the top of her head down to her neck. The grisly act left her holding half of her skull, blood cascading down in torrents. Tears streamed down her face as she presented the dreadful offering to her mother. "Just... don't hurt my siblings," she sobbed, her tortured plea reverberating in the chilling silence.

Mother took half of her head and placed it atop the cake, but with a critical eye, she assessed its placement. "This topping doesn't quite enhance the essence of my creation, truth be told," Amma remarked with an air of discontent. "I'm sorry, kitten, but I must do this."

She picked up the knife and, with a swift, decisive slash, Lily's head was severed and placed atop the cake. The lifeless body of Lily dangled and swayed like a pendulum, blood cascading down from the severed neck like a waterfall. The crimson stream flowed down from the apex of the cake. Reena sank to her knees, weeping uncontrollably, with one eye and half of her facade.

"Don't cry, honey; the cake is all for you," Amma said soothingly. She expertly sliced a pristine cake triangle and placed it on a plate, then approached Reena and extended the nightmarish confection to her.

"Enjoy," Amma said with a chilling smile. Reena stared at the cake, the eyeball toppings seeming to follow her gaze. *(It's all your fault...)* Overcome by a surge of despair and fury, she erupted in a scream. In an instant, her eyes snapped open, and she found herself lying on her bed, drenched in sweat.

Lily and Bhushan jolted awake, their faces etched with fear as the piercing scream reverberated through the room. "AHH... What happened?" Bhushan asked, his voice trembling with alarm.

Reena, turned to her siblings, her voice quivering with the remnants of her terror. "Nothing... It was j-just a nightmare," she stammered, trying to mask the fear still gripping her.

"Do you want me to call Amma?" Bhushan asked, his concern evident in his voice.

"No, never, it's alright," Reena replied, settling back onto her bed. Her siblings followed suit and returned to their beds. Yet, sleep eluded Reena for the remainder of the night. She lay awake, paralyzed by paranoia, the haunting remnants of the nightmare lingering in her thoughts, and a profound fear of losing her siblings to her mother.

CHAPTER-14

The Conflicted Heart

In the morning, the cheerful laughter of children playing outside filled the air. However, Reena remained in her bed, unable to escape the lingering shadows of the haunting nightmare from the night before. Questions plagued her mind, casting doubt on whether the disturbing dream might foreshadow her future.

Her contemplation was then abruptly interrupted by the sound of footsteps. Peeking out from her room, she saw her mother heading toward the exit, her familiar basket in hand.

Once her mother had departed, Reena remained seated on her bed, her mind still adrift in rumination. After a period of reflection, an inexplicable pull led her toward the enigmatic pink door. She crossed the checkered floor and stepped into the room to confront Nindhi. He lay sprawled on the sofa, his hands fully restored but his legs conspicuously missing, evidently severed by Amma. Though no words were exchanged, Reena felt a complex blend of pity and solace for him. It was the first time she had seen him without legs, yet he remained nonchalantly relaxed, his arms propped behind his head, while a book floated effortlessly above his chest.

"How are you holding up, Nindhi?" Reena asked.

"Alive!!" Nindhi replied coldly, his focus unwavering on the book floating above his chest, deliberately avoiding Reena's gaze.

Moving closer, Reena said, "I came here to apologize. I can't offer you any help."

"That's alright, Reena. I understand. Maybe you're not the one meant to help me. Perhaps it's someone else."

"Someone else?" Reena asked.

"Leave it, Reena. Just tell me, why did you come here?" He asked, closing his book and letting it float back to the table. Supporting himself with his hands, he adjusted his position on the sofa, his gaze unwaveringly fixed on Reena.

"I just came here to apologize, Nindhi. I wish I could help, but I can't," she replied.

"Alright, apology accepted. You can leave now," he said. Despite his words, Reena remained, unable to silence her growing turmoil. After a moment of silence, she finally burst out. "I had a nightmare...a horrifying vision... o-of Amma baking a cake with the limbs of my brother and sister. She had extracted Bhushan's eyes to use as cake decorations. S-She baked a cake exactly like the one depicted in the comics, but instead of flour and strawberries, the ingredients were the flesh and eyes of my siblings. Bhushan's regenerative power provided an endless supply of eyes to decorate the cake. The sight was horrifying. It was so sickening," Reena cried, her voice quivering with anguish.

Nindhi listened intently, his eyes locked onto Reena's with a piercing focus. "That wasn't just a nightmare; it was a glimpse of your future," he declared solemnly. A chill of terror gripped Reena's heart at the thought of her nightmare manifesting into reality—an outcome she desperately wished to avoid.

"Why are you treating me with such hostility, Nindhi?" Reena snapped, trying to mask the storm of emotions roiling just beneath her composed exterior.

"Reena, look at me. I've been confined here for years, enduring a relentless cycle of pain, isolation, and despair. Each day is a struggle against hunger, as Amma only feeds me mugas twice a week. I'm even driven to consume my own flesh to stave off the hunger. Do you honestly think your future will be any more bearable than mine?" Nindhi's voice trembled with the burden of his grim reality.

Reena stood in shock, her world disintegrating with Nindhi's revelations. "I don't know," she confessed, her voice trembling. "But the possibility terrifies me. I've known my mother for years, and she always took good care of us... We don't know anything about the outside world. I-I can witness the brutality of what Amma did to you. It's beyond cruelty. I was hoping that, maybe, if I'm lucky, she won't do anything like this to me and my siblings." Overwhelmed, Reena sank to her knees. Nindhi watched her in silence, as the harsh reality of her situation began to settle in. Despite her fear, she still enjoyed a semblance of freedom, a stark contrast to Nindhi's grim confinement.

"I-I know I sound foolish, but maybe it's because... I don't want to confront the crisis I'm facing. I cling to the hope of a future that may not even exist, as it momentarily soothes my heart. But I don't know how long I can endure this existence. Each day, I'm gripped by paralyzing fear, with an incessant ache gnawing at my heart. Such profound terror is entirely strange to me... I don a mask each day, feigning normalcy while the unbearable weight of my reality crushes me," Reena gazed at Nindhi with tear-filled eyes and sobbed, "All I yearn for is to escape this wretched existence, but I can't... No matter how many times I drive a blade into my flesh, my wounds mend as if by sorcery."

Nindhi sensed the profound turmoil within Reena. He extended a gesture of comfort, murmuring, "Reena, it's alright. I am deeply sorry for the anguish you are enduring. The tumultuous emotions that churn within you are the harsh tributes, the burdens that life bestows upon those who come of age."

Wiping her tears, Reena met Nindhi's gaze. After a contemplative pause, he continued, "I've come to believe that hope is one of the most formidable forces in existence... Indeed, it stands among the most potent of all. It's the beacon that kept me alive, even in the darkest time when my grip on sanity seemed to falter... I endured," Nindhi said, his eyes gleaming with a spark of hope. "I believe... We can escape this inferno."

Reena snapped her gaze toward Nindhi, her face a canvas of silence.

"After years of waiting on the precipice of surrendering my freedom, I was ready to give up. But then you arrived... and I couldn't bring myself to relent. Because... you were my last beacon of hope."

Reena absorbed Nindhi's words, a mix of surprise and disbelief on her face. "I was... the last beacon of hope.?"

"You'll be surprised to hear the story of how I summoned you. Call me delusional, but I believe it."

"Summon me here?" She asked, her voice tinged with curiosity and surprise.

"Yes, let me share a mystical tale," he replied with a wistful smile.

CHAPTER-15

The Lamb and the Godman

Reena placed herself across from Nindhi, and he commenced with the tale.

After I was imprisoned, I was utterly shattered. Consumed by hopelessness, I found myself ensnared in nightmarish introspections. Every seven days, when Amma visited me to serve my limbs, all I wished for was death, yet it eluded me. I waited and waited, feeling as though my soul might depart from my body, but it remained tethered. It was an unbearably dark period, steeped in despair. Years passed, and my pleas for escape from this torment grew more desperate. I was teetering on the edge of madness, having developed a grim habit of consuming my own flesh. Then, one day, in a dream, I glimpsed a scene from my past—a time when I was allowed to read books. It was the only book with a tattered cover and missing initial pages, rendering the title and author unknown. Yet, the book spoke of something extraordinary—how to reshape one's life and harness vitality through the power of imagination. It spoke of how, even in the harshest circumstances, the power to reshape one's life resides within oneself. Initially, I found the author's belief in such fantastical notions of imagination transforming reality to be far-fetched. Being a wizard or a witch entails handling many aspects of existence, but life itself remains evasive, even to the mightiest. Despite this, the author was proposing something seemingly outlandish. I was skeptical, but somehow, I resolved to give it a try.

The book posited a provocative argument regarding the belief in God, suggesting that genuine power resides in the intellect and ingenuity of humans. From his perspective, I surmised that the author was likely an atheist, someone who dismissed the notions of god and devil. Perhaps our existence was beyond his understanding, leading me to strongly disagree with his hypothesis.

However, he discussed how people prayed in temples, oriented their prayers in specific directions at home, visited shrines, sacrificed animals in the name of deities, worshipped statues, and saw themselves as superior to others. He categorized all these practices under one term: "Fallacy." People engage in these practices to seek happiness in their lives, yet they spend their entire existence in terror. Praying to God promises certain outcomes, adding a veneer of glamour to their lives. However, a constant, underlying fear is instilled—the fear of defying God. The belief. They believe that the problem may resurface in their lives, or dire consequences may befall them if they dare to rebel against God. Their entire existence is dictated by the notion of a creator; they surrender their souls to self-proclaimed Godmen, who act as puppeteers, manipulating their fears. Terrible acts are perpetrated in the name of God. The fear instilled by their godmen blinds them—so profoundly that they would willingly sacrifice their own children or themselves for their venerated deity. The concept is called "The Lamb and The Godman." The lamb symbolizes innocence—representing you and your siblings—while the Godman embodies cunning, supreme power—epitomized by Amma. In this dynamic, lambs and Godmen are eternally at odds, destined never to coexist in harmony. The lambs are nurtured by the Godmen until the moment of sacrifice arrives. At that point, the lamb is offered up to satiate the hunger of the Godman. This fate is imminent for you, Reena, just as it once was for me. But Amma's actions surpass those of any Godman. Beyond instilling fear, she seeks to dominate you and your siblings. She will butcher you, almost every day, inflicting upon you the most excruciating pain imaginable. While the lamb may die peacefully after sacrifice, you, Reena, will endure ceaseless torment—every second, every minute, every hour. And when you plead for death to relieve you, it will evade you, for eternity. And she demands that you accept it all with a smile, merely because she is the one who raised you.

Nindhi paused, awaiting a response from Reena. She remained silent, her face etched with visible terror, yet her lips stayed firmly sealed.

However. Nindhi began. The author of this tattered book spoke of a profound magic in life—something far more powerful than the false gods: Imagination. "Imagination is the true prayer" the author claimed. Just sit with your eyes closed, feel good about yourself, and fantasize, the film of your desired life—what you wish for most.

In the depths of my despair, a revelation dawned upon me—a concept of true prayer and the re-creation of life through the power of imagination. I was uncertain of the origin of this insight, but in my desperate quest for salvation, it appeared as my beacon of hope. In my mind's eye, I began to conjure a vivid narrative, akin to the films I had seen on television, immersing myself in its palpable reality. Closing my eyes, I envisioned an ethereal scene where an angel gracefully emerged through the door, offering me a chance to escape this prison. In my imagination, I resided in a quaint cottage by the beach, where the rhythmic waves serenaded my days, and I could indulge in the simple pleasure of eating watermelons and revelling in the beauty of nature. Far from this nightmarish fortress, I conjured visions of meeting new souls by the serene beach and embarking on adventures to different cities. I nurtured this fantasy for years, though my reality remained unchanged. Yet, I persisted, delving deeper into my imagination, for it was my only solace. These vivid daydreams offered a fleeting escape, a respite from the relentless torment of my existence. At least in my mind, I was living the life I longed for. But as the years dragged on, my frustration grew; the reality I yearned for remained elusive. I teetered on the brink of despair, ready to abandon my dreams as nothing seemed to change. Then, one day, you entered this room... Believe me, no one had ever crossed this threshold before, except Amma. I was astonished that my imagination had finally manifested into reality. Reena, I believe you are the angel I envisioned, the one destined to rescue me from this agony. We can escape this place together and forge our own destiny, but only if you trust me and follow my lead.

Reena was taken aback by Nindhi's words. She responded, "I-It could just be a coincidence!"

"It might be, or it might be not. I'm willing to take my chances... Do you have another choice, Reena?" Nindhi's words hung in the air, leaving Reena speechless.

"Amidst these hardships, I've come to grasp the profound power of imagination and hope. Whether you choose to join me or not, it's alright. Perhaps you may not be the angel I envisioned, but I will find my way out, with or without you. The choice is yours: Be the angel of my liberation or become a prisoner behind the pink door."

"But if the lambs are being sacrificed," Reena questioned, "how is the world beyond any different? It's just like Amma described—wolves preying on lambs."

Nindhi looked at Reena thoughtfully before replying, "The world beyond isn't merely a place of joy and splendour. No... from the books I've read and the films I've seen, the world is a tapestry woven with both light and shadow. In the world beyond, wolves and godmen do prey upon lambs. Yet, if a lamb possesses the means to save itself, it can. Here in the castle, however, such freedom is denied. My yearning to escape lies in one thing—freedom. It's the only thing I crave, the one thing these sombre castle walls can never provide. Freedom is the liberty to pursue your passions, to savor your favourite foods, and even to die in the place of your choosing. Freedom is all I desire."

"But what if we fail? The witch in the mirror was the most horrendous thing! I-I don't even know sorcery... How am I... you are supposed to confront her? What you're proposing seems hopeless, Nindhi... What if we never manage to escape and en... end up dying here?" Reena asked, her voice quivering with fear.

"If this is where my journey concludes, let it be with hope, not fear. Let me give her the fiercest battle of her lifetime, until my last breath, ensuring that I have no regrets in the end," Nindhi declared, his eyes blazing with resolve.

Reena said nothing; she rose and quietly exited the room. A wave of reassurance washed over Nindhi as he reclined on the sofa, a smile gracing his lips. Reena, lost in her thoughts, paused just outside. After a moment's contemplation, she reentered the room and declared, "Guide me towards freedom, Nindhi."

CHAPTER-16

Guliver's Travels

Reena reclined in the swivel chair nestled within the clandestine workshop, immersed in reading a book entitled "Conservancy from Dark Arts." As her reading finished, with a soft sigh, she closed the book and placed it aside. Her fingers danced through the air, weaving intricate patterns that mimicked the sinuous movement of a serpent. With a delicate flick, she cast a spell on a flower pot, nestled in a small corner garden, causing it to float effortlessly above the ground. Maintaining her gestures, she guided the levitating pot toward herself. Suddenly, a jarring thud echoed, disrupted her focus and the flower pot plummeted to the floor, shattering into fragments. Reena let out an irritated grunt. Investigating the source of the disturbance, she discovered the fallen book, Conservancy from Dark Arts. After returning it to the table, she carefully collected the shards of the broken pot and transferred the bud into a new vase.

She walked over to one of the workshop's walls and added the one-hundred-fifty-seventh tally mark to the growing count. Her actions reflected her unwavering dedication and consistency in her work. The wall was adorned with graffiti that read "ESCAPE 300," marking their collective goal of breaking free within three hundred days.

Then, she picked up "Gulliver's Travels" from the book rack. Placing it on the table, she stood nearly three feet away, dramatically waving her fingers. The book responded by floating gracefully. With another wave, "Conservancy from Dark Arts" levitated towards her and hovered to her right, just before her eyes. Opening to page three hundred forty-five, she read, "Join your thumbs and index fingers to perform a defence shield."

Executing the instructions meticulously, Reena interlaced her thumbs and index fingers, forming a diamond-shaped gesture with her hands. Concentrating on "Gulliver's Travels" she conjured a shimmering pink bubble around it, manifesting a protective shield.

Excitement surged through Reena as the protective shield successfully formed around "Gulliver's Travels." Eager to delve deeper, she turned the page of "Conservancy from Dark Arts" and read, "Hold the gesture near your chest to create a shield around yourself." She followed the instructions, but despite her efforts, the technique of shielding herself eluded her grasp. Hours slipped away as Reena immersed herself in mastering the intricacies of the shield charm. Despite her relentless dedication, success remained just out of reach. Later, her attention turned to the winged tent, where she meticulously adhered to Nindhi's detailed instructions. Over the span of one hundred and fifty-seven days, she tirelessly dedicated herself to perfecting the flying tent. Utilizing a cauldron, she meticulously crafted materials, concocted potions, and assembled the essential components to construct and enhance the tent. The wings were successfully mended, and the navigation steering ball was meticulously designed. Currently, she was deeply engrossed in the creation of a defence cannon wand and an astral crystal.

Most of Reena's time was devoted to the workshop, where she tirelessly honed her magical skills. She scavenged materials from her surroundings, occasionally pilfering a few items from her mother's room. As her curiosity grew with each passing day, so did her strides toward victory. After her work sessions, she would join Nindhi, engaging in detailed discussions about the flying tent and offering him some mugas in hopes of curbing his habit of consuming his own flesh. She often requested extra portions and saved some for Nindhi to eat.

However, Nindhi preferred his flesh, finding it more flavorful than the gooey alternative. She dedicated time to interacting and playing with her siblings and engaged in conversations with Amma while maintaining her cheerful facade each day. As she made progress toward her goal, her fear gradually waned. However, given the time-consuming nature of building the tent, she began contemplating alternative plans.

After a gruelling day of work, Reena managed to complete half of the cannon wand. Exhausted, she set the wand aside near the tent and reclined in the revolving chair. With a wave of her fingers, Gulliver's Travels floated toward her, and she lost herself in its enchanting tale. While reading, a folded parchment slipped from the book, catching her eye. She retrieved the yellowish-brown parchment, which consisted of three pages, and was about to examine its contents when a gnome-like wooden doll in the workshop whistled, signalling Amma's imminent return. Reena quickly gathered her belongings and exited the workshop.

The very next day, within just a few hours, Reena cheerfully completed the other half of the cannon wand. As she reflected on her swift progress in mastering sorcery, she contrasted it with the earlier days when she relied on enchanted manual tools like hammers and saws. Despite the satisfaction of completing the cannon wand, the rest of the day was consumed by relentless attempts to perfect the astral crystal. Its creation proved elusive, as she faced repeated disappointments and setbacks.

She remembered Nindhi's warning about the difficulty of crafting the astral crystal. Frustrated and distracted, Reena reclined in her chair, took a deep breath, and paused. Her gaze then shifted to the folded parchment she had discovered the day before in Gulliver's Travels. She picked up the parchment and began to read. As she delved into the text, her eyes widened in astonishment. After finishing the first two missives, she paused, her heart fluttering with apprehension. When she unfolded the third page, a wave of wonder swept over her, leaving her breathless and spellbound.

Reena hurried to the workbench and seized a quill. Pulling her revolving chair closer to the desk, she began to scribble furiously on the paper, lost in her thoughts for hours. The room was filled with the sound of her quill scratching across the paper and the occasional crumpling of discarded drafts. Eventually, she scribbled a note on a piece of paper, which she placed alongside the folded parchment. After tucking both into her pink pouch, she made her way to see Nindhi.

In Nindhi's room, they both settled on the floor and began discussing the remaining work on the tent. Despite being without arms, Nindhi's face brightened with joy as Reena shared her progress on the cannon wand.

"Haven't you yet uncovered the method for crafting the astral crystal to power the tent's engine?" Nindhi inquired.

Reena met Nindhi's gaze and said, "It's proving to be the most formidable task. My attempts have been fraught with failure. We need a dragon's fang, crystal eyes, and bug flowers to craft it... but I have no clue where to find any of them."

Nindhi suggested, "Perhaps you might need to sneak into Amma's hidden garden or room and retrieve some of the items."

"I can't risk sneaking into the garden," Reena protested. "I've already searched her room, and the items were nowhere to be found. The things I took serve no purpose in making the crystal,"

"Have you tried another method?" asked Nindhi.

"In crafting the crystal? I've tried before," Reena replied, her frustration evident. "I took a break after countless failures and then shifted my focus to the other parts of the tent. Now that everything else is complete, this astral crystal is still a real pain in the neck."

"If you fail to create the astral crystal, There will be no escape," said Nindhi, concern etched on his face.

An uneasy silence hung in the room. Both Nindhi and Reena felt the weight of the moment. Aware of the immense effort Reena had invested in the escape plan, Nindhi chose to stay silent, unwilling to add to the tension.

"What if there's another way?" Reena suggested.

Nindhi looked at her curiously and asked, "Another way?"

"I'm not sure if you'll agree, but escaping from this place is consuming far too much time and effort," Reena proposed. "What if we shift our focus to annihilating the witch instead of trying to flee?"

Nindhi's eyes widened as Reena's words sank in. A seed of doubt began to take root in his mind. The girl who had once been tearful and adamant that her mother wasn't a witch, now suggested her assassination. "Do you truly mean it?" Nindhi asked, raising his eyebrows in surprise.

Retrieving the parchment from her pouch, Reena nodded and handed it to Nindhi. The parchment hovered in mid-air before him, unfolding itself as he began to read.

Thousands of years ago, a miraculous child was born and given the unique name Shukranjan. As he grew, he became a fine young man with dark hair, a sharp-pointed long nose, and big eyes with blue irises, missing pupils. He was well known for his helpful nature and readiness to defend the weak. The values instilled by his parents shaped him into a man of social standing. As he matured, he began to discover his magical powers and with the passing years, he grew stronger and more creative with his abilities. Between the ages of fourteen and twenty-one, his powers helped countless people lead better lives. Some revered him as a God, while others viewed him as a potential threat, but none dared to challenge him.

At the age of twenty-one, a deep desire to explore the world bloomed in his heart. Shukranjan decided to embark on a journey, but the mode of travel was a significant concern. One day, he seized a broom and had the sudden idea of enchanting it to fly. Infusing it with his magical power, he sat on the broom, and soon he was soaring above the clouds.

During his travels, Shukranjan visited various countries, offering his help to those in need. He faced and defeated terrifying beasts, liberating people from horror with his powerful Adikalin Wand. Eventually, he found love in Albion and chose to retire from his adventurous life to pursue a peaceful existence. At the age of twenty-eight, he married. Shukranjan and his beloved Igraiine were blessed with ten sons and seven daughters, all inheriting the gift of sorcery and the family expanded. Their arcane power was bequeathed through the ages, and as successive generations of magically gifted children emerged, the Wizard Society was established, forging a legacy of enchantment and wonder.

Centuries passed, a new generation emerged to lead the Wizard society. Committed individuals dedicated their efforts to creating diverse forms of magic for the welfare of the community. The governance of the Wizard society fell into the hands of two siblings, Neoma and Gnows—a sister and brother duo known for their exceptional creativity and wisdom. Despite their vision of collaboration with the society of non-magical people, the Ordinarium Society and living in harmony, they faced rejection from the Church of England, under the reign of King James I. Leading to significant opposition from a substantial portion of the society. In response, the wizard society chose to live in seclusion, hidden from the eyes of the wider world.

However, driven by a fervent belief in the Daemonologie of witchcraft and an intense personal interest in witch-hunting, James I devised a sinister plot. He masterfully orchestrated the Church's influence, where its leaders were swayed by his machinations. The Church, steadfast in its adherence to Biblical doctrine, was persuaded that witchcraft was a blight upon the moral fabric of society. They believed it posed a profound threat to the spiritual well-being of both individuals and the community at large, contended that witches and wizards were in league with the Devil, their malevolent powers capable of blighting harvests and spreading miseries throughout the land. In defiance of these allegations, Neoma persistently penned her arguments under the pseudonym Marlin Cavendish. She diligently contributed her articles to the Ordinarium Society, striving to preserve harmony and challenge the prevailing orthodoxy.

The King and the corrupt factions within the Church felt their authority challenged by Neoma's leadership and Shrewd tactics. Outraged by a woman steering a powerful society, they branded her with the title of "Evil Witch." Eager for an opportunity to dismantle the wizarding realm, they awaited the perfect moment to strike. Fueled by relentless rumours propagated by the Church, a wave of mass hysteria surged through the common populace. The seeds of fear and suspicion, sown by those in power, took root and spread, destroying the minds of ordinary people with dread.

Consumed by paranoia, the authorities ignited the Pendle Witch Trials, mercilessly executing innocent women at random. They were accused of being covert agents for the Wizard society, allegedly responsible for spreading afflictions. The witch trials persisted for years, stoked by relentless propaganda aimed at tarnishing the reputation of the sorcerer's community. Despite Neoma's earnest appeals conveyed through desperate letters, the Church and authorities remained indifferent, systematically executing hundreds of innocent women under the chilling slogan, "Witchcraft: A Manifestation of Evil Against God."

Society fractured into discord. The relentless immolation of countless women inflicted suffering far greater than any supposed witchcraft ever could. Families were shattered—mothers, sisters, daughters, and wives were lost in the flames, igniting a groundswell of rebellion among the populace. The resistance surged as people rose against the abhorrent injustice. Yet, the church and the entrenched authorities wielded their power with an iron grip, making them seemingly invincible. In retaliation, the church branded the dissenters as witches, denouncing them as traitors to God. The grim atrocities persisted unabated until a pivotal moment arrived. A courageous woman named Marry Dyler, a fervent rebel against the witch trials, managed a desperate escape, albeit at a tragic cost—her children had sacrificed their lives to ensure her freedom. Marry was utterly devastated, her spirit irrevocably shattered after the loss of her family. After enduring days of concealment and starvation in the forest, one day, she encountered a shadowy figure with one eye. Fueled by a burning rage and an insatiable desire for vengeance, she forged a dark pact with the devil, bartering her soul for unparalleled power. Marry transformed into something hideous—a merciless monster, a cannibal witch known as Daemonara. In a single night, she unleashed havoc upon the entire town, with churches shattered and houses drenched in red. In the ensuing upheaval, the majority of the authorities and the church's high-ranking officials were slaughtered. However, her thirst for vengeance did not end there. Now under the devil's thrall, she commenced the abduction of innocent children. With each heinous deed she perpetrated, Marry's power grew exponentially. Blessed by the devil, she gave rise to an army of Daemonaras. Every night, a coven of dark witches, riding their brooms, descended upon the towns, abducting children, slaughtering mankind, and at times, reducing entire towns to rubble and dust.

After the devastating genocide and widespread abductions of innocents, both the church and the rebels implored the Wizard Society for aid. The wizards, willing to support the Ordinarium Society, rallied an army under Neoma's command to confront the Daemonaras. However, magic alone proved insufficient against the formidable foe, culminating in the fierce Battle of Eldritch Vale. Despite the sacrifices of many sorcerers and sorceresses, the Daemonaras continued to gain strength. It was a fierce struggle of magic versus dark magic. During the gruelling Eldritch Vale War, Gnows embarked on a perilous journey with his comrades in search of a solution to the dark cannibal threat. After more than a hundred days of struggle, he discovered the Phoenix flower, distinguished by its curly leaves and blooms that resembled flickering flames. Through extensive research, Gnows devised the "Phoenix Spell Bomb." For several days, wizards and humans alike deployed these spell bombs against the Daemonaras, leading to their swift and decisive downfall. Before long, the majority of the cannibal witches were eradicated, while a few managed to conceal themselves from the outside world. Consequently, peace was restored to the Ordinarium Society. A truce was signed, and the Wizarding Society became allies with the Ordinarium world, eventually choosing to retreat back into seclusion.

Nindhi was in a state of stupefaction. "This is..."

"Unbelievable, right?" said Reena. "Amma lied about the outside world. I believe the non-magic people, the Ordinarium society, are still living in harmony."

"Where did you find it?" Nindhi inquired.

"Does it matter?" Reena replied. "I have something better to suggest... I've come up with a plan."

"Plan?"

"Yeah," Reena said, her eyes gleaming with a newfound revelation. "The letter makes it clear that Amma was one of the

Daemonaras who terrorized towns. I suspect she fled when they were vanquished by the wizard society in the Battle of Eldritch Vale."

"Alright! Listening," said Nindhi.

"I believe Amma is hiding from the wizard society, but she still needs food to survive."

"So?"

"So, we're her lifeline," Reena continued, her eyes fixed on Nindhi. "She intends to create an endless supply of human flesh through us, allowing her to live comfortably in the castle without the need to hunt in the towns. If she were to do that, she'd be pursued and eliminated by the wizards. Which means she is hiding out of fear."

Nindhi was taken aback by Reena's theory, acknowledging its startling plausibility. "Reena, it actually makes sense... brilliant. But what do you propose we do about it?""

Reena nodded. She turned the page of the floating parchment and pointed to an illustration of a jar, accompanied by descriptive text.

"Phoenix spell bomb!"

"Yes, the craft is known to me," said Reena.

"Known to you? How?" He asked, his eyes widening with surprise.

"It was taught by the One-Eyed Master," Reena explained. "This is one of the specialties I recalled from my lessons in dreams. The methodology is detailed on the next page."

Nindhi turned the page and found diagrams filled with crudely drawn figures and labels. "So, you're suggesting that we create the Phoenix Spell Bomb to eliminate Amma?"

"Yes."

He turned to Reena, his brow knitted in apprehension. "Reena, I'm concerned that you're underestimating Amma. She's a shrewd and formidable witch, unlike any we've faced in tales. I know her well, and this assassination attempt carries a considerable risk of failure."

"We won't," Reena said with resolute confidence. From her pouch, she produced another folded parchment, unfolding it with precision and spreading it out on the floor. Nindhi leaned closer, intrigued. The parchment was covered with whimsical stick figures, each line reflecting an air of novice artistry.

"What is this?" Nindhi inquired, his confusion evident.

"This," Reena declared, "is my strategy."

Examining the parchment, he gestured toward a drawn figure with his eyes. It was a stick figure with spikes on its head, menacing triangular eyes that looked wicked, and a wide mouth lined with fangs, all scribbled with curly dark lines that nearly filled the space with black.

"What is it?" Nindhi asked.

"It's Amma," She answered.

"And what is in that dark part?"

"It's blood drooling from her mouth," Reena explained innocently.

The next moment, unable to contain his laughter, Nindhi found himself rolling on the floor, tumbling across the honey and scarlet surface.

"Why are you laughing?" Reena demanded, her irritation growing. Nindhi, caught up in his uncontrollable mirth, remained oblivious and continued to convulse with laughter.

"Stop it!"

(Ha..haha....hahaha..ha..)

He snorted once, twice, thrice; the laughter persisted unabated.

"Alright, laugh it up. I'm leaving," Reena huffed, turning her back to Nindhi and sitting with her arms crossed, a scowl etched on her face.

(Ha..haha....hahaha..haha..)

"I'll leave for real!" Reena barked, her face flushing crimson with anger.

"Sorry, sorry... I'm serious now," Nindhi said, rising from the floor and giving Reena a solemn look, pressing his lips tightly together to stifle his remaining laughter.

"One day, somewhere far from this place, my drawings will flourish with grace. Then we'll see who's laughing, Nindhi!" she declared, jabbing a finger at his face, her voice brimming with determination.

"Okay, okay, sorry," said Nindhi, composing himself. "Please, begin the explanation."

Reena cast a glance at the parchment. "I'm confident this plan is impeccable. Once I've explained it, I'll be open to your feedback," she said, her irritation still palpable. Nindhi nodded, intrigued, suppressing his giggles.

Pointing to the first drawing, she began, "Look at this. This is Amma." She gestured to the distorted stick figure. A laugh bubbled up from Nindhi, but he quickly sobered as Reena shot him a glare sharp enough to cut glass.

"I'm familiar with the rhythm of Amma's routine," she began. "So, once the Phoenix Spell Bomb is prepared, in her absence, I'll slip into her chamber. There, beneath her mattress, within a timeworn cardboard, I'll nestle at least three spell-bomb jars, untouched by her vigilant eye. These jars will be enchanted to ignite with celestial flames only at my command."

Nindhi was about to pose a question, but Reena interrupted him, instructing him to hold his queries until she had finished her explanation.

Reena shifted her finger to another crudely drawn figure, showing a stickman of Amma yawning with a blood-dripping mouth near a poorly illustrated bed. "So, at night, when Amma falls asleep, she'll be off guard and from the window's perch, I shall keep watch," she continued, tracing her finger over a cheerful face peeking through an ill-drawn window. "Her room will be locked from the outside... I'll whisper the incantation, and then—Boom! In deep and restful slumber, the witch will meet her demise. If, by some chance, she manages to escape the confines of that room, the flames will be swift to pursue her. In mere moments, she shall be nought but ash."

"Do Phoenix flowers bloom in your garden?" Nindhi inquired.

"No, but I recently discovered their seeds and decided to plant them," Reena replied. "The good news is they'll grow faster than usual—within ten to fourteen days—thanks to the special manure I concocted from ficus branches, mud, and a proliferation potion."

"Will the exploding enchantment be effective on the Phoenix Spell Bomb?" Nindhi asked.

"Yes, it will," Reena confirmed. "Historical accounts validate it; Gnows used it himself."

"How long will it take to craft a Phoenix Spell Bomb?" Nindhi asked.

"About a month," Reena replied.

A heavy silence hung in the air as Nindhi pondered her words, his response slow to come.

"Look, I understand that time is of the essence, and you might be thinking, 'What if our assassination attempt fails?' But I will continue my efforts on the astral crystal, even if it means devoting less time to the Phoenix Spell Bomb. I have unwavering confidence that this plan will succeed," Reena asserted, her eyes sparkling with determination.

"Alright, let's move forward with it."

Reena lifted her gaze to meet Nindhi's smiling eyes. The next instant, Nindhi was enveloped in the warm embrace, his head resting contentedly on her shoulder.

"A higher likelihood of success is attributed to your plan," Nindhi mumbled, his eyes closed as his cheek softly brushed against her shoulder.

She then released Nindhi, her eyes shimmering with emotion. "I—I thought you would never agree to this," she confessed, her voice quivering slightly.

"Your plan carries weight," Nindhi agreed, his tone solemn yet resolute. "Though it might seem cowardly, yet dangerous to strike the witch while she slumbers, the potential outcome justifies the crapshoot."

"Are you attempting to evoke guilt in me for eliminating the witch who inflicts suffering upon you?" Reena inquired, raising her eyebrow.

"No, never," he replied. "I admire your strategic mind. It holds great promise for success." He looked at Reena with genuine admiration.

"However, I'm curious about one thing," asked Nindhi "From where you discovered the parchment?"

"I stumbled upon it within the pages of the book "Gulliver's Travels," replied Reena nonchalantly.

Nindhi's eyes widened, transitioning from a state of cheerfulness to one of shock.

"What happened?" asked Reena. "Are you alright?"

"Well... Gulliver's Travels is one of my cherished books, and I've read it thrice. It was the book I was reading when Amma imprisoned me," he explained, his eyes remaining wide in astonishment.

"So?" asked Reena

He turned towards Reena, fixing his gaze upon her.

"Within its pages, this parchment has never been encountered by me."

CHAPTER-17

Lurking in the Shadows

Reena immersed herself in the arduous task of crafting the Phoenix spell bomb. The endeavour commenced as the first phoenix flower unfurled its fiery petals in her garden. Through relentless effort, meticulous testing, and unwavering perseverance, she perfected the creation over the course of twenty-four days. Eventually, the Phoenix Elixir was successfully concocted. The potion was carefully decanted into a small, spherical glass jar, adorned with an intricate skull design, which she had discovered in one of the antique cupboards.

Reena dedicated herself to the arduous pursuit of making the Astral Crystal and mastering the Conservancy from Dark Art. Progress with the Astral Crystal remained both challenging and tedious, but her magical abilities experienced significant advancement. She had mastered the art of creating a protective shield around the Ambo and making it levitate, yet generating a shield to envelop herself remained a formidable challenge.

Nindhi was deeply impressed by her magical accomplishments. He marvelled at her progress, especially since, despite his own efforts, he still struggled to levitate a mere table and found crafting a shield to be a persistent challenge, the only skill he had truly perfected was the crafting of magical instruments. While all the progress Reena made over time brought her joy, today her excitement soared to the seventh sky, making her bounce on the balls of her feet. Pouring the elixirs into three jars, she chanted the mantra to activate them. The jars glowed purple, and bubbles rose in spirals, resembling a little tornado, in each jar. The Phoenix Spell Bomb was now successfully crafted.

Ecstatic, Reena was eager to showcase her creation to Nindhi and finalize their strategy for the witch's downfall, which she intended to execute that very day. After carefully placing one of the Phoenix Spell Bomb jars into her pouch, she dashed towards Nindhi with a renewed sense of urgency..

Entering the room, she burst with excitement. "We did it, Nindhi!"

Nindhi, reclining on a sofa, shifted his gaze abruptly as Reena entered. A book levitated above his chest, while a lantern floated gently beside him. Before Nindhi could utter a word, Reena dashed toward him, her eyes gleaming with exhilaration. She brandished the Phoenix Spell Bomb triumphantly. "Look, Nindhi! I did it! We did it! Soon, we'll be as free as birds."

The book gently settled onto the table, while the lantern continued to hover above, casting a warm, ethereal glow over them. Although Nindhi wished to grasp the Phoenix Spell Bomb, his missing fingers rendered him unable. Nonetheless, his heart swelled with joy. The hope he had cherished for years was finally materializing. Tears began to stream from his wolf-like eyes. Overcome with emotion, he leaned into Reena and embraced her, sobbing uncontrollably. "At last, this tormenting nightmare will come to an end... M-My heartfelt prayer has been answered. This is the dawn of our freedom."

Reena wiped away his tears and declared, "Today, we shall set our plan into motion and kill the witch at once and for all!"

"KILL THE WITCH!?" an unfamiliar voice reverberated from the dark corner of the room. A chill of apprehension cascaded down Nindhi and Reena's spines as they turned toward the shrouded corner, their eyes straining to pierce the darkness. The sound of approaching footsteps intensified, their rhythmic echo melding with the mounting tension. Gradually, a shadowy figure emerged from the dim recesses, its form shrouded in obscurity. As it stepped into the scant light, a chilling scarlet smile illuminated its face. The floating lantern, once casting a gentle glow, plummeted to the ground, shattering into a myriad of fragmented pieces.

The room was swallowed by darkness, the unsettling void briefly interrupted before chandeliers burst to life with a magical flare. Reena and Nindhi beheld the figure now clearly revealed before them. Their jaws fell agape, and their hearts tightened with dread. Frozen in place, they found themselves unable to move, utterly transfixed by the figure's menacing presence. Then, Nindhi stammered, his voice quivering with fear, "A-A-Amma Meiga!" Reena crumpled to the floor, her eyes wide with terror, fixed on the formidable figure of Amma Meiga, draped in a red saree, looming ominously before them.

"Ah, my precious little kitten, are you truly astonished to see me here?" Amma Meiga purred, her eyes locking onto Reena with a chilling, predatory gaze.

"A-Amma, you didn't go to w-work today?" Reena fumbled.

"Darling, my schedule is rather unoccupied. I frequently visit my fellow witches for some lively company. Dealing with children can become rather dull and repetitive. Pretending to genuinely care for all of you can only be maintained for so long."

"Nindhi was right! He was right all along!" Reena exclaimed.

"Ahh, my dear kitten," Amma Meiga said with a malevolent smile, "I realized there's no need for pretence now. As you can see, in this domain of mine, I wield the power to spook anywhere within these walls." She bent slightly, striking a theatrical pose, and said, "Allow me to demonstrate."

"Snappy, isn't it?" the voice echoed with a chilling undertone. Reena and Nindhi whirled around in alarm to find Amma Meiga now standing behind them. The swiftness of her movement left them disoriented, their minds racing to understand when she had shifted her position.

Amma advanced with menacing grace, each step amplifying the terror in their hearts. Nindhi was terrified, not for himself but for Reena, overwhelmed by the impending danger, grappled with a frantic sense of helplessness, his thoughts racing but failing to provide a solution. As she drew nearer, Amma lowered herself, her hands poising gently over their heads.

"You know, kittens, I am profoundly, deeply disappointed in you. Children are like tender shoots, nurtured and cultivated by their mothers with the hope that they will one day bear fruit. Yet, it seems plants are never meant to become rebellious. You, my children, were never meant to be mere weeds," Amma said, her gaze shifting from Reena to Nindhi. After a deliberate pause, she added, "The betrayal is unforgivable, Reena," her eyes locked onto Nindhi, emanating a merciless and frigid demeanour. "I was heartbroken when I discovered you pilfering essences from my chamber, concealing your thefts with an illusion spell. Seriously? ...You were never meant to betray your mother." She turned her icy gaze back to Reena, her voice dropping to a chilling whisper. "You were meant to grow... and provide me sustenance, to offer me... your flesh!"

Reena's heart pounded erratically, and terror surged through her veins, rendering her body quaking uncontrollably. The room descended into darkness, as malevolent eyes materialized on the walls—eyes of searing acid, weeping rivers of crimson. Sinister grins appeared, revealing rows of jagged teeth, and a haunting laughter reverberated through the space, amplifying her dread.

Nindhi, his gaze locked on Reena, who was sprawled on the floor in a frenzy of terror, stood up resolutely. "Let her go!" he demanded, his voice firm despite his trembling hands. "You have me already, willingly offering my flesh. Let her go! There's no need to harm Reena or her siblings. Release them, and I will remain here forever, like a loyal plant, bearing fruit for its master. But if you hurt Reena, I'll cease consuming the mere mugas you feed me, and my limbs will no longer regenerate to your satisfaction."

"You have no authority to command me," Amma grunted.

"This is a plea, Amma," Nindhi implored, his voice wavering with desperation. "Please." His eyes flickered toward Reena, paralyzed with fear on the floor and then turned back to Amma and continued, "You need me, and you know it. Reena isn't ready to be your "plant" yet; she's still in the process of becoming one. If you harm her, you risk losing my cooperation, and my limbs won't regenerate as needed. You rely on me, and you know it."

Amma fixed her gaze on Nindhi, then began to pace in slow, deliberate circles around them, her expression morphing into one of chilling contemplation. After a tense silence, she finally spoke, her voice eerily composed, "You have cornered me, Nindhi," she conceded. "You are correct." She glided over and positioned herself behind Nindhi, placing her hands on his shoulders in a mockingly affectionate manner. "Well, you know I have relished your flesh for years, and I have one last thing to say."

Reena felt a wave of relief as the malevolent eyes slowly faded from the walls. Turning her attention back to Amma and Nindhi, she watched as Amma raised her left hand, closed her eyes, and began murmuring something under her breath. In her grasp materialized a dark katana, its tsuba intricately designed like a spider. With a swift, seamless arc, she manoeuvred the blade effortlessly. A sickening thud resonated as something hit the ground, blood pooling and spreading across the floor.

The splatter of blood spattered across Reena's face, leaving her shaken by the abrupt turn of events. The decapitated soma crumpled to the floor. Her gaze shifted to Amma, who was frenetically wiping the sword clean with her saree. "I never found your flesh to my liking," she sneered with a chilling smile. A severed head rolled towards Reena. Her blood-spattered visage turned towards the head resting near her knee. Sheer terror was etched into her eyes, her entire body trembling with dread. The reality was almost too ghastly to comprehend. Nindhi lay lifeless on the floor, his once-vibrant presence now extinguished.

CHAPTER-18

Worse than Death

A gruesome canvas painted with blood was witnessed on the footing. As the sun dipped below the horizon, so did the hope for liberation dissolve into the growing shadows. Reena, slumped upon the blood-soaked ground, stared numbly at Nindhi's severed head. Her eyes, glistening with unshed tears, mirrored the deepening sorrow and desolation. She clung desperately to the illusion that Nindhi would miraculously awaken, whispering reassurances that he would be alright. Yet, stark reality set in; Nindhi's head lay motionless, a poignant testament to the finality of death. Unbelievably, after enduring years of pain and suffering, he succumbed to mortality. She reached for Nindhi's head, her trembling hands gently closing his eyes in a final, tender farewell. Tears streamed down her face in surges, each drop mingling with the bloodstained surface of Nindhi's lifeless visage. The anguish she felt was a deeper wound than any physical pain she had ever endured.

Amma sneered, "Aww, did you lose your loved one, little kitten? How tragic. But fret not, for you shall lose much more." With a dismissive flick, she wiped her katana clean on her saree, then stalked towards Reena. Grasping her by the hair with a vicious yank. "Save your tears for your siblings, dear. Save them for the suffering that awaits," Amma hissed, her voice dripping with malice. Reena, paralyzed with fear, could only stare at Amma's menacing figure and a blade in her hand.

Amma noticed Reena's horrified gaze fixated on the sword. "Oh, admiring my weapon?" she taunted, brandishing the blade with a theatrical flourish. "This is a cherished gift from the abyss. Every esteemed witch and wizard possesses one. This blade is dear to my soul." With a sinister grin, she turned her back on Reena, sensuously tracing her tongue along the cold steel. "I abhor bloodstains on it, especially those from such revoltingly vile flesh," Amma spat disdainfully on the floor. Seething with fury, Reena's hand plunged into her pouch, emerging with the Phoenix Spell Bomb. With a swift, determined motion, she hurled the Phoenix Spell Bomb with all her might. It struck Amma with precision, erupting into a fierce blaze that enveloped her in searing flames. A blood-curdling scream erupted from Amma as the fire consumed her. Reena stood, a cold resolve settling over her as she watched the witch's fiery demise. She wiped her tears away with her trembling hand, her voice a fierce cry of vengeance, "DIE, WITCH!"

As Amma heard Reena's anguished cry, her screaming abruptly ceased. Yet, she remained standing amidst the inferno, unscathed. "Do you honestly believe," she intoned, her voice dripping with contempt, "that a mere wretch like you could bring an end to me?"

Reena watched in horror as Amma remained unharmed, even as the flames engulfed her. The Phoenix spell bomb had proven ineffective, leaving Amma untouched. As the fire dissipated, Amma stood before Reena, a chilling smile etched across her face. Their eyes locked, and a wave of terror swept over Reena.

"How are you still alive?" Reena's voice cracked with desperation as she fell to her knees, tears streaming down her face. "How can this be?"

"I begin each day with a chalice of my fire-warning potion, my dear. It's been my shield against countless assaults," Amma said with a malevolent grin. She approached Reena, her footsteps echoing with menace, and with ruthless precision, drove the sword into her left eye, the blade emerging from the back of her skull. A piercing scream erupted from Reena's throat, her anguished cries filling the room as she thrashed on the ground like a serpent in agony. Amma swiftly withdrew the blade, leaving behind a gaping, grievous wound. Reena convulsed in agony for a while before collapsing onto the floor. Her laboured breaths echoed in the room as tears flowed from one eye while blood trickled from the other. Within minutes, however, the regenerative magic took effect, flawlessly restoring her eye without a trace of the previous wound.

"Devil's eye, you're a piece of art, my kitten," Amma remarked with a sinister smile. "This clears up the mystery surrounding the bloodstained dress I discovered in your cupboard." She waved her hand theatrically, and the chain soared through the air, coiling tightly around Reena's neck—the very same chain that had once bound Nindhi. Reena fought desperately against the constricting chain, invoking every breaking spell she had mastered in her study of the Conservancy from Dark Art. Yet, despite her efforts, she could not overcome the chains' relentless grip. Her knowledge of magic, once a beacon of hope, now seemed powerless to free her.

"The chain is infused with powerful enchantments," Amma hissed, her voice dripping with disdain. "It's impervious to the feeble efforts of an amateur like you."

Reena, defeated and despondent, slumped on the floor, her strength sapped. She wept uncontrollably, her earlier defiance crumbling into despair. Amma, with cold satisfaction, grasped the chain and forcefully pinned Reena against the wall. Pointing the sword at Reena's face, Amma delicately traced the blade along her cheek, drawing a stream of crimson. Leaning in with a sinister smile, she licked the blood from the blade, savouring its metallic tang.

"It's exquisite," Amma purred, her voice dripping with pleasure. "Your blood is far more delectable than Nindhi's, and your healing power is quite extraordinary. I'll be able to savour your flesh three times a week—one more day than I did with Nindhi."

Reena remained silent, her hope extinguished, surrendering to the dire situation. Amma glanced at Nindhi and remarked, "I considered roasting and feasting on his entire body, but I refuse to ingest his tainted flesh. I suppose, I should bury him." Seizing Nindhi's head and body by the leg, she dragged him out of the room, leaving a trail of blood in her wake. Moments later, a mop floated in, diligently wiping the floor, erasing the crimson trails.

Reena sat in the room, her thoughts consumed by the relentless unfairness of her life. What had she done to deserve this? She longed to cry more, but she knew deep down that tears would alter nothing. She yearned to escape, but she was ensnared. She even contemplated death, but that, too, eluded her. "What kind of existence is this?" she whispered to herself, her voice tinged with despair.

Meanwhile, Amma dragged Nindhi's body to the rear of the house. She callously flung the lifeless form and severed head into a freshly dug pit. Staring down at the remains, she muttered, "Rest in peace, tainted meat." The shovel autonomously began filling the grave, completing the task in mere minutes. With a snap of Amma's fingers, the grass regrew, and the ground appeared undisturbed as if it had never been touched.

Amma returned to her room, resting briefly before heading back to the pink room with a large kitchen knife. As she stood before Reena, a barbecue setup materialized from thin air. Gripping her knife, Amma moved towards Reena, seizing her wrist and tearing down the sleeves of her kurta.

(No no no....... I beg you don't do it.... don't don't don't... please don't)

Seizing Reena's right arm, Amma pressed the cold blade against her bare skin. "Hush, kitten," she whispered with a chilling calm. Reena, paralyzed with fear, pleaded desperately, "No... I beg you, don't do it... please, don't." Her body quaked uncontrollably, her pleas echoing through the room.

Amma chortled, her laughter echoing sinisterly as she playfully traced the edge of the knife across Reena's skin. She relished the fear that danced across Reena's face, her eyes glinting with malevolent satisfaction.

"In the grand theatre of mortal existence, what do you think becomes of the gluttons and the chickens, even as they plead for mercy? You are my quarry—a divine offering from nature's cruel embrace," she declared with a chilling smile. Laughing maniacally, she drove the knife into Reena's arm, beginning to carve with deliberate, torturous precision. From the bottomless slit of her arm, the blood gushed, cascading into a magically conjured bucket that appeared beside her. Overwhelmed by the searing agony, Reena's anguished cries filled the room. "Ahhh... I beg you, please don't... don't do this... don't..." Amma, unfazed by Reena's pleas, revelled in the macabre symphony of her screams. There was an unsettling pleasure in the sound of her torment. With a sinister calm, she continued her gruesome work, methodically slicing through her arms. As she worked, she hummed a melody, her movements deliberate and unhurried. The process, painstaking and grim, took about three and a half minutes to complete.

Amma carefully placed the severed arms on the grill, the flames crackling to life beneath them. As she set about the preparation, the aroma of the cooking flesh began to fill the room. Reena lay there, her breaths shallow and laboured, barely clinging to consciousness. The relentless pain had left her barely aware of her surroundings. Reena endured a torment beyond any she had ever known—an excruciating agony that transcended the physical pain of losing her arms and the relentless bleeding. It felt as if she had been thrust into the very bowels of a living hell, her suffering a relentless and consuming inferno.

Reena managed to lift her head just enough to witness her severed arms smoking on the grill. The scene was hauntingly reminiscent of a grotesque vision she had once had—a nightmare where Amma was baking a cake. Nindhi's ominous words about her grim future echoed in her mind, adding a chilling layer to her despair. Gazing at her shoulders, she saw that they had miraculously healed, but she was left arm-less.

Amma gathered the necessary ingredients for her macabre meal and then turned her attention to Reena. "Oh, my dear," she said with cheerfulness, "I can see you must be quite bored in your current predicament. Allow me to provide some entertainment." Donning a chef's hat and a crisp white apron, she faced Reena with a hauntingly cheerful grin. Her emerald eyes sparkled with a glint as she continued, "Welcome to my cooking show."

CHAPTER-19

The Blazing Hope

"Never did I foresee my arms, reduced to this state," Reena mused, her thoughts awash with horror. "Severed, mutilated, butchered. I could never have fathomed my existence plunging to such abysmal depths, particularly by the hands of the woman I once called Amma. The pain is mercifully absent at the moment, but I know it will return with a vengeance as the bones regenerate. The chains around my neck felt like the weight of despair itself, and my severed arms sizzled on the grill. What have I done to deserve such torment?" Reena's mind was echoing with anguish.

"Did Nindhi ever share his tale?" Amma inquired, attempting to spark a conversation. Reena stayed silent, the remnants of hope dwindling within her.

(clank clank) She banged the spatula with the barbeque kettle.

"I abducted Nindhi from a small town when he was just a child," Amma continued, flipping the arms sizzling on the grill. "I crafted a sense of belonging within these opulent walls and nurtured him. He was my cherished little kitten. I imparted knowledge to him, and furnished him with books and films, hoping to tether him to the castle indefinitely. But I was gravely mistaken; it only fueled his curiosity to rise above the confines of this castle. Eventually, he decided to leave me. I adored him... Nindhi, his tantalizing flesh... Mhhh... I bestowed upon him the gift of regeneration. All I required in return was his meat for my sustenance... but he grew resentful. He began to loathe me. I remained silent and ceased all discourse with him. When the perfect moment presented itself, I imprisoned him."

Reena sat propped against the wall, her posture slack and defeated, listening with hollow eyes.

"At first, his flesh was delectable, but over the years, it grew repugnant. The reasons eluded me, but the shift was undeniable. I came to realize the necessity for fresh sustenance and the acquisition of new progeny. I devoted myself to you as well, though not with the same fervour as I did for Nindhi. I withheld certain privileges from my new charges, intent on avoiding the errors of the past."

"At one point, I considered shrouding the pink door in a hex, but trust must be mutual. I wished to test the allegiance of my kittens."

"What loyalty do you expect when, in the end, you only seek to butcher us?" Reena wailed. "Look at me—I cannot die; my wounds perpetually mend," she lamented, her voice trembling as she recalled her futile attempts to end her suffering. "I am convinced it's a curse to be deprived of the release of death."

"This isn't mere butchery, Reena!!" Amma hissed, her eyes fixed on her cooking as she performed the final flips with a spatula. "You are still alive and regenerating your limbs, at best. It's merely a matter of enduring a bit of agony to supply me with essence. I would have mitigated the pain if it were within my power, but alas, magic has its bounds. There's nothing I can do to ease your suffering."

Reena's attention waned as Amma busied herself with the cooking. The only sound in the room was the sizzle of the grill and Amma's occasional hums of satisfaction. After a moment, she seized the bucket of Reena's blood, its contents sloshing with each movement. She poured the blood over the cooking meat, savouring the rich, iron-laden aroma that wafted through the air, enhancing the flavour of her grim culinary creation. "There was once a time when I had more sisters than I do now," Amma mused, basting the sizzling arms. "We used to hunt together, revelling in the thrill of the chase and the shared camaraderie. Those were the days I cherished most. But as fate would have it, many of them perished. To survive, I was forced to retreat into the shadows, journeying far from those days of glory. And now, here I am, ensconced in this castle with you, a solitary remnant of those once vibrant times."

The meal was prepared. The barbecue kettle transmuted into an elegant square table, draped in a pristine white cloth, a shimmering silver vase brimming with crimson roses, and a golden cutlery stand. An ethereal knife floated into Amma's grasp, gleaming ominously in the subdued light. With surgical precision, she commenced slicing the arms into meticulous, spheroidal segments, her movements deliberate and methodical. Placing the neatly sliced pieces on the plate, she artfully arranged them. A plush chair materialized behind her, and she seated herself gracefully. "Do you know what felled my fellow sisters?" she inquired, her gaze locking onto Reena's.

Reena remained silent, her gaze moved towards Amma.

"Their savage behaviour and stubbornness! it sealed their fate," Amma said, her tone dripping with disdain. "They refused to evolve with the advancements in mysticism, clinging to their uncivilized ways, and thus met their demise."

Reena observed Amma savouring a morsel, her eyes fluttering shut in blissful contentment. "Exquisite," she purred. "Your flesh is remarkably tender and delectable." Reena diverted her gaze to the floor, an unsettling discomfort settling over her as she witnessed Amma feasting upon her own flesh.

Amma said with a sinister smile, "You might even find yourself feeling a pang of loneliness. But fret not, your younger sibling is on his way. In just a few years, you two will be playing a game of seven stones with chains around your necks."

Reena's face paled at the horrifying prospect. Her voice trembled as she implored, "You've found my flesh to your liking, haven't you? You even said it surpasses Nindhi's. Please, spare Bhushan from this dreadful fate."

"Ah, my dear kitten," Amma purred with a malevolent grin, "I possess your siblings as well. Their destinies are entwined with service to me, just as yours has been. I cannot afford to squander such delectable flesh."

Silence fell once more, the futility of Reena's pleas clear to all. It seemed a pointless endeavor to beseech her mother any further.

Amma chewed thoughtfully, savouring each bite before speaking, "I was wondering how you managed to create the Phoenix spell bomb."

Reena remained mute, her silence a testament to her rebellion against Amma.

Amma took another bite, her eyes gleaming with satisfaction. "Ah, as anticipated, you choose to remain silent about it," she murmured between chews. She, then, gazed at a gleaming fork in her hand, her expression shifting to one of mock contemplation. "Ah... and what should I tell your siblings about your disappearance?" she asked playfully. "Do offer me some guidance or shall I say, that their self-centred sister left them here to endure my torments?"

Consumed by fury, Reena ached to lunge at Amma, to grasp her throat and strangle her with whatever strength she had left. But her hands were gone, leaving only the blaze of her anger in her eyes. With a voice trembling with rage, she screamed, "YOU WRETCHED CRONE! I WILL MAKE YOU PAY... I SWEAR... I WILL DESTROY YOU!"

"Is this the outcome of my nurturing? How ungrateful," Amma remarked. "This proves that Nindhi was never a worthy companion for you. Despite his youthful appearance, he was far too mature to be your friend... The results of the Mugas are indeed remarkable, wouldn't you agree?" Amma, absorbed in her feast, savoured each morsel with delight before Reena's anguished eyes. When she had finally finished, the table and all its elaborate accoutrements vanished into thin air.

"Very well, I'll devise a plan," Amma declared, rising gracefully from her seat. As she moved toward the door, she paused and glanced back with a wry smile. "Oh, and by the way," she added, gesturing toward the wall on Reena's right, "that's actually a lavatory. You'll have to pass through it to get there. For now, farewell, until hunger beckons again." With a final click, Amma locked the room from the outside, sealing Reena's fate. Overwhelmed by a wave of despair, Reena felt the weight of her desolation. With Nindhi gone and her options dwindling, she was adrift in uncertainty, grappling with the bleakness of her next steps. The last vestige of hope flickered in the form of the enigmatic tree. Reena, her heart heavy with despair, silently prayed that her younger brother Bhushan would discover it. She clung to the fragile hope that he would unravel the truth about Amma and finish the task left incomplete, rescuing her from the looming catastrophe.

Meanwhile, Bhushan and Lily's concern for Reena's disappearance deepened. They scoured every corner of the castle, their worry growing with each passing moment. Their desperate search for Reena stretched into hours, driven by the urgency to find her after such an unsettling absence. While searching for Reena, Bhushan dashed outside the castle, his anxiety propelling him forward. After a thorough inspection of the grounds, he halted at the Ficus tree. As his hand made contact with the gnarled bark, an unforeseen force enveloped him, drawing him deep into the tree's enigmatic depths. The portal within the tree had been left ajar, a careless oversight by Reena in her eagerness to show Nindhi the Phoenix spell bomb.

Bhushan found himself sprawled on the floor. As he rose, he surveyed the vast room with its sinuous walls and captivating ambience. The familiar bookshelves and furnishings caught his eye, but his attention was drawn to an intriguingly shaped triangular structure standing out in the room. Fascinated, Bhushan approached the triangular structure and examined it meticulously, calling out for Reena, hoping she might be hidden inside. The silence that greeted his inquiry left him disheartened. After a while, he left the tree and resumed his search, determined to find his sister.

"Bhushan," a voice echoed through the air. He turned to see Amma beckoning him inside. It was dinner time, and the family had gathered at the dining table—a rare occasion since Amma had been more distant recently. She was ladling mugas into bowls.

"Dinner tonight looks exceptional," Amma remarked. "It has a more vibrant colour than usual," she added, as she continued to ladle the contents into bowls with a measured grace.

"Where's Reena, Amma?" asked Lily.

Amma glanced at Lily and narrowed her eyes. With an exaggerated gasp, she feigned a look of concern. "She isn't with you?" she inquired, her voice laced with surprise.

"No," Bhushan replied.

Lily asked anxiously, "Is she losth?"

"No, no, she must be around here somewhere, honey," Amma reassured with an air of nonchalance, continuing to ladle the vibrant mugas into the next bowl. "She'll come any minute now."

"Amma," Bhushan exclaimed, his eyes alight with excitement. "The tree outside is absolutely enchanting." He remembered the tree he had neglected to mention earlier, the wonder of it still fresh in his mind. "It's like a hidden sanctuary within... There are countless books, shelves, plants, and even a peculiar bird designed from cloth... It's quite expansive. Why didn't you share this secret with us before?"

Amma was completely perplexed by Bhushan's revelation. A sense of unease crept over her, casting a shadow on her otherwise composed demeanour. She pushed the bowls filled with mugas with one of her fingers, causing them to clatter dramatically against the table.

"Finish your dinner, honey, and then I'd like to hear your story," Amma said with a smile as she rose and marched outside the house.

As she approached the tree, her eyes glowed with an eerie green light, meticulously scrutinizing it. She uncovered a cloaking enchantment, crafted to veil its existence from her. The profound secret of Reena was now fully exposed. Amma summoned her twisted wand, crowned with a zombie-like butterfly, and dispelled the enchantment. As she stepped inside, she was greeted by a vast workshop brimming with arcane books and entities, a hidden trove she had remained oblivious to for years. With a darkly satisfied expression, she made her way back to the castle and resumed her seat at the table.

Once the children had completed their meal, Amma's gaze grew intense as she fixed her eyes upon them. With a swift motion, she twirled her wand in the air, conjuring a mesmerizing spell. A spectral green light wove from the children's foreheads, drifting toward the wand with an almost ethereal grace. She deftly extracted the recent memories from their temples, her task facilitated by the memories' recent formation and their fragile anchoring in the brain. The process was seamless as if she were delicately plucking blossoms from a barely rooted stem. Once the memory extraction was complete, Amma directed them to retire to their rooms, her voice smooth and commanding, assuring them that she would find Reena. The children obediently made their way to their chambers.

Amma glided through the pink door into Reena's room, her demeanor calm and composed. "Darling," she began, her voice laced with a cold reassurance, "I'm aware of the tree."

"What tree?" Reena attempted to act clueless.

"Your beloved tree, my dear. The one harbouring your cherished witchcraft workshop."

Reena's heart raced as a wave of dread swept over her. The revelation that Amma had uncovered the workshop—so meticulously concealed within the tree's protective enchantment—sent shivers down her spine. Her once secure refuge now seemed like a nightmare come to life, her fears manifesting with every dark thought.

"I haven't the faintest idea what you're referring to," Reena fibbed.

Amma offered no reply, moving towards the door. Just before her departure, she paused and turned, saying, "There's a delightful surprise waiting for you, kitten. I'll return shortly to fetch you."

Amma retreated to her chamber, reclining on her bed with mounting irritation. She retrieved a crystal ball from an old carton in her cupboard, where it had lain dormant for years. Placing it on the bedside table, she began to peer through the orb, observing her children with a watchful gaze. As Amma waited for her children to fall asleep, her patience waned. Despite her efforts, they remained restless, consumed with worry over Reena. She considered using an enchantment to lull them to sleep but realized it would interfere with the hypnotic spell she had previously cast. Amma herself was yawning from the prolonged concentration on the crystal ball. After an extended wait, Amma finally saw her children succumb to sleep. With a grim satisfaction, she moved to Reena's room. At the door, she raised her hand, and the chain unfastened from the wall, coiling into her grip. With cold, unfeeling intent, she hauled Reena from the room, dragging her along with the same indifference one might show a mere varmint.

Reena, though reluctantly, complied with Amma's directives, matching her pace with each step. Amma guided her outside, positioning them before a tree where they maintained a deliberate distance. As Reena observed Amma's calculated actions, a profound sense of dread settled in her stomach, hinting at the dark machinations that were unfolding. Raising her hand high, she summoned her butterfly wand, whose eyes shimmered ominously. Directing it towards the tree, she began intoning an ancient mantra. The eyes of the butterfly glowed with spectral light, and a vivid green fire burst forth like a comet. A fierce gale assailed Reena, causing her to collapse to the ground. As she struggled to her feet, the relentless wind whipped her hair into her face, blurring her sight. Clearing her eyes, Reena beheld the tree engulfed in flames, set ablaze by Amma's enchanted wand. Amma stood amidst the inferno, her laughter echoing maniacally through the chaos. Her silhouette was a dark, menacing figure against the tumultuous backdrop of the roaring flames. Desperation surged within Reena, and she screamed in anguish, understanding that everything contained within the tree represented her final vestiges of hope. Years of research, painstakingly compiled by Nindhi and Reena's relentless quest to uncover secrets, were consumed by the inferno blazing before her. Collapsing to her knees, she wept bitterly upon the scorched grass, her tears streaming uncontrollably only to be whisked away by the unyielding wind. In that harrowing moment, it dawned upon her that her final hope—the possibility of Bhushan rescuing her—was nothing more than a forlorn fantasy. Her cries reverberated through the air, a haunting testament to her despair and broken spirit, as she longed for a miracle to rescue her from this infernal plight. Before her sobs could even subside, Amma began to drag her away, inexorably pulling her from the remnants of her shattered hopes. Unfazed, Amma allowed the tree to fall prey to the conflagration, its flames devouring its perplexing entities. As Reena resisted Amma's relentless grip, she was inexorably dragged back to the pink door room, where she was once more tethered to the wall, her defiance fading into submission.

"Good night, kitten," Amma sneered and departed. Heading directly to the children's chamber, she found Bhushan and Lily ensconced in a peaceful slumber. With a flick of her wand, she began intoning incantations. A sinuous, emerald-hued mist unfurled from the wand, coiling around the heads of the unsuspecting children, casting a spell that promised further mischief. She wove a fabricated narrative into their dreams, a memory meticulously crafted to intertwine with her malevolent scheme. As the spell's power waned, she stood amidst the room, basking in the satisfaction of her perceived victory.

"The tale of Reena has reached its conclusion," Amma grinned.

CHAPTER-20

Everything in its Right Place

The morning broke with a serene beauty for Amma. She awoke enveloped in tranquillity, confident that everything was up to snuff. Rising with the dawn, she prepared her breakfast, savouring the meat from Reena that she had meticulously carved the night before. As she cooked, she hummed one of her cherished self-penned witch songs: *Cook the flesh of mortals true, Savour the feast with a rhythm askew. Witchy melodies in the morning's grace, A darkened tune, a haunting embrace.* Placing her breakfast on the bed, she savoured it while immersing herself in one of her favourite storybooks. *The Last Witch on Earth* wove a dark fantasy tale of a witch who survived against the odds, and revived the witch society by transforming humans into witches. The story, complemented by a glass of exquisite blood, was an integral part of her morning ritual.

She finished her breakfast, mindful that it was time for the children to awaken. Each deliberate step toward the dining table brought her closer to the final stage of her intricate scheme. Taking her place at the table, she settled into her chair, awaiting the arrival of the children with calm anticipation.

Bhushan and Lily stirred from their slumber, their first worry being Reena's unexplained absence. Troubled by a disquieting dream he kept to himself, Bhushan methodically searched the room, his concern growing with each passing moment. "Whereh.. is Reena?" Lily asked, her voice laced with unease. "Perhaps she's at the dining table, awaiting us for breakfast," he suggested, though his uncertainty was evident in his tone.

They moved down the corridor and reached the dining room. There, Amma sat at the table, her sobs resonating through the room. Her head was buried in her arms, and her grief was palpable, filling the space with a deep, sorrowful echo. Bhushan and Lily rushed to her side, their eyes searching the surroundings for any sign of Reena. With growing worry, Lily asked, "Amma, why areh yohh cryinh? Whath has happenh?"

"Reena... S-She was running away," Amma rose, stammered through her tears. "I called out to her, but she didn't heed my cries! I pursued her, but she crossed the threshold of our house... and came face-to-face with the one-eyed monster. It... it seized her and devoured her right before my eyes! I was utterly helpless, incapable of saving my precious kitten. What a terrible mother I am!" Amma sobbed even more intensely, her body quaking with sorrow.

Bhushan was stunned by Amma's tale, realizing it mirrored his own haunting dream. "That's exactly what I dreamed last night, Amma. Typically, my dreams of the one-eyed monster involve it devouring everyone, but this time, it was Reena alone. I saw her... it was consuming only her, just Reena," he exclaimed, his voice trembling with the weight of the revelation.

"I hadh the same dreamhh," Lily cried. The children mourned, never anticipating that Reena would meet such a tragic end. She fled on her own and met her demise while trying to escape. Bhushan was deeply troubled, recalling Reena's unstable state of mind before her disappearance. Yet, a question began to stir in his thoughts.

"Amma, how did Reena manage to reach the boundary wall?" He asked. "None of us have ever managed to get that far before."

"I don't know... Ask your father... ask him!" she burst out, tears streaming down her face again. "He's the one who built the wall for your protection. I don't have no clue about it." Amma slumped back against the table, her cries growing more insistent. Frustrated with Bhushan's probing, she wept loudly, hoping to drown out his questions. "I'm not even sure how I managed to bypass the wall, but I had to, for your survival, for this family, I only wish your father had entrusted me with the proficiency." She started to cry even louder, using her tears as a shield against Bhushan's questions. This was her typical strategy for avoiding discussions about the wall and what lay beyond it. Bhushan watched his mother's dramatic display, a wave of guilt sweeping over him. He found himself unable to ask another question. The weight of Reena's death, perhaps due to her solitary and unusual behaviour, pressed heavily on him. "I should have told you, Amma. I knew Reena wasn't sane anymore... I should have confided in you," he sobbed intensely, standing beside Amma. The weight of his inaction, the failure to step in and assist Reena, was more than he could bear.

"It's not your fault, my dear," Amma reassured Bhushan, rising from her chair to envelop him in a comforting embrace. "I-I can't fathom why she felt the need to flee from such a loving family. With a sweet sister like Lily and a caring brother like you, Bhushan, she should have felt secure and cherished. I... I don't even know if she was okay... to begin with... to feel the need to escape. It's my fault; I failed to protect my precious child. My own selfishness blinded me, and now one of my kittens is dead. I've failed you all!"

"You are the best mother anyone could ask for... don't ever say otherwise. Everything you did was to protect us," Bhushan insisted, tears shimmering in his eyes. Amma hid her face in her hands, a secretive smile tugging at her lips. Bhushan's reaction confirmed that her strategy was working and the final stage of her plan had succeeded. She began to cry, her face obscured, her performance perfectly executed.

Suddenly, the conversation veered to Reena, and the siblings began to lay the blame squarely on her for the tragedy. If only she hadn't fled, they argued, the disaster might have been averted. In the exchange between their mother and the siblings, Reena became the focal point of their accusations. Amma feigned panic, the final touch of her performance. "Promise me you'll never venture beyond the wall," she implored, her voice trembling. "I've already lost one kitten... I-I can't bear to lose another!" She cast anxious glances between Bhushan and Lily, her hands gripping their arms with desperate intensity.

The children solemnly vowed to abide by Amma's request. She drew Lily into her embrace, wrapping her arms around both Lily and Bhushan. Together, they wept in mutual sorrow before quietly taking their places at the dining table. None of them had an appetite; the weight of the news hung heavily on their hearts. Nonetheless, Amma insisted they eat, determined not to let them miss a meal. Skipping meals would hinder the development of a sufficient meat supply, and the children didn't wish to add to Amma's distress. Bhushan, in particular, was consumed by anger towards Reena, his emotions twisted by Amma's manipulative influence. Hurt and irate, he ate his food with a hardened heart. He had urged Reena to confide in him if anything troubled her, but her fierce independence meant she never sought help. Anger, guilt, and sadness swirled within him, a tempest of emotions he could not quell. The entire day hung heavily over both of them, immersing them in an ocean of sorrow. It felt as though a piece of themselves had been irrevocably lost. Amma opted to forgo her usual time with fellow witches that day, determined to offer her children a tangible sense of her presence and care. She kept a watchful eye on everything, remaining vigilant in the wake of Reena's actions, despite her witchly instincts reassuring her that there was no immediate danger. The witch's keen intellect possessed an uncanny ability to unravel and resolve every challenge.

Several days passed, and Reena remained ensconced in the pink room, seated by the wall as she meticulously carved tally marks into its surface. Using her own blood as ink, she painstakingly recorded each count. At times, she had to wait for two or three days for her fingers to regrow before she could draw all the tally marks she had mentally tracked. With a bite to her finger, she etched the marks, a routine that had grown painfully familiar. Reena's limbs healed with remarkable speed, usually within two to three days, a sharp contrast to Nindhi's protracted recovery time of nearly a week. Amma was profoundly pleased, finding herself even more content than before, thanks to a steady supply of high-quality meat. The tally marks on the wall were a constant presence, but Amma scarcely reacted to them anymore; after all, a simple tally mark held no threat to her. Reena also noticed a change in the basket she once carried, which had previously been used to transport meat for her fellow witches. The difference now was that, whereas the basket once contained Nindhi's meat, it now held Reena's.

As time wore on, Amma returned to her usual self, no longer burdened by caution. She took pleasure in the company of her children, her fellow witches, and especially in the abundance of food. Today marked the seventy-fifth day of Reena's captivity, her sorrow deepening with time, though now more subdued and less apparent. She had grown accustomed to the routine, no longer protesting or voicing complaints. Even when Amma served her limbs, Reena no longer wept. She consumed the Mugas with reluctance, doing so only to safeguard her siblings' well-being. Once, in a moment of desperation, she attempted to consume her own flesh but recoiled at the repulsiveness of the act. With Amma providing Mugas daily, hunger was no longer a concern for Reena.

Amma approached her, beaming with delight. "I am so pleased with you, Reena. Do you see the glow on my face?" She placed her hands on her cheeks and twirled like a child. "All thanks to you, my dear kitten." After slicing her hands, Amma handed Reena the Mugas and left. Reena consumed it in a manner reminiscent of a dog, due to her temporary lack of hands. Once she finished, she lay down, her thoughts heavy with memories of Nindhi.

Nindhi had confided in her about how he found solace in imagining the world beyond, finding brief moments of happiness within his thoughts. Though he knew escape was futile, his imagination offered a temporary reprieve. Inspired by his words, Reena tried to follow his lead. She closed her eyes, picturing the world outside the house and the pink door that kept her confined. Yet, her thoughts quickly spiralled to the haunting memory of Nindhi's death, causing her to open her eyes abruptly. The harsh reality struck her: imagination offered no escape; instead, it only deepened her torment. "You were wrong, Nindhi," Reena murmured to herself. "Your faith in the power of imagination was in vain. It didn't set you free, and it won't free me either."

Lying on the ground and staring up at the ceiling for a while, she closed her eyes once more. In an attempt to escape mentally, she began to conjure joyful visions. In her imagination, Reena and Nindhi were running away from the witch's grasp, hand in hand with her siblings. The awareness of its fantastical nature brought a faint smile to her face, yet she savoured the illusion, finding solace in the comforting falsehood. For the first time in a long while, a genuine smile touched her lips as she continued to weave her fantasy. She envisioned them basking in pink cake by sunlit shores, adorned in whimsical, multicoloured, pointy hats—an image reminiscent of a comic. Despite Nindhi's death, he remained alive in her heart, and this expansive dreamscape brought a deeper, more genuine smile to her face.

Somewhere within Bhushan and Lily's realm, the acceptance of Reena's loss gradually wove itself into their daily reality. Over time, the heaviness of their sorrow lifted, and they found themselves absorbed in the rhythms of ordinary life. Laughter once again took centre stage as Amma crafted a small wooden sanctuary for them to play in. The death of the Ficus tree was attributed by Amma to a lightning strike, casting an initial shadow of sorrow over the children. Nevertheless, She built the "Toy House" elevated safely from the ground, filling it with a delightful array of toys. In this whimsical haven, the duo found solace and spent much of their time. While occasional pangs of sadness for Reena lingered, most days were now brightened with cheerful moments.

One day, Amma visited Reena with a new purpose, not for meat. Standing before her with a smile, she reassured Reena that the past was now behind them. However, she had removed the couch from the room as a form of punishment following the discovery of the workshop inside the tree. The tree had been successfully scorched. Recognizing the quality of Reena's meat, she decided to grant a reward. With a flick of her wand, she conjured a new sapphire and cream sofa into the room.

"Comfortable enough?" Amma inquired, but Reena remained silent. Without waiting for a response, Amma hurriedly left the room, seemingly on her way elsewhere.

Reena carved another tally mark into the wall, marking her five hundred forty-two days of captivity under the witch's control. Seated on the new sofa, her expression remained lifeless and vacant. Despite everything, the sofa offered a comforting embrace, prompting her to recline and close her eyes. In her mind, she envisioned a world where she was free from the witch's grasp, surrounded by her siblings and her departed friend.

With her eyes closed, she immersed herself in fantasies of soaring through the skies in a tent with Nindhi and her siblings, savouring a brief surge of excitement and joy. In these daydreams, she escaped her grim reality, embracing the whimsical adventures of her cherished comic book characters.

This was her daily escape, a fleeting respite that brought a brief smile to her lips. However, the sound of the doorknob turning abruptly shattered her momentary peace, casting a shadow of grim across Reena's face. She steeled herself for the possibility of Amma's return, bracing for another gloomy extraction session. But in the next heartbeat, her expression shifted from bother to sheer astonishment— Someone familiar stood before her.

In disbelief, Reena questioned the reality of the scene before her, wondering if she was lost in a hallucination. As she attempted to rise, she faltered and collapsed to the floor, only to be steadied by Nindhi's reassuring hand. His words resonated with hope and promise: "I've come to rescue you, Reena."

CHAPTER-21

Unexpected Arrival

Reena couldn't trust her eyes; the figure before her appeared almost ethereal. She rubbed her eyes repeatedly with her forearm, yet the vision of Nindhi supporting her persisted. The undeniable reality stared back at her, reflected in her peacock eyes with a vividness that left no room for doubt. She scrutinized his features—his wolf-like eyes, the familiar contours of his nose, and his hair, now longer and neatly combed. He seemed healthier than she remembered. Her eyes drifted to his kurta, a rich burgundy adorned with a checkered pattern on its collar. She questioned if this vision was a mirage conjured by her daily flights of imagination or a cruel torment imposed by the witch.

Nindhi leaned in, wrapping Reena tightly around her waist, and offered a warm smile. Reena gently touched his face with her right hand, missing three fingers, and whispered, "Nindhi." As he observed her hand, he noticed a faint bruise from a bite that healed before his eyes. His gaze then shifted to the tally marks etched on the wall.

"Reena, let's make our escape," he implored, his grip tightening around her waist. "I've come to rescue you." Reena heard Nindhi's remarks, but suspicion gnawed at her mind. Could this be another of the witch's cruel deceptions? Overwhelmed by frustration and doubt, her face flushed with anger. She mustered all her strength to push Nindhi away, but with one of her hands missing, she lacked the force to dislodge him. He lost his balance and stumbled back a few steps. Reena, unsteady herself, toppled over, colliding with the sofa before crashing to the floor. Struggling to rise, she reached for the sofa, but her efforts were in vain. With her missing limbs, she found herself unable to grasp hold.

"YOUR TRICKS WON'T FOOL ME, DAMNED DAEMONARA!" Reena howled, her voice filled with defiance.

"Reena, it's really me, Nindhi. I've come to rescue you," he reassured her, his voice earnest and filled with urgency.

"Don't you dare deceive me, you murderous witch! Nindhi died before my eyes—YOU KILLED HIM!" She cried.

"Reena, I am Nindhi," he said, leaning closer. "I understand it's difficult to believe how I survived, but you must trust me. I came to rescue you. For our escape's sake, come with me."

"I don't believe you," Reena snapped, her voice sharp with distrust.

"You must believe me, for I am the one to whom you entrusted your only secret," Nindhi said with a knowing glance. "You spoke of the teachings imparted to you by the one-eyed master in your dreams."

Reena was taken aback, her eyes widening in disbelief.

"Nindhi, is it really you?" She gasped, tears streaming down her cheeks. He gently grasped her shoulder, lifting her up, and enveloped her in a warm embrace. "It's all right now. We're going to make it through this. Today, we're breaking free from this inferno together."

Nindhi reached into the pouch he carried and retrieved a small bottle of yellow liquid. With meticulous precision, he dispensed three drops onto the chain. The liquid reacted swiftly, causing the chain to dissolve into a wisp of yellow smoke, thereby freeing Reena from its grasp. Helping her to sit on the sofa, Nindhi reached into his pouch and produced a pink, square-shaped candy adorned with an intricate flower engraving. He placed it gently in Reena's mouth, offering a small gesture of comfort amidst their harrowing escape.

"Eat it, Reena!" he urged. Reena swallowed the candy, and immediately her severed arms began to glow pink, their regeneration swift and painless. She moved her fingers tentatively, clenched her fists a couple of times, and then gently touched his face, again, her touch both tender and reassuring.

"Let's go," he said. "We need to get out of here."

"Wait, Nindhi," Reena asked, her curiosity piqued, "how did you survive? Your head... it was severed."

"We're running out of time, Reena. We need to go. I'll explain everything once we're safely out of here," Nindhi urged. Reena nodded in agreement but halted as they neared the exit. "No, I can't just leave like this," she insisted.

"Why not?"

"My siblings—I need to find them; we can't leave them behind," Reena protested. Nindhi, understanding her concern, handed his pouch to her. "You know how to use its contents. If you run into the witch, this will help you," he said urgently. "Meet me outside, and make it quick."

Nindhi started rushing towards the main door.

"Wait, Nindhi," she called out, again, her voice tinged with concern. "How do you plan our escape?" Shadows of worry and unease enveloped her.

He offered her a reassuring smile, which brought Reena close to a sense of relief. With that, Nindhi dashed out of the house, while Reena hurried toward her room. Her heart pounded with every step. What if Amma discovered her absence? But there was no time to waste. She reached her bedroom door, a warm smile spreading across her face. Bhushan, lost in play with his toys on the bed, looked up in surprise. His eyes widened in disbelief at the sight of Reena standing before him, alive and well. It was almost too surreal to grasp.

"Reena!" he exclaimed, rushing toward her. He enveloped her in a tight embrace, his voice quivering with emotion. "I thought you were dead. Amma said... she said you had fled beyond the boundary and you were devoured by the one-eyed monster."

"Bhushan, she deceived you. The grim reality is that she's a cannibal witch, a Daemonara. She imprisoned me in the pink room, where she devoured my limbs daily. Her cruel scheme was to do the same to you and Lily, once you turned thirteen."

Bhushan, his eyes a whirl of confusion and fear, struggled to grasp the full extent of the situation. Yet, an instinctive trust in Reena tugged at his heart. Without hesitation, he resolved to follow her, setting aside his doubts for the moment.

"Where is Lily, Bhushan?" Reena asked.

"Playing outside."

"Okay, let's get her. We are leaving this place," Reena said, her voice steady with resolve. Grasping Bhushan's hand, they sprinted down the corridor towards the exit. "Going somewhere, my kittens?" The shrill voice echoed through the hallway. Bhushan halted abruptly, glancing around in panic, but Reena, with unwavering determination, pulled him forward. She kept running towards the exit. They both charged towards the doorway, only to be met with a resounding slam as the main door shut before them. They skidded to a halt, breathless. Reena gripped the door handle with both hands, straining with every ounce of her strength, but the door remained immovable. Turning back, Reena saw Amma perched on a chair above the dining table, her ankles crossed with an air of casual authority. She sipped from a glass filled with a deep red liquid, then regarded them with a chillingly composed demeanour. "It appears my earlier warnings didn't quite sink in... And where, might I ask, do you think you're going, my little kittens?"

CHAPTER-22

Valiant Cowboy

"Amma, why did you mislead us about Reena's demise? She's still alive!" Bhushan demanded, his face flushed with outrage.

"Because, to me, she's as good as dead," Amma replied with a casual sip from her blood-filled glass. "She betrayed me, and now she's nothing but a ghost of the past." Taking another languid sip, she fixed Bhushan with a sinister gaze, sending a chill down his spine. Running her tongue sensually over her lips, Amma continued, "Forget about her, Bhushan. Come stand by my side. I'm sure you wouldn't want to end up in the pink room before your time. It's a place of unspeakable horrors."

Bhushan was paralyzed with fear. Amma's demeanour had shifted dramatically, now more menacing than the ghouls, phantoms, and werewolves from the stories. Quivering uncontrollably, he hesitated, torn between moving toward Amma and staying put. But Reena's resolute grip on his hand pulled him back to reality. "Bhushan and Lily are coming with me," she declared with unwavering determination. "We're leaving this horrid place!"

"No, I won't permit it," Amma declared, her eyes locked onto Bhushan. "The world beyond is fraught with danger, teeming with monsters." Despite the revelation of her deceit regarding Reena's fate, she remained resolute, attempting to sway Bhushan with her warnings. "Should you choose to join me," she continued with calculated calmness, "I'll fill your toy house with an abundance of toys and spare your life." A glimmer of hope sparkled in her eyes, believing she could persuade Bhushan to stay willingly, only to later erase his memories with her magic.

"Monsters! Monsters are not beyond the boundary but right here within these walls," declared Reena. She shifted her gaze from Bhushan to Amma and exclaimed, "And it's you, our mother, Amma Meiga, the Cannibal Witch."

The glass shattered against the wall above her head, spraying fragments in all directions. Droplets of blood splattered onto her yellow floral lehenga. Reena's gaze shifted from the blood-stained wall to Amma, who stood defiantly atop the table, her eyes blazing with fury. Anger burned in her emerald eyes as she realized her attempts at manipulation had failed. With a glare at the shattered glass and then at Reena, Amma spoke through gritted teeth, seething with rage.

"I don't know how you managed to evade the prison room, but escaping from my house... that won't happen," she snarled, her glare piercing through them.

Reena braced herself for the looming confrontation, swiftly reaching into the pouch. Suddenly, two shadowy, tentacle-like serpentine tails lunged toward her, coiling around her and squeezing like a vice. The pressure forced the bag from her grasp, causing its contents to spill onto the floor.

Reena's gaze fixed upon her mother. Amma's hair had morphed into serpentine tendrils, evoking haunting memories of the ghastly reflection she'd glimpsed in the mirror shard. Amma's sinister grin widened as she tightened her grip, the tentacles secreting a corrosive slime that began to dissolve Reena's clothing. Her skin seared, and her bones crunched under immense pressure, but her ability to heal sustained her, though it fought a losing battle against the relentless damage. Despite her regeneration, the dark, grotesque tendrils inflicted such harrowing harm that Reena couldn't fully recover, leaving her in a constant state of agonizing repair.

Bhushan was engulfed in a profound sense of unease and terror, helplessly witnessing the unfolding nightmare. Fear gripped him tightly as he watched his mother's once-soft hair transform into sinister black tendrils, ensnaring and harming her own beloved daughter. The anguished cries of Reena spurred him into action. Bhushan hurried towards her, his heart pounding, determined to save his sister from the monstrous grip. With steely resolve, Bhushan grasped one of the coiled tendrils and tried to pry it away from Reena. A piercing cry of agony tore from his throat as searing pain coursed through him, and wisps of smoke began to rise from his burned palms. Releasing the slick, writhing appendage, he stared in horror at his charred hands, smoke still curling from the scorched flesh.

He writhed in agony, his focus snapping back to Reena, whose tormented screams filled the air. Desperately, he reached into his pocket, which was always stocked with stones. Retrieved one and aimed for Amma's eye, but the searing pain in his burnt hands caused him to misfire, striking her forehead instead. Amma, stunned by the unforeseen impact, turned to face Bhushan, who stood resolutely clutching his slingshot.

A tentacle surged from Bhushan's left, propelling him airborne before he crashed violently to the ground. Reena watched in horror as Bhushan lay sprawled on the floor, his neck twisted and cheek bleeding. The brutal impact had scorched his left eye and cheek, causing his eyeball to bulge from its socket.

"Bhushan... no... no!" Reena's anguished scream cut through the air.

"Poor thing, he must have succumbed to his mother," Amma remarked with icy detachment, redoubling her assault on Reena.

Reena, bracing against the relentless onslaught, tried to summon a protective shield. However, her nascent abilities were insufficient against the overpowering force of the coiled tentacles.

Meanwhile, Bhushan lay sprawled on the floor, his eyes locked onto the scene of his mother's merciless torment of Reena, as his own strength waned and his life force slowly ebbed away.

"Look, Reena, the consequences you've unleashed upon your brother. Cease conjuring that good for nothing shield and surrender," Amma admonished.

"Never!" Reena exclaimed defiantly.

"Don't test my patience, kitten. I wish no end to you," Amma said with feigned tenderness.

"D-Death... death is preferable to living as your prisoner," Reena declared.

Yet another tentacle rose, winding around Reena's neck, wisps of smoke rose, squeezing the life out of her. Her face darkened to a ghastly purple, and her breath was choked from her lungs. The piercing screams that once filled the room had been extinguished, stifled by the relentless grip of asphyxiation.

"If you think an easy death is in store for you, think again. I was lenient before, but now you'll see my true nature," Amma snarled.

Reena's breaths grew ragged and her vision dimmed as Amma's form blurred into a dark haze. Desperately, she wished for Amma to relent, but the witch appeared to take sadistic pleasure in the suffering she inflicted.

"This will be a lesson you won't soon forget... Now, let's take you to the pink room," Amma declared, her voice laced with malice.

As Amma dragged Reena toward the prison room, a translucent marble filled with azure liquid flew through the air. Instinctively, Amma flicked the marble with one of her tentacles, sending it crashing into the exit door. The impact triggered an explosion of blue flames, the door shattering into fragments and a shockwave rippling through the room. The tentacles around Reena loosened, their grip faltering as Amma turned in bewilderment toward the source of the disturbance. Her eyes widened in shock as she saw Bhushan standing before her. His neck had miraculously healed, though his face was marred by a bleeding wound and his eyeball was half out of his socket. Bhushan stared in disbelief at the explosion caused by a small, azure marble that had fallen from Reena's bag.

"Devil's eye, how can you heal at such a young age? You're barely eleven!" Amma exclaimed, her voice a mix of astonishment and frustration.

"RUN, BHUSHAN!" Reena's desperate cry echoed through the room.

Two menacing tentacles lashed out at Bhushan. Acting on Reena's urgent command, he sprinted towards his bedroom, his heart racing with terror. He charged forward with every bit of strength he could muster, only to slam into the door of his room and collapse onto the floor. Casting a hurried glance over his shoulder, Bhushan noticed the tendrils hovering at a cautious distance, reluctant to pursue him further. He quickly got to his feet, slammed the door shut behind him, and locked it tightly, securing himself within the room.

"This fresh batch of mugas-eating brats is yielding splendid results," Amma exclaimed joyfully, her tentacles coiling around Reena, again. "Let's pay him a visit. My hair lacks the reach to touch him from this distance."

As Amma spoke, she began advancing towards Bhushan's bedroom. Yet, dragging Reena proved difficult; she clung resolutely to one of the oriel windows with a hand that had managed to slip free from the coiled tendrils during the explosion. Amma grappled with the resistance, her efforts to pull Reena away from the window proving arduous.

"Release it, you wretched juvenile!" Amma barked in frustration. But Reena remained resolute, steadfastly refusing to yield. "I won't allow you to harm him," she declared through clenched teeth, her defiance unwavering.

Amma's fury escalated as she tightened her tentacles around Reena and the hand grasping the window. With a vicious squeeze, she inflicted excruciating pain, eliciting a shrieking scream from Reena's throat.

(Arrhhh.....Arh...Arh......Arrrhhh)

Bhushan's heart ached at the sound of Reena's anguished scream, a fierce urge to help her clawing at his insides. Despite this, he felt paralyzed by Amma's overwhelming power. Wincing with pain, he staggered toward the cupboard, his reflection in the glass appearing distorted and blurry. As he drew nearer, he squinted, hoping for a clearer view, only to be confronted with the brutal reality of his injuries. His fingers traced the contours of his battered face, recoiling as blood stained his trembling hand. Fear seized him as he looked upon his reflection—an unrecognizable, grotesque visage staring back from the reflector's depths. Overcome with horror, he collapsed to the floor.

(Arrhhh....Arrhhhhh.....Arh...Arh......Arrrhhhhhhhhhhhh)

The anguished cries of Reena echoed through the castle, amplifying the sense of distress. Bhushan, paralyzed by panic, acted with desperate resolve. With a wrenching effort, he forced his dislocated eye back into its socket. A guttural scream erupted from his throat as he wrestled with the excruciating pain, his body wracked with agony.

Both Amma and Reena heard the agonized scream. "It seems your younger brother is enduring quite the ordeal," Amma remarked with cold detachment. "Let's go and assess the situation." With a violent yank, Amma tore the window from its hinges, sending window glass scattering across the floor. Despite the destruction, Reena acted quickly, grabbing onto a supporting pillar beside the shattered window. The pillar, embedded firmly between the walls, provided a solid anchor, and Reena clung to it with an iron grip.

"Oh, for devil's sake," Amma spat in frustration, her face contorted with rage. She redoubled her efforts to wrench Reena from her grip. With an exasperated glare, she warned, "I have no desire to end you, but if you continue to test my patience... so be it." Amma lashed her tentacles towards Reena's throat once more, applying an unrelenting grip that seemed intent on extinguishing every last breath from her lungs. Unlike the previous attempt, this constriction was brutally efficient, carrying an unmistakable menace that suggested Amma was poised to snuff out Reena's life for good.

In the interim, Bhushan's face had miraculously mended, his reflection in the Almirah bearing no trace of the earlier wounds.

He steadied himself and cautiously peered into the corridor, searching for a chance to aid Reena. However, snake-like tendrils of acidic menace lay poised, obstructing his path. His trembling fingers retrieved four marbles from his pocket, the fear of confronting Amma intensifying with each moment. The relentless echoes of Reena's screams were turned into creepy gargles, amplifying Bhushan's terror, making it nearly impossible for him to muster any courage. He hesitated to strike at the writhing tentacles directly, fearing that his efforts might be futile against their deflective menace.

After a few minutes of agonizing contemplation, inspiration struck Bhushan. Resolute, he moved toward the narrow hallway, preparing to confront the tentacles. Yet, fear seized him, and he retreated to his room. His hands trembled uncontrollably, rendering his aim unsteady and unreliable. Anxiety overwhelmed him, especially as Reena's gurgling suddenly ceased—Is she dead? The thought gnawed at him. Despite the impulse to rush out and help her, he found himself wandering in a panic. His gaze fell upon his hat lying on the bed, a small semblance of normalcy amidst the chaos.

He seized his cowboy hat, placed it firmly on his head, and glanced at his reflection in the Almirah. The blurred outline of his hat seemed to dispel his fear, replacing it with a surge of newfound confidence. Clutching three marbles between his fingers, he readied one by anchoring it between his thumb and index finger. Venturing outside with resolute determination, he confronted the tentacles with a fearless grin, symbolising the spirit of a valiant warrior. Raising his slingshot with unwavering resolve, he unexpectedly aimed it at the ground. The shot struck the floor, erupting in a brilliant blue explosion that forced Amma to withdraw her tentacles.

As the azure smoke swirled and billowed upward, Bhushan seized the fleeting opportunity to dash towards the dining room. Emerging from the smoke with a burst of agility, he caught Amma's eye. In response, she unleashed another wave of her monstrous tentacles. Yet, Bhushan nimbly sidestepped the onslaught, evading her vicious attack with practised skill. He hurled another marble at Amma's feet, triggering a chaotic explosion that sent chairs soaring through the air, splintering into pieces amidst the swirling blue smoke. Amidst the pandemonium, Bhushan darted behind a hefty chair nestled in a corner for cover. Peeking out from his hiding spot, he made eye contact with Reena, who resolutely clung to a pillar, her defiant stance a stark contrast to Amma's relentless advance.

Amma, blinded by the sudden onslaught of smoke, frantically searched for Bhushan in the haze. Meanwhile, Bhushan's eye fixed upon the massive chandelier suspended from the ceiling, now swaying gently from the shock waves of the explosion. Through the blurred silhouette of Amma emerging from the mist, an idea ignited in Bhushan's mind. With precision, he took aim at the chandelier, devising his next move. However, Amma, having spotted him in the corner, unleashed another assault with her tentacles, intent on crushing him.

The tentacles were closing in, but just in time, the shot was unleashed. The marble slapped the chandelier, triggering a powerful explosion. Despite the tentacles ensnaring him, Bhushan bore the crushing force in silence, his gaze fixated on the chandelier as it began to plummet. He beheld a vivid vision—Amma's deflection of the marble triggering the prior explosion. And then the chandelier plummeted, crashing down onto the witch's skull, striking her with brutal force to the floor. "Suffer that, wretch," he murmured, a defiant smile etched across his face.

CHAPTER-23

The Deliverer

The tentacles relinquished their hold, liberating both Bhushan and Reena. Bhushan expelled blood with a raspy cough as he broke free from the serpentine grasp. Surveying his torn and battered skin, he witnessed his wounds mending miraculously, filling him with astonishment. At first, he dismissed it as ordinary, recollecting how, in his younger days, even the smallest scratches would linger for days. Now, he mused, perhaps this swift regeneration was simply a byproduct of growing up. He retrieved his hat from the floor, dusting it off before setting it back on his head. As he rose to his feet, he turned his gaze towards Reena.

Reena crumpled to the ground. "Reena!" Bhushan sprinted to her side and shook her, desperate to awaken her. After a few agonizing winks, Reena's eyes fluttered open. She gazed at Bhushan, attempting to rise, but her strength had waned. Collapsing to her knees, she coughed up blood, wracked with the agony of her crushed ribs and arms. After taking three deep breaths, she experienced a miraculous recovery, her body mending itself completely. Rising once more, she whispered, "The candy Nindhi gave me amplified my healing abilities."

Rotating on her heels, they both shifted their focus to the witch sprawled on the floor beneath a shattered table and a fallen chandelier. Her tentacles lay lifelessly, sprawled around her, while her spine and neck were contorted under the crushing weight of the massive chandelier. She bled profusely, the sight of her suffering stark and undeniable.

"Is she dead?" Reena inquired.

"Indeed, no one could withstand such a devastating blow," Bhushan remarked with a sense of gravity.

Suddenly, a low, guttural growl reverberated through the room, making the siblings flinch. To their astonishment, the witch's tentacles began retracting, transforming back into strands of hair, slithering toward her head.

"What's happening?" queried Reena.

"She might be dying... I think," Bhushan replied, his confusion palpable.

In an instant, the body sprawled on the floor began to rise. Reena and Bhushan starred in stunned disbelief, their jaws hanging open and hearts racing as they witnessed a horrifying transformation. Amma's form twisted and reshaped, pulsating and dissolving into a grotesque and nightmarish entity before their eyes.

"What's happening?" Bhushan asked.

"Something dreadful! RUN!" Reena urgently shouted, gripping Bhushan's arm.

They dashed towards the doorway, now a gaping, blasted hole. Reena paused briefly at the threshold, swiftly collecting the scattered items from her pouch. She crouched down to gather the objects scattered across the floor. Meanwhile, Bhushan joined her, picking up a small glass orb and a jar of pitch-black substance. Rushing over to Reena, he found her still on the floor, absorbed in the task of collecting the items.

Bhushan stood beside her, waiting for her to rise and hand over the retrieved items. He glanced back and saw the witch's height increasing, her head nearly brushing the ceiling. A tentacle, resembling that of an octopus, emerged from her twisted face as her skin underwent a grotesque transformation, melting and morphing into a twisted, honeycomb-like pattern. Multiple eyes began to appear eerily on her visage. Her transforming hand grasped the heavy chandelier and hurled it towards the adjacent wall, causing a catastrophic collapse. Bhushan's heart skipped a beat as he leaped over Reena and bolted out of the house. From a safe distance, he frantically shouted, "Run, Reena!"

Reena quickly stored the items in her pouch and sprinted toward the breach. Once at a safe distance, she whispered a mantra under her breath. With a dramatic flourish, she crossed her hands and wove them through the air, causing the bricks from the gaps to stretch and fuse together. The hole was sealed. Bhushan, staring in astonishment, approached Reena and extended the jar and sphere he had retrieved.

"I've got plenty of questions, but they can wait until we're out of here," Bhushan said, his astonishment clear in his voice.

Reena meticulously placed the items back into her pouch. Bhushan, peering inside with a mix of curiosity and awe, observed the array of enigmatic artifacts nestled within.

"Where's Lily?" inquired Reena, her hands continuing to sift through the contents of the pouch.

"She should be in there," Bhushan replied, indicating the toy house.

"Alright," Reena nodded decisively. "Stay alert." She handed him a clutch of marbles, instructing him to remain vigilant for any signs of Amma and to act swiftly at the hint of danger. With that, she set off to find Lily.

Hastening towards the toy house, Reena ascended its ladder and slipped inside. Bhushan remained outside, stationed near the toy house with his slingshot drawn, eyes fixed on the wall Reena had sealed. His heart pounded with anxious anticipation, bracing for any sign of Amma's imminent breach.

"She's not in here," Reena called out from the toy house, peeking her head out before starting to descend.

"How do we escape from here?" Bhushan queried.

"My ally will arrive shortly, but our immediate priority is to find Lily," Reena declared as she descended the ladder.

Reena and Bhushan dashed off in opposite directions to search for Lily, but their efforts were thwarted as a chilling voice reverberated through the air. "Kitteeens."

The siblings were rooted to the spot, their movements frozen. Their eyes followed the source of the voice, and there stood Amma, a humanoid figure emerging with Lily cradled in her arms. The child's face was illuminated by a serene smile, finding solace in her mother's embrace. Amma advanced towards them with a graceful, menacing stride.

"You know, Lily, your siblings have been quite mischievous. They've really upset me," Amma said. However, her words fell on deaf ears. Her hair flowed with the breeze, and her demeanour was deeply unsettling. Both Bhushan and Reena found their eyes drawn involuntarily to Amma's nude body, her voluptuous figure fully visible. Despite this, Amma remained oblivious to her lack of clothing, seemingly unaware, as her body transformed from a monstrous entity back into human, which had destroyed her clothes.

Both Bhushan and Reena were compelled to inform Amma of her nakedness, but their primary concern was their own safety. Bhushan aimed his slingshot at Amma, only for it to be skillfully plucked from his hand, along with the marbles he had been holding, and floated into Amma's grasp. In one swift motion, she crushed both the slingshot and the marbles, causing a blue mist to rise from her wounded hand, which then healed almost instantly.

"Didn't I mention, I wield authority over my domain?" Amma grunted.

As she continued her stride, Amma raised her hand and chanted a mantra. A katana materialized in her right hand, leaving both siblings astonished. Reena recognized the weapon instantly—it was the same black, spider-like sword that had severed Nindhi's neck.

Amma halted at a measured distance and proclaimed, "Move toward the pink door immediately, or this little piggy here... will be slaughtered." She menacingly pointed the sword at Lily. Reena and Bhushan, their hearts pounding wildly, stood paralyzed with helplessness. Bhushan might not fully grasp what a "pig" is, but he understood that Amma's threats were dire and could jeopardize Lily's life. Filled with dread, he and Reena watched in horror as Amma gripped Lily by the leg, dangling her upside-down like a pendulum. She pressed the sword against the child's delicate throat, causing Lily to emit piercing screams of terror.

The cries brimmed the air, sending waves of terror through Bhushan and Reena. The grim scene before them left them paralyzed with dread, unsure of how to respond.

"Ugh! I detest children and their incessant cries," Amma grumbled irritably. "Now, start moving before her fragile little head hits the ground." With a dramatic flourish, Amma swung Lily's dangling form towards them, the sword poised menacingly at her neck. The siblings, hearts pounding, began to move as Amma directed them towards the sealed hole. Amma then turned her attention to the wall. With a swift motion of her wrist, a bolt of vibrant green light erupted from the sword, tearing a hole through the barrier. Reena froze, her eyes locked on Amma, her mind racing with thoughts of the assistance Nindhi was supposed to offer.

"I'm not bluffing; I'll sever her head this instant," Amma snarled, her gaze locked on Reena. Resolutely, Reena advanced toward the blasted opening, though her steps were cautious and hesitant.

"Faster," Amma yapped.

As Reena moved forward, she subtly reached into her pouch. Amma, however, was sharply attuned to her actions. With a deft motion, she drew the sword against Lily's neck, eliciting a bead of blood. Lily's cries grew more intense, their echoes piercing the tense silence.

"Don't even entertain the thought, you foolish imp," she snapped, her voice dripping with menace. "Relinquish your pouch at once!"

Reena obeyed, unfastening her pouch and casting it toward Amma. The pouch levitated briefly before descending softly to rest at Amma's feet.

"Good kittens, now proceed."

"Why are you tormenting Lily? Spare her; she's just a child, innocent and vulnerable." Reena pleaded, her voice quivering with desperation.

"Innocent?" The witch's laughter turned sinister as she lowered her sword. "NO ONE IN THIS WORLD IS INNOCENT!!" Her gaze hardened, her face flushing with fury. "Not even children. You haven't truly witnessed the human world as I have. I've seen countless creatures slaughtered for sustenance and pleasure, birds hunted for sport, and children mercilessly tormenting insects and small animals for their amusement. Do you honestly believe such deeds can be considered innocent?"

"Humans are multifaceted; their concern is often confined to their own kind and community. They erupt with wrath when their own are threatened, yet revel in the misfortunes of others. That's what my sisters endured. That's the grim reality of the Ordinarium world."

"Your sisters were slaughtering them," Reena cried.

"Just as they do to the animal realm," Amma roared. "This is the nature of this accursed, wretched world. If only animals were astute enough to rise up against them, humankind would have been doomed long ago. They are just fortunate, unlike me and my sisters."

Reena shuddered at Amma's ominous words, a cold dread creeping over her at the thought of the outside world. Bhushan, too, was taken aback by the revelation. Under Amma's stern command, they made their way toward the house, their steps heavy with reluctant compliance. In the midst of their march, Reena suddenly halted, a sharp instinct telling her something was amiss. She turned sharply toward Amma, who was poised to speak, when an unsettling, ghostly movement erupted from the ground, sending a chill through the air.

The motion was so sudden and forceful that as it surged across the ground, a shockwave rippled outward, overwhelming everyone with its intensity. The sheer force of it caused everyone, including Amma, to be thrown to the ground in a collective collapse. The sword slipped from Amma's grip, and Lily tumbled to the ground, liberated from her clutches. Seeing the opportunity, Reena shouted, "Bhushan, grab Lily!" Bhushan quickly sprang into action, rushing to Lily's side, and swiftly scooping her up before making a hasty retreat.

As Reena lifted her gaze to the sky, a yellow tent with bat-like wings ascended with regal grace. A triumphant smile touched her lips as she murmured, "You did it, Nindhi. Let's escape this place together."

CHAPTER-24

The Sparkling Orb

Amma rose from the ground, her eyes locked on the airborne spectacle soaring high in the sky. Yet, to her surprise, the tent pivoted like a boomerang, hurtling back in her direction. The witch's eyes locked onto the enigmatic figure peering through the front window of the descending tent. She squinted, endeavouring to identify the figure navigating the tent. Recognition was obscured by the individual's attire—a helmet and brown leather goggles. "Nindhi?" The name slipped from her lips, imbued with astonishment and incredulity. Despite the disguise, Amma recognized him from his partially exposed face. As the tent approached, it unleashed jets of blue light from the enchanted round shield mounted at its front. The beams hurtled toward Amma, nearly striking her, but she nimbly sidestepped, avoiding the oncoming assault and fell to the ground once again. Rising from the ground, she stared at the tent in astonishment, her jaw dropping in disbelief. Her eyes struggled to accept the sight before her.

"Unbelievable! How in the world is he still alive?" Amma gasped in astonishment. She had decapitated him with a katana, a method deemed infallible for eradicating those wielding the power of Mugas. Yet, the enigma of his survival would have to remain a mystery for now, as she was under siege from an aerial assault. Clutching her wand with determination, she unleashed a relentless torrent of spells against the tent. Blazing streams of emerald light erupted from the wand, only to dissipate harmlessly against the protective shield encasing the craft. After a brief but intense scrutiny, her eyes sparkled with the revelation of an optimal spell. With both hands firmly gripping the wand, she directed it at the tent and began to intone a potent mantra.

As Amma trained her focus on the tent, Reena's anxiety mounted, dreading that their escape could be compromised if the tent were obliterated. Her gaze darted to her pouch, now lying perilously close to Amma's feet. Summoning her enchantment, she willed the pouch to levitate and drift back towards her. Drawing forth the crystal orb from her pouch, she activated it, releasing a mesmerizing cascade of vibrant lights that swirled within the sphere. As Amma remained absorbed in her focus on the tent, the sphere rolled silently towards her, coming to rest beneath her legs. The crystal orb erupted in a brilliant explosion, scattering myriad lights that coalesced into a radiant cocoon around Amma. Reena observed the witch tormenting, captured under the brilliant cocoon. Her spider-like hands clamped over her ears and piercing screams reverberated through the luminous sphere, her form ensnared within its dazzling confines.

Nindhi observed the witch's incapacitation. He deftly piloted the tent, bringing it to a halt at a secure distance, its wings flapping incessantly. Amid the vibrant, wind-swept grass, Reena, Bhushan, and Lily dashed towards the tent's rear. Nindhi tossed down a ladder, and one by one, they ascended, the tent hovering just above the ground. As Reena climbed, she keenly observed the intricate network of ropes connecting the wooden base to the wings and canopy of the tent. Once all three were on board, the tent took flight. However, a new obstacle loomed—an impending challenge to penetrate the formidable shield enveloping the witch's stronghold.

With a swift pull of a lever, the tent emitted an ethereal azure glow from within. The circular shield at the front of the tent blazed to life, radiating a brilliant aura that projected silver streaks resembling shooting stars. The tent collided with the castle's mystical protective barrier. Those within the tent were jostled, instinctively clutching the handles embedded in its surface. Nindhi grasped the tent's steering orb with unwavering resolve, his brown gloves adorned with a radiant azure lightning bolt pattern. His determination to escape was unmistakable. With the distinct sound of a clutch, he yanked another lever, his teeth clenched in concentration. The silvery cocoon of light surrounding the tent expanded, its brilliance searing through the castle's protective shield. A dark hole was left in its wake as the tent successfully breached the barrier.

"We've made it!" Nindhi exclaimed, raising his hands in triumphant jubilation.

CHAPTER-25

The Tent and The Broom

Amma remained entrapped within the orb of incandescent lights, bursting like a constellation of firecrackers around her. Shrieking at the top of her lungs, her vision was overwhelmed by the dazzling brilliance, while the echoing cacophony assaulted her temples. Her desperate attempts to break free from the sphere proved futile, and after an agonizing eternity, the enchantment's effects finally abated. Collapsing to her knees on the ground, she panted heavily in anguish. Miraculously, the bruises inflicted by the spell had vanished. Glancing upward, her eyes fixated on the sky where a gaping dark chasm bore witness to the tent's breach. The edges of the void glowed intensely, radiating a fiery luminescence. Fury consumed her from head to toe, reaching a boiling point where she no longer desired to confine them to the pink room; her sole inclination was to obliterate them all. Raising her right hand, a broom flew toward her, drawn irresistibly like a powerful magnet to her grasp. As she seized the broom, she suddenly became aware of her own nakedness. She had been engaged in combat unclad all along. So engrossed was she in capturing the scoundrels that her vanished attire went unnoticed. With an irksome expression, she struck her broom against the ground, conjuring a swirling cloud of dark smoke that enveloped her. When it dissipated, she was clad in an ebony robe, a golden belt cinched around her waist, and a pointed, weathered witch's hat. Mounting her broom, she kicked off the ground and ascended towards the rift in the shield.

Meanwhile, inside the tent, Bhushan found himself in an unfamiliar predicament, a bewildered outsider to the unfolding events.

As he watched Reena conversing with Nindhi, their voices reverberated in the ambient air. He endeavoured to grasp the complexities of their discussion. However, the only discernible topic he managed to glean was their dialogue concerning "mugas." Succumbing to confusion, he abandoned his efforts to comprehend the conversation and redirected his focus, contemplatively surveying the interior of the tent.

The interior unfurled, as far more expansive than the exterior would imply. The azure fabric walls billowed gently with the breeze, flowing in synchrony with the ambient air around the tent. An intricate lattice of posts and beams constituted the structural framework, while low wooden walls, rising only to Bhushan's waist. Plush cushions embellished the seating area where they lounged. Lily was nestled beside Bhushan, her head resting gently on his lap, a serene smile adorning her face as she slipped into slumber. Bhushan responded with a tender stroke of her hair. His gaze wandered upward to the tent's ceiling, adorned with an array of suspended lanterns that bathed the space in a warm, golden luminescence. Bhushan marvelled at the ambience, immersed in the soft murmur of Nindhi and Reena's exchange. His eyes were drawn to the epicentre of their discussion, which revolved around a towering, mechanistic pillar standing conspicuously in the heart of the tent. This pillar served as the centrepiece of the tent's interior, commanding attention with its imposing presence.

Bhushan rose from his seat, driven by a compulsion to explore the enigmatic mechanical pillar. With great care, he replaced his lap beneath Lily's head with the cushion. As he began to stand, a handle materialized on the wooden post nearby, leaving him in awe. In the course of a single day, he had been exposed to an astonishing array of magical marvels. Grasping the handle, he rose to his feet, and as soon as he let go, the handle vanished as if it had never been there. He stared at the spot for a moment, then moved toward the mechanical pillar for a closer examination. The pillar was cylindrical, its internal workings akin to a pulsating engine. On one side of the pillar was a square aperture, as tall as Bhushan's shoulder, intricately adorned. Turning his attention to the source of the conversation, he observed a figure clad in a helmet seated in a chair that pivoted with his movements. Two broad windows, draped with a gossamer-like translucent fabric, framed the view before him, and the figure appeared engrossed in surveying the surroundings. Encircling him were a multitude of levers embedded in the base of the tent, poised for action. Bhushan recognized the levers, recalling them from an illustration in one of Amma's storybooks. His attention then shifted to Reena, who stood beside the helmeted figure, leaning against the eccentric chair and deeply engaged in a serious discussion.

Approaching them, Bhushan interjected, extending a finger toward Nindhi as he inquired of Reena, "Who is he?"

"It's quite a tale, Bhushan. At the moment, he's Nindhi, the one who rescued us," Reena responded.

"And what's this?" Bhushan inquired, gesturing toward the levitating orb on the Tent's instrument panel, where Nindhi's hands were positioned.

"This is the steering orb. I use it to navigate the tent," Nindhi explained.

"What are these?" Bhushan queried, pointing at the hanging ropes from the ceiling surrounding Nindhi.

"Those are integral to the tent's structure," Nindhi replied, sensing Bhushan's curiosity.

"And wha—"

"Enough," Reena interrupted with a grunt, "we'll provide explanations when we're out of danger."

"Why? Why must I wait when you have all the answers?" Bhushan retorted sharply.

"Because Bhushan... the danger posed by Amma still looms over us. Once we're out of harm's way, we'll fill you in," Reena replied, her tone equally firm.

Bhushan regarded Reena in silence for a moment before abruptly turning away and hastening back to his seat. Settling onto the cushion, he concealed his face beneath his hat. Reena found herself taken aback; Bhushan had never exhibited such behaviour before.

Approaching him, she seated herself beside Bhushan. After observing him for a moment, she gently removed his hat, revealing tears streaming down his cheeks.

"Bhushan," she called softly, tenderly wiping away his tears.

"I...I just want to understand, after so many years of love and tranquillity, after countless moments of joy and harmony, why Amma now seeks to destroy us?" He sobbed, leaning into Reena and clinging to her tightly. "Why, Reena, why?"

A surge of sorrow for her siblings enwrapped Reena. She looked at Lily, peacefully sleeping, and then enfolded Bhushan in her warm embrace. "Bhushan... I—I don't have all the answers, but I am determined to shield us. I want to defend you and Lily and forge a new life in a more promising place."

"I believe we are out of danger," a voice reached Reena's ears. She turned to find Nindhi standing there. Kneeling beside them, he rested a reassuring hand on Bhushan's shoulder, who looked up at him with a mixture of hope and weariness.

"Well," Nindhi began, "Your Amma, who was once my Amma as well, is a malevolent figure. She seeks to consume you when you come of age, and she imprisons people within pink..."

The tent was struck by a violent jolt, sending everyone inside reeling and crashing onto the wooden floor.

A wave of astonishment surged through everyone in the tent, mingling with the echoing cries of Lily. Nindhi scrambled to his feet, determined to return to the pilot seat. Yet another sudden jolt threw everyone tumbling about the tent like a loose ball. Crawling swiftly on all fours, Nindhi hastened to the chair, seated himself with urgency, and fastened his seatbelt. Another wave of turbulence erupted, triggering the tent's safety mechanisms. Wooden tendrils emerged from the posts, coiling around the waists of Reena, Bhushan, and Lily, anchoring them securely. Lily's cries escalated as one of the wooden tendrils ensnared her waist.

Nindhi pressed a button, and a crystalline orb rose from the instrument panel, casting an external view of the tent into the space.

"Devil's eye... Amma is assaulting us!" Nindhi exclaimed, his voice filled with alarm.

Reena placed her hand upon the wooden tendril, and a soft pink luminescence emanated from her touch. With a deft movement, she extricated herself from its embrace and rushed towards Nindhi. As she watched the crystal orb, it revealed Amma in hot pursuit, soaring on her broom. With one hand clutching the broom and the other wielding the wand like a sword, she unleashed a barrage of green lights upon the tent.

Nindhi pressed another button, and a curious arrangement of small purple crystal orbs, aligned in a precise row upon a wooden block, materialized.

"What's this?" inquired Reena, curiously.

"These are the shield indicators," Nindhi explained. "Observe, two are already shattered," he indicated with a pointed finger. "So, we're down to only ten shields." (crank) "Well, make that nine now. I'm worried she might obliterate our tent at this proximity," Nindhi confessed, his anxiety becoming palpable.

Another violent surge of turbulence shook the tent, compelling Nindhi to swiftly yank one of the levers. With one hand resting on the steering orb, the tent surged forward with the swiftness of the wind. The orb whirled toward the front, and Reena was jolted violently, sending her sprawling to the ground.

Nindhi gazed intently into the crystal orb, noting that the witch was pursuing them with a velocity akin to the wind. To protect the tent from her relentless assaults, he deftly manoeuvred through the air in a serpentine pattern. Fueled by fury, Amma unleashed a relentless barrage with the singular aim of demolishing the tent. Yet the tent skillfully evaded most of her onslaughts, thwarting her every effort.

Lily's piercing cries echoed hauntingly within the tent.

Rising to her feet, Reena clung desperately to Nindhi's chair. "Is there nothing you can do about this incessant turbulence?" Reena exclaimed.

"Oh, right... right," Nindhi murmured, pressing another button on the console. The interior of the tent was suffused with a gentle purple glow. "That should prevent any more turbulence."

Lily's cries grew increasingly frantic, yet she received no attention from Reena and Nindhi, save for Bhushan, who was fervently trying to comfort her.

(Amma.....Amma....Mamaaa)

As Nindhi focused on piloting the tent, Reena's gaze remained riveted on Amma's relentless pursuit through the crystal orb. "For a moment, I believed we had evaded her," Reena remarked.

"She's a veritable nightmare," Nindhi replied, a veil of apprehension cloaking him. They were soaring high, and any damage to the tent could precipitate a deadly fall from such a height.

"I think it's time to deploy the cannon wand," Reena suggested.

Nindhi gazed at Reena contemplatively for a moment.

"What? Please don't tell me we're lacking a cannon wand," she said, her voice tinged with disbelief.

Nindhi pressed another button on the instrument panel, and a cannon wand materialized at the rear of the tent, its barrel aimed towards the sole entrance. They hastened to the back of the tent and approached the formidable wand.

Reena examined the cannon wand with keen scrutiny. It was markedly different from her own creations, adorned in a vibrant gold and blue colour scheme that resembled a toy from the Toy House. The wand boasted an eerie fox-head design with jewel-like blue eyes, and a Y-shaped handle at the rear that resembled the grip of two oversized wands. It also featured a seat akin to Nindhi's pilot chair.

""I drew inspiration from a war film for its design," Nindhi exclaimed, glancing at Reena, who regarded him with a bemused expression. "Nevermind," he muttered, a hint of embarrassment in his voice.

He then turned his gaze to Bhushan, who looked on in astonishment at the cannon wand, having never encountered such an object before.

"Bhushan, Reena mentioned that you're adept at aiming. I need you to man this cannon wand," Nindhi instructed.

Bhushan's face brightened with a smile, the wooden tendrils released him and without a moment's hesitation, he took his seat and gripped the handles of the cannon wand with determination.

"But Bhushan is no wizard," Reena objected. "Considering it's a matter of our safety, I don't think..."

Another jolt reverberated through the tent, sending Reena and Nindhi sprawling onto the floor. Nindhi quickly scrambled to the counter, noting with concern that only seven shield orbs remained.

(Amma...Amma...mammmaaaaa...)

"Hey, you promised we wouldn't be tossed around!" Reena exclaimed.

Nindhi rushed over to Bhushan, directing his hand toward the tent door. The cloth barrier swung wide open as the blue luminescence of the lightning bolt pattern on his glove flared to life. He stared at Amma through the open door, observing her assault from a distance. Turning to Bhushan, he began to explain the operation of the cannon wand with a sense of urgency.

"It's alright, Bhushan. You can manage this wand," Nindhi reassured him. "Just remember what I've said, set your target and press the buttons atop the Y-shaped handle."

Reena felt a surge of irritation towards Nindhi for dismissing her concerns. After ascribing the features of the cannon wand to Bhushan, Nindhi made his way back to Reena.

"Are you disregarding me?" she snapped.

"Reena, I understand your concern, but we simply don't have the luxury of time..."

Another violent jolt shook the tent. Nindhi raced back to the counter to inspect the shield orbs, relieved to find that there were still seven remaining. Turning his attention to Bhushan, he observed with satisfaction that Bhushan was maneuvering the cannon wand with considerable skill.

(Ammaa... Amma... Amma...)

"You must be proud of your brother; he's managing it exceptionally well," Nindhi remarked. Reena glanced at Bhushan, who was skillfully deflecting every assault Amma hurled at the tent.

"But... how is it penetrating the tent shield?" Reena inquired, her curiosity piqued.

"It's all part of the Spellcraft-engineering," Nindhi replied

Another violent bout of turbulence rattled the tent. At the helm, Nindhi was jolted by the sharp sound of a sudden crack. He swiftly inspected the shield orbs and discovered that only six remained.

(Amma...Amma...mammmaaaaa...)

"I CAN'T DO IT!" Bhushan shouted, pounding both fists against the cannon wand in frustration.

"Why? You're performing admirably," Reena said.

He turned his head towards Reena and pointed a finger at Lily. "I don't know if anyone has noticed, but Lily has been crying incessantly. Her wails are piercing through my skull... Aiming demands intense concentration!" he exclaimed.

Reena had completely forgotten about Lily. She glanced at the infant, who was wailing inconsolably, her cries echoing, "Amma... Amma... umaaaaa." Rushing over, Reena freed Lily from the wooden tendrils and carefully moved her away from the tent door, placing her at the side, where the control counter was situated. She endeavoured to soothe Lily, assuring her that they would soon escape the peril and that a better place awaited them all. Yet, Lily remained stubborn, her cries for Amma unabated, yearning for the comforting embrace of her mother. Despite Reena's heartfelt attempts to comfort Lily, she was unable to calm the child. After a moment of contemplation, Reena placed her hands gently on Lily's temples. "I'm sorry, Lily," she murmured, as her hands radiated a soft pink glow. Lily slumped onto the wooden floor of the tent, unconscious.

"Did you use the Torpified Charm on her?" came Nindhi's voice from behind.

"Yes," Reena replied. She then glanced at Nindhi, who was deeply engrossed in navigating the tent.

"It's alright," Nindhi reassured. "Hopefully, we'll have found peace before she awakens."

"Hmm," Reena responded coolly. She grabbed one of the blue pillows and gently placed it under Lily's head. Almost immediately, a wooden tendril emerged from the post and tenderly encircled Lily

She approached Bhushan and halted beside his chair. Observing the witch pursuing them with heightened ferocity, she noted that it was Bhushan who was valiantly launching the counterattacks. Amma was diligently countering the twin jets of blue light fired from the eyes of the wolf-headed wand. Despite the witch's formidable prowess, Bhushan's efforts to knock her out of the sky proved futile, as she deftly deflected each assault from the cannon wand.

"Bhushan, do you think you can bring her down?" asked Reena.

"I don't know; she's deflecting every attack I launch," Bhushan replied with concern.

"She's far more powerful than we ever imagined," Nindhi acknowledged, overhearing their conversation from his pilot seat. He turned his head and added, "The attacks from the cannon wands are typically difficult to counter, even for formidable witches, yet she's neutralizing them with a mere flick of her wrist." Anxiety was etched across his face.

Nindhi executed a sharp manoeuvre with the tent, causing a jolt that unsettled Reena. This sudden shift offered Bhushan a chance to target the witch from the side. He pressed the button on the cannon wand, and jets of blue light shot forth, striking Amma and exploding around her like a shower of fireworks. However, as the dazzling fireworks faded, a swirling aura of green energy enveloped Amma. She then pivoted towards the tent and began her counteroffensive. She twirled her wand, summoning six emerald-glowing, dragon-like creatures with butterfly wings, which swooped menacingly towards the tent. Bhushan reacted swiftly, managing to neutralize four of the fierce, winged dragons, while the tent's shield successfully repelled the remaining three. Having just vanquished four of the creatures with the cannon wand, Bhushan shifted his gaze towards Amma and saw another swarm of six dragon-like entities charging relentlessly toward them. Gripping the handles of the wand firmly, he took aim. Three streams of twin blue light erupted from the wolf-headed wand, obliterating the entire swarm of creatures. Reena, thoroughly impressed, stared in awe as Bhushan, panting heavily and drenched in sweat, took a moment to catch his breath.

The relentless cycle of attack and defence continued unabated. At times, Bhushan would unleash a barrage of strikes while Amma concentrated on repelling them, only for their roles to shift in the next moment. The unremitting exchange of blows was wearing Bhushan down. His hands, clutching the wand handles, trembled with exhaustion. Yet, fueled by the urgent need to protect himself and his family, he pressed on, pushing himself beyond his limits.

Amma, wearied by the unending conflict, felt her pride bruised as she struggled to capture the troublesome children. In a moment of exasperation, she soared into the sky. Bhushan and Reena watched her ascend, and Bhushan, determined, endeavoured to elevate the cannon wand as high as he could. He fired several shots at Amma, but she remained out of his reach. Seizing the respite as Amma's attacks ceased, Bhushan lowered the cannon wand, releasing the handles. He glanced at his hands, which were red and bruised, and felt a surge of relief as they healed almost instantly.

"Reena, come here," Nindhi beckoned urgently.

Reena rushed over to Nindhi, who directed her to gaze into the crystal orb. She complied and observed Amma climbing ever higher into the sky. From Amma's vantage point, the tent appeared to diminish below as she ascended to the very zenith.

"Is she abandoning us?" Inquired Reena.

"I—I don't think so," Nindhi replied, his voice thick with uncertainty. Amma continued her ascent, eventually coming to a halt high above. From her lofty perch, she surveyed the moving tent below. With her eyes shut tightly, she began to twirl her wand in a sweeping motion above her head, murmuring a mantra under her breath.

"What is she doing?" Reena asked, her voice laced with apprehension.

"Devil's eye, WE GOTTA RUN!" Nindhi shouted urgently. He yanked another lever, causing the tent to surge with an electric blue radiance. Its bat-like wings spread wide like an eagle's, ignited in azure flames. The tent hurtled forward at breakneck speed, trailing a luminous streak akin to a shooting star.

As Amma spun the wand above her head, the clouds began to churn menacingly overhead. The sky darkened, and the wind howled with escalating ferocity. Inside the tent, an eerie stillness gave way to a palpable sense of dread that gripped everyone within. The tent hurtled through the air at a breathtaking velocity, causing a noticeable pressure to press against everyone's faces and chests, despite the protective enchantment surrounding them. Reena's persistent inquiries about the escalating situation went unanswered, as Nindhi remained steadfastly silent, his attention solely devoted to manoeuvring the tent as far from the threat as possible.

Amma's eyes fluttered open, now blazing with an electric scarlet intensity. The dark, swirling clouds above her danced in tandem with the wand's movements, pulsating with vivid crimson light and emitting a series of ominous, thunderous rumbles. With a decisive thrust of her wand, Amma directed the swirling dark cloud, crackling with scarlet electric light, toward the tent. The cloud metamorphosed into a monstrous, serpentine behemoth, its mouth agape to reveal a flickering torrent of crimson lightning seething within. The fearsome apparition surged forward with the swiftness of the wind, pursuing the fleeing tent with a relentless, predatory determination. Bhushan reclined in the cannon wand's chair, his eyes shut and his hands rhythmically clenching and unclenching as he sought some semblance of relief. A sudden tremor shuddered him from his trance. He opened his eyes to see the lanterns suspended from the ceiling trembling in unison, casting flickering shadows that danced ominously across the tent. Repositioning himself in the chair, Bhushan scanned the horizon with growing unease. His gaze fixed on a looming, dark, and ominous cloud that advanced with alarming speed. Squinting against the encroaching darkness, he called out, "Something's coming this way," his voice sharp with urgency. The menacing cloud surged forward, its approach marked by searing red flashes that momentarily blinded him. Leaning forward for a clearer view, Bhushan's eyes widened in horror as he beheld the dark cloud unfurling its maw. Within its gaping, nebulous jaws, sharp, cloudy fangs emerged, and a crackling surge of electricity buzzed ominously within its throat. Bhushan's jaw fell slack in sheer disbelief.

"We're doomed," he lamented, his voice heavy with despair.

CHAPTER-26

Behemoth

The serpentine behemoth surged towards them with menacing speed. Bhushan, now tense and vigilant, gripped the handles of the cannon wand once more. Twin jets of blue light erupted from the wand, streaking towards the dark creature in relentless pursuit, yet it seemed impervious to the assault. Reena, standing beside Nindhi, was paralyzed by sheer terror, she clung to his chair with all her strength. Wholly absorbed in steering the tent, Nindhi kept one eye fixed on the window ahead and the other on the crystal orb, which now displayed the giant serpent in place of Amma in pursuit.

Momentarily, the shadow loomed over Bhushan, and his gaze shifted upward, reloading him with terror. The colossal serpent was on the verge of taking a sizable chunk out of the tent, with Bhushan caught in that imminent portion. The jets of twin lights ceased, and a piercing scream escaped his throat. The serpent snapped its jaws menacingly, but the air was all it caught. Redirecting its attention to the tent now veering south, the serpent was outmanoeuvred by Nindhi's skilful navigation. Before they could be engulfed, Nindhi executed a sharp turn, narrowly escaping the deadly clutches.

The serpent's luminous eyes narrowed with malevolent intent. It arched its sinuous upper body, preparing to strike again. With a renewed burst of speed, it lunged menacingly toward the tent, undeterred in its relentless pursuit. Bhushan, who had briefly felt his racing heart settle, now experienced a fresh surge of dread as he realized the dark leviathan was still hot on their trail. Grasping the cannon wand's handles with renewed determination, Bhushan resumed his relentless assault on the behemoth serpent. Each blast of blue ray from the wand struck out against the massive creature. Despite his efforts, the serpent closed in, its gaping jaws poised to engulf the tent. Yet, with a deft manoeuvre, Nindhi veered sharply northward, narrowly evading the serpent's grasp once more.

Shake it off! Shake it off!" Bhushan bellowed with a fervent urgency.

Nindhi was paralyzed by his own terror, rendering him speechless. The illumination within the tent morphed into a foreboding crimson, accompanied by an incessant, alarming buzz that reverberated through the confined space. Reena and Bhushan instinctively clutched their ears, wincing in discomfort.

"What's this infernal racket?" Reena yapped.

Nindhi offered no reply, his focus unwavering as he concentrated on steering them to safety.

Amidst the cacophony within the tent, an hourglass emerged from the instrument panel. Its glass chamber contained a verdant liquid that had dwindled to less than half its capacity. As Nindhi beheld the hourglass, an unmistakable expression of anxiety etched itself across his features.

Reena's voice pierced through the din, "What's that?" Yet Nindhi remained silent, his gaze steadfast on the crystal orb, where the image of the giant serpent loomed closer, its menacing form growing ever larger.

Bhushan relentlessly engaged the formidable serpent, unleashing a torrent of twin azure jets of light from the cannon wand. Slowly, the serpent retreated, melding into the roiling dark clouds. Despite the temporary reprieve, he remained on high alert, his eyes meticulously scanning the tempestuous skies for any looming threats, resolute in his determination to shield his family from the encroaching malevolence.

As the dark creature remained absent, a wave of relief washed over Bhushan. "I vanquished it! I witnessed its demise within the clouds," he exclaimed with pride and satisfaction. Reena and Nindhi caught wind of his declaration. "Are you certain?" inquired Reena, her voice tinged with both hope and doubt.

"Indeed, it has remained motionless for quite some time," Bhushan confirmed, his voice echoing with a newfound confidence.

Nindhi, catching wind of their conversation yet harbouring his doubts, kept his gaze fixed on the crystal orb. There, a shadowy silhouette began to materialize from the depths below. His face contorted with alarm as he urgently manoeuvred the steering orb to the left, veering the tent away from the looming menace. Reena, standing close to Nindhi, peered towards the left window and beheld a towering formation of clouds, serpentine in its shape, crackling with scarlet lightning as it surged upwards. Although the tent narrowly escaped the immediate threat, it was now caught in a violent whirlwind, spinning uncontrollably and being buffeted by ferocious gusts. Inside, everyone was tossed about, helplessly whirled in the tempest's wake. Reena, unsteady and without any support, was enveloped by the wooden tendrils that materialized from the tent's surface, forming a protective embrace. After enduring around seven or eight tumultuous spins, Nindhi managed to bring the tent to a halt by deftly steering the orb and halting its chaotic rotation. Amidst the billowing dark clouds, Nindhi grasped one of the strings hanging from the tent's ceiling and tugged it firmly. This action summoned a fresh layer of clouds, enveloping them in a dense, protective shroud. The tent came to a complete stop.

"Devil's eye... That sudden assault from below took me completely by surprise," Nindhi exclaimed, breaking his silence.

"Why has the tent stopped ?" Reena inquired.

"We've run out of energy, Reena. A refill is imperative," Nindhi responded, gesturing toward the empty hourglass on the counter. His eyes then shifted to the crystal orb, where the giant serpent was relentlessly prowling amidst the clouds, its electrified howls and ominous buzzing filling the air.

"We need more than just energy," he mumbled.

"Nindhi, I'm sorry, I thought it was killed," Bhushan cried.

"It's alright; stay vigilant," he reassured Bhushan.

Nindhi then unfastened his safety belt and stood up, his eyes fixed on a small, intricately carved wooden ball. With a deft motion, he pressed it, and two delicate wooden wings unfurled from it, shimmering with a soft, golden hue.

"What is this?" asked Reena.

"The Mirage Boomerang," Nindhi clarified, his voice tinged with urgency. He swiftly moved to the window and cast it forth. The boomerang arced through the air, briefly vanishing before reappearing as an exact replica of their own tent, now airborne. Nindhi and Reena observed as it sailed into the distance, drawing the serpent's attention away, which promptly gave chase to the illusory decoy.

Returning to his seat, Nindhi secured the seatbelt.

"How do you always know exactly what to use and when? How do you manage to have the perfect solution for every conceivable situation?" Reena enquired, her voice brimmed with curiosity and suspicion.

His chair swivelled to face Reena, and he shot her a look laced with irritation. "It's called preparation!!" He snapped, his gaze fiery.

A heavy silence settled over the tent as Bhushan stared at them in wide-eyed astonishment from his seat.

"Now, Reena, listen to me," Nindhi said, taking a deep breath to steady himself. "We are in a perilous situation right now, and all discussions can wait. Your questions will be answered once we are out of this imminent threat. We don't have much time left. The cloud charm will dissipate soon, and the behemoth may return to pursue us before it does. So please, follow my instructions carefully."

"Alright," Reena replied.

Nindhi pressed a button on the instrument panel, causing the wooden planks to shift and reveal a sizable square storage compartment beneath. With a commanding tone, he directed Reena to retrieve four diminutive wooden barrels, each scarcely larger than her foot. As Reena set the barrels on the surface, she watched in astonishment as the storage compartment vanished in a flash. The four diminutive barrels began to expand rapidly, growing to a height that reached up to her waist.

As Reena's gaze lingered on the barrels, a metallic clank echoed through the tent. She turned to see that the door of the central metal pillar had swung open, exposing two broad, rectangular funnels. The blue funnel perched at the top, with the green one stationed below, presented a puzzling sight. Confused, Reena glanced at Nindhi, who, without shifting his focus from the crystal orb, instructed her to fill each funnel with two of the barrels.

Released from the tendril's embrace, Reena struggled to lift the barrel, so she resorted to a charm that made it hover effortlessly after removing its small wooden lid. The barrel floated towards the metal pillar, tilting to let the verdant liquid flow into the green funnel. The distinct aroma of the liquid triggered a sense of familiarity in Reena. "Is this mugas?" she asked, her curiosity piqued..

Nindhi responded with a hint of irritation, "Yes." Reena, noting his tone, continued with the task, pouring the mugas into the funnel with precision.

"The first barrel is completed," Reena announced after a moment's effort.

"Good, move on to the next one," Nindhi instructed, his eyes fixed intently on the crystal orb.

Reena levitated the next barrel and began pouring its contents into the green funnel. The liquid soon flowed steadily, filling the funnel to its brim.

"Good," Nindhi affirmed. "Now pour the remaining two barrels into the blue funnel."

Reena began emptying the green liquid into the blue funnel. As she worked, Nindhi's attention remained riveted to the crystal orb. He noticed a turbulent shift in the clouds, as they started to converge ominously towards their tent.

"Done."

Nindhi cast a frantic glance at Reena and cried, "It's coming our way! Hurry, the next barrel!" He pivoted swiftly back to the counter, his hands yanking two strings hanging from the ceiling. They flared to life with a brilliant green glow, casting an urgent light across the tent. As he redirected his attention to the crystal orb, the giant serpent was closing in with relentless speed. Nindhi's gaze sharpened on the shadowy form that loomed ominously above the serpent. A chill traced along his spine as the dark silhouette became increasingly discernible.

The dark shadow resolved into a formidable figure: Amma, perched atop the Behemoth serpent. She guided the serpent with a commanding presence from her broomstick, steering it with malevolent intent directly towards them.

"Reena, she's upon us!" he shouted urgently. "Hurry with the filling!"

"Almost done," Reena replied, her voice trembling. The levitating barrels wobbled, spilling some of the liquid onto the surface. Meanwhile, Amma steadied her wand, pointing it menacingly at the tent.

"SHE'S SPOTTED US!" he bellowed. "HURRY UP, DEVIL'S EYE!"

"ALMOST DONE... ALMOST DONE," Reena cried, struggling with the stubborn barrel. She couldn't fathom why this one seemed to be resisting her efforts. Amma chanted a mantra, and a tempestuous gust of wind erupted from the tip of her wand, tearing through the clouds and revealing the tent that had been concealed.

"Hiding time is up, kittens," she hissed, urging her serpent minion to surge forward with renewed fervour towards the exposed tent.

"HURRY UP, REENA! DOOMSDAY IS UPON US!" Nindhi cried, his voice laced with dread.

"ALMOST FINISHED," she cried out.

Amma was closing in on the tent, her monstrous serpent's jaws agape, poised to engulf them. Inside, the three occupants were seized by a paralyzing fear.

"FINISHED!"

Nindhi rapidly engaged a button, and a thunderous rumble reverberated through the tent as the metal pillar's door sealed shut. With a decisive motion, he twisted the steering orb sharply to the left. The serpent's jaws snapped shut, but the tent narrowly eluded being engulfed. The force of the serpent's collision sent the tent spinning once again, buffeted by the gale of wind.

Nindhi gripped the top of the steering orb with both hands, his knuckles white with strain. With a surge of determination, he halted the tent abruptly in mid-air. As the serpent loomed closer, he yanked a lever, and the eagle-like wings flared to life in a brilliant azure glow. Steadying himself, he thrust the steering orb forward, propelling the tent ahead with renewed urgency.

A sudden jolt resonated through the tent, causing everyone inside to be tossed about. Nindhi wrestled with the steering orb, but the tent's structure remained stubbornly unresponsive. Meanwhile, Reena, once again, cocooned in the protective embrace of the wooden tendrils, felt a strange and unsettling sensation creeping over her skin. Peering at her arms, she observed her hair standing on end. Both Nindhi and Bhushan were similarly affected by the phenomenon. Nindhi gazed in astonishment at the crystal orb, his jaw dropping and his heart skipping a beat. The behemoth serpent had clamped its jaws tightly around the tent. Its fangs clashed against the shield, sending reverberations through the tent. The vacuum of energy stored within its paunch began to draw the tent inward. In a matter of moments, the tent was engulfed by the serpent and consumed by the dreadful scarlet electricity crackling within.

The hairs on the children's skin stood erect, piercing like needles as the tent hurtled through the serpent's gaping maw toward its stomach. Electricity crackled and buzzed around the tent, pressing against its shield. The tent swayed and spun, ensnared by the vacuum pulling it inward. The immense pressure weighed heavily on Reena and the others, compressing their chests and making it difficult to breathe.

They felt as if their arms and legs were being twisted into knots, while their stomachs and heads were being stretched like rubber. Amidst the chaos, Nindhi's eyes darted to the shield orbs, which were rapidly cracking; only two remained intact. The tent continued to drift, finally reaching the tail of the colossal serpent. Suddenly, the behemoth fragmented into a swarm of smaller serpents with butterfly wings. The crimson creatures ascended briefly before descending upon the tent with the velocity of a storm, colliding with relentless ferocity.

All the scattered swarms bombarded the tent with a cacophony of explosive sounds. Inside, everyone covered their ears as the tent endured extreme turbulence. Nindhi, ever vigilant, kept his eyes shut against the blinding flashes of lightning that illuminated the tent's interior. Gradually, the bombardment ceased, and the acrid smoke from the explosions began to dissipate.

Nindhi opened his eyes and glanced at Reena and Bhushan, discovering them unscathed yet levitating. His focus then shifted to Lily, who lay cocooned and resting on a floating pillow. A wave of astonishment washed over him as he became aware that he, too, was lifting from his chair, only to be held in place by the safety belt. Looking upward, Nindhi beheld a sky darkened by roiling clouds and littered with the remnants of shattered posts and beams. A piercing scream sliced through the tumult, and he turned to see Bhushan's horrified expression. His gaze followed Bhushan's line of sight to one of the torn tent wings, now drifting away from the ravaged structure. The tent's beams and posts were still in the throes of disintegration, with splintered wood and debris being swept away from the tent by the relentless forces of the wind.

"We are dead!!" Bhushan cried out.

The crushing pressure on their chests grew more intense, as though an immense boulder was compressing their ribs. The tent, reeling uncontrollably, began its rapid descent.

The shrieks of terror from Reena and Bhushan pierced through Nindhi's ears with an almost physical force. Reena's fear was palpable, a raw, visceral manifestation of despair. After enduring so many trials, the prospect of plummeting to their deaths seemed a cruel and unjust fate. If death had to come, it might have been preferable in the relative safety of the pink room; but now, amidst their desperate escape, it was an outcome both unacceptable and profoundly distressing. Reena's gaze darted frantically around her, her chest constricted with a tightening panic. The wooden tendrils, which had offered her a semblance of safety, began to dissolve and retreat into the tent's wooden veneer. As the last of the protective tendrils vanished, she crumpled onto the tent's surface with her hope waning.

Reena gingerly lifted herself, her fingers tenderly rubbing her jaw, which had struck the surface with considerable force. Her gaze shifted to Nindhi, who met her eyes with a reassuring glance. As she looked upward, she was astonished to see that the tent's ceiling had been miraculously restored, as if by some unseen force. However, the structural integrity of the wooden beams and posts had been severely compromised. Only six posts remained intact—three on each side—leaving the tent precariously supported.

"What happened?" Reena asked, her voice tinged with astonishment.

"No need to worry," Nindhi replied, refocusing on the tent's controls with unwavering resolve. "I managed to restore the damage."

Reena stood nearby, still rubbing her jaw, and watched Nindhi with curiosity. "How?" she asked, her tone tinged with wonder.

"Well, it's the enchantment," Nindhi explained, eyes fixed on the controls as he steered the tent towards the north. "I sacrificed many of the tent's features to construct the new wings. As you can see, numerous beams and posts are missing. The wood was sent upwards to build the new wings, transferred with the Bequeath Charm and the mugas you poured into the blue funnel."

"And what of the fabric draping the wings?" Reena inquired.

"It's now a deep azure," Nindhi gestured towards the tent's draped walls, which had shifted from blue to a warm golden hue. "The fabric was integrated into the Bequeath Charm, and I deliberately allocated additional material, which has been instrumental in the reconstruction of the new wings."

Reena glanced at the crystal orb and observed the tent, now adorned with azure wings instead of the previous yellow.

"Brilliant, saving our necks."

"But there is one issue, Reena," Nindhi continued, "our shields are depleted, and these wings, though functional, lack the strength and enchantments of the previous ones. This means we can't propel the tent at full speed. We'll need Bhushan to remain ever-vigilant for any threats."

Reena spun around urgently, her gaze locking onto Bhushan. She was met with a harrowing sight: Bhushan lay slumped over the cannon wand, his hands hanging lifelessly. Blood dripped from the wand, and it was clear that Bhushan's head was the source. A jagged splinter of wood had impaled his skull, provoking a blood flow.

Reena was struck with terror, her heart pounding as she feared the worst—Bhushan might be dead. With trembling hands, she hurried to his side and carefully removed the splintered wood from his head. To her relief, the wound began to close and heal almost immediately, a clear sign that Bhushan was just unconscious. As Reena tried to revive Bhushan, a burst of red light struck the cannon wand with devastating force, causing severe damage to its front. The impact sent a resounding thud through the tent, and the wolf-like head of the wand crashed to the floor, leaving the weapon significantly impaired.

Reena gazed out in disbelief as Amma hurtled toward them, her wand blazing with wrathful intensity. The fury in Amma's eyes was palpable, her frustration spilling over as she declared, "I can't believe you... you mere pests are still alive, even after such an attack."

Amma twirled her wand with a fierce flourish, unleashing a streak of red light that cut through the air like a lightning bolt. The powerful beam hurtled towards the tent with deadly intent, but as it neared, it was abruptly absorbed and neutralized by something unknown.

The witch's eyes narrowed in concentration as she scrutinized the tent more closely, discerning the thin, pink barrier that enveloped it. Her gaze then fell upon Reena, who was the source of the enchantment. With a pink luminescence radiating from her eyes, Reena's hands were pressed together in a namaste-like gesture, maintaining the protective shield that guarded the tent.

The witch accelerated to match the tent's pace, swiftly closing the gap. With a sinister flourish, she unleashed a barrage of crimson lightning bolts towards the tent, each one crashing into the resilient pink shield with no effect. Meanwhile, Nindhi, ever vigilant, expertly manoeuvred the tent, guiding it away from Amma's relentless assault. Despite the protective shield, the tent's performance had waned significantly. Amma, having persistently attacked from behind, now soared above and positioned herself directly in front of the tent, blocking its path.

With a sweeping flourish of her wand, Amma summoned forth dragon-like apparitions, composed of shimmering red light and delicate butterfly wings. These fiery entities surged towards the tent with unrelenting force. The transformation of her attacks from emerald to scarlet mirrored the growing tempest of her rage, a reflection that did not escape Nindhi's notice.

Despite the tent's deft manoeuvre to the left, narrowly avoiding the onslaught of red lightning creatures, a critical vulnerability remained. The frontal shield, sacrificed in the creation of the new wings, was now absent, leaving the tent exposed and defenceless against attacks from the front. Undeterred, Amma pressed on with unyielding ferocity. Through the crystal orb, Nindhi observed her transformed visage: a grotesque honeycomb pattern distorted her features, and three additional eyes had emerged upon her forehead, glowing with malevolent intent.

It became evident to Nindhi that Amma's internal strife was manifesting physically; her struggle to contain her inner turmoil was causing her inner demon to claw its way to the surface.

"Reena," Nindhi called out urgently.

"Yes?"

"You've done remarkably well so far, but we must remember that we cannot endure another formidable spell like the behemoth serpent. We must ensure she doesn't have the chance to summon such a force again," hei urged.

"I'm unable to launch an attack without a wand; my only function here is to sustain the shield," Reena grumbled. "And to complicate matters, Bhushan lies unconscious, with no indication of when he might awaken."

"Then we are facing a dire predicament," Nindhi remarked, his gaze fixed on the horizon as he deftly manoeuvred the tent downwards, narrowly avoiding the cascade of red lightning bolts that Amma hurled from the front. Nindhi was acutely aware of the strain on Reena's energy as she laboured to sustain the protective shield around the tent, all the while evading the relentless assault.

Amma pursued them relentlessly, sending three more streaks of light from her wand before soaring above the tent once again. Reena urgently alerted Nindhi of her ascent, prompting him to focus his attention on the crystal orb.

"Hold tight," Nindhi instructed, executing a swift manoeuvre to swing the tent around. With the force of a tempest, he directed their course straight at Amma. She narrowly dodged his aggressive charge, spiralling away in the air.

Meanwhile, within the confines of the tent, Reena was disoriented and drifted helplessly toward one of the tent's posts. As she collided with it, a crack in her concentration caused the protective shield to waver and then vanish entirely.

Amma, having reoriented herself on her broom after a series of dizzying spins, observed the tent's new position above her as it sped away. Noticing the absence of the protective shield, she swiftly flicked her wand, unleashing another bolt of lightning toward the tent. However, just as before, the bolt was repelled, forming a shimmering sphere around the tent.

"Stay wary!" Reena cried, her head whipping towards Nindhi. Her glowing pink eyes, now eerily reminiscent of the ghouls from Amma's grim tome, only added to her urgent warning. "Reckless manoeuvres like this will bring about our defeat sooner than we could ever imagine," she shrieked in alarm.

Amid the fierce clash between the tent and Amma, Bhushan slowly regained consciousness. He lifted himself from the cannon wand, gently massaging his throbbing head. After retrieving his hat from the floor and placing it back on his head, he turned his gaze towards Reena. She was seated a short distance away, her eyes glowing with an intense pink hue.

"What has happened to you?" Bhushan asked, his voice trembling with a mix of concern and astonishment as he gazed at Reena.

"She is maintaining a protective shield around the tent, Bhushan," Nindhi explained, deftly manoeuvring to avoid yet another crimson projectile hurtling towards them.

Bhushan's gaze was drawn to the tent door, where he saw Amma swiftly approaching from the left. A chill crept down his spine.

"She's still on our tail!" he exclaimed.

"Bhushan, we need to confront Amma; if we don't, our time will run out soon," Nindhi urged.

"Alright," Bhushan said, preparing to activate the cannon wand. However, his attention was diverted by an unexpected sight on the floor.

"Hey Nindhi, the cannon wand is damaged," Bhushan called out, rising from his chair and examining the device. "Half of the wolf's face is wrecked, including the eye. Will it still function?"

"I'm uncertain; we must attempt to improvise," Nindhi replied, deftly manoeuvring the tent to avoid another attack.

Bhushan scrutinized the wand with keen eyes and discerned that its severed head could indeed be reaffixed. He lifted the cumbersome fragment with considerable effort, and despite faltering twice, he persevered. After his third attempt, he succeeded in rejoining the wand's head to its body with a satisfying click.

Settling back into his chair, he fastened the seatbelt with a sense of urgency. With a quiet plea, he pressed the activation button, murmuring, "Please... please... work well, work well." The lone eye of the wand flared with a brilliant glow as he released a focused beam of azure light towards the target.

The beam of blue light surged through the narrow gap in the shield created by Reena, swiftly closing behind it. The attack took Amma by surprise; as she was in the midst of countering it, the blast struck her hand, sending her spinning away from the tent.

"Excellent shot! Aim for her broom next time," Nindhi exclaimed.

"Understood," Bhushan replied, his eyes shining with the compliment.

Amma's hand was scorched and bleeding. She halted some distance away, gripping her broom tightly with her uninjured hand to maintain her balance. Her visage had become increasingly grotesque, and her burned and bleeding hand, which still clutched the wand, had morphed into a spider-like claw as she lifted it above her shoulder for further inspection. Two additional eyes emerged on her forehead, her lips stretched grotesquely, and her teeth elongated into razor-sharp fangs. As she gaped her mouth open, it seemed she could effortlessly rend the head of an adult with ease.

A piercing scream erupted from her throat, and she charged toward the tent, her eyes blazing with fury. Bhushan braced himself, ready to target her broom, but was momentarily distracted as a barrage of red light comets streaked toward them. Despite his attempt to intercept them, the red comets proved faster than expected. However, their advance was thwarted when Reena swiftly sealed the breach she had created for the cannon wand.

The barrage hurtled toward the tent with lightning speed. Bhushan's jaw dropped as he watched the jets of red light slam into the protective shield. The shield rippled violently under the unyielding assault, reminiscent of colossal raindrops splashing on a once serene pond. He stood poised for another attempt to strike the witch, but it seemed that the opportunity had slipped away. Amidst Amma's relentless assault on the shield, a solitary red comet found its way through the protective barrier, crashing into the central pillar of the tent. The reverberating explosion drew Nindhi's gaze, and he quickly swivelled his chair to investigate. He found a significant dent in the metallic tower, but, to his relief, it seemed to remain functional despite the damage.

He cast a concerned look at Reena, observing her laboured breathing and the evident signs of exhaustion etched across her features. Her once vibrant visage now appeared worn and emaciated, with the contours of her skull becoming more noticeable as if her skin were a taut fabric stretched across the underlying bones, revealing every crevice and cut beneath.

Her eyes, once vibrant and sparkling pink, now teetered on the brink of closure. Nindhi quickly discerned the reason; one of Amma's comets had penetrated their defences due to Reena's momentary lapse in concentration.

Nindhi shifted his gaze to Bhushan, fear etched deeply on his face. Turning his attention to the wavering pink shield, he felt a sense of urgency. The shield teetered on the brink of shattering, and the looming consequences were dire.

"We can't afford to prolong this indefinitely; we must strike her down before she strikes us," exclaimed Nindhi. With a decisive manoeuvre, he sharply altered the course of the tent. The rippling of the comets over the shield ceased momentarily, once again outfoxing Amma, but only for a few fleeting seconds.

"Do you have any strategies, Nindhi?" asked Reena, her voice barely a whisper. Her dry, bleeding lips quivered as she teetered on the brink of collapse.

"I do, but it's a gamble," Nindhi responded, his voice steady but laced with urgency. After a momentary pause, he added, "Yet, with careful execution, it could lead us to victory."

CHAPTER-27

Bewitched

The witch's assault intensified, a testament to her complete descent into madness. Each strike echoed her spiralling lunacy. The cannon wand's defensive fire faltered, leaving the tent vulnerable, while Reena's strength waned with every attack, the shield quivering on the brink of collapse. "What plan do you propose?" she inquired weakly.

Nindhi, about to reveal his plan, but first, he directed Bhushan to rise from the cannon wand and follow his declaration. Bhushan complied promptly, retrieving a sack and a bowl from the tent's storage compartment—the same place where Reena had fetched the barrels to fuel the tent. Pouring the contents of the sack into the bowl, revealing the shimmering essence of mugas, Bhushan carefully fed Reena with a spoon. With each spoonful consumed, her vitality surged, and her body began to rejuvenate. Nindhi sensed a noticeable fortification of the shield, a glimmer of hope in the midst of their dire circumstances.

Having consumed half of the mugas-filled bowl, Reena declined further, deeming it an inappropriate time to finish the meal. She was feeling better, her strength returning. Bhushan placed the bowl on a surface, and both Reena and Bhushan shifted their gaze towards Nindhi. "Speak now," urged Reena. However, Nindhi was engrossed in scrutinising the crystal orb and attempting to sidestep Amma's assaults. "Amma's broom is bewitched; if we can get close enough, I can rupture it. But our effectiveness is limited to a specific range," he disclosed without making eye contact with his beleaguered team.

Attentively, both Reena and Bhushan absorbed his words. Bhushan's astonishment was palpable. "You are indeed a brainiac," he exclaimed, springing onto the balls of his feet. Reena, her strength renewed, nodded in agreement, her eyes reflecting a mix of determination and desperation. "If the broom breaks, we won't be pursued by Amma anymore," Bhushan marvelled. Reena, though surprised, maintained an expression of stoic concentration, her focus unwavering as she laboured to uphold the shield.

"But there's a complication," Nindhi countered.

"A complication?" Bhushan inquired.

"Throughout this ordeal, I've been strategizing our approach to vanquish the witch," Nindhi explained, skillfully manoeuvring the tent to the left. "I explored every conceivable option to ensure her downfall. Consequently, I placed an exploding hex on her broom. While I anticipate she will follow us if we try to flee, the real difficulty lies in closing the distance to her."

"How close do we need to get?" Bhushan asked, his curiosity laced with apprehension.

"As close as possible," replied Nindhi. His words were absorbed in a profound silence by both Reena and Bhushan. He continued, "There's one more crucial detail. I can't trigger the explosion while the shield is active, so it will need to be deactivated."

After delivering this crucial information, Nindhi paused briefly before adding, "I require someone to man the steering orb. I can't juggle the incantations and the controls simultaneously. The tent can navigate itself, but with the witch on our trail, trust in its autonomy is precarious." For a moment, a hushed silence fell over the group as they contemplated whether Nindhi was jesting or had lost his grasp on reality. Soon, the gravity of Nindhi's words sank in, and it became clear he was serious. The silence stretched for a few seconds before they collectively began to deliberate on who would take control of the steering orb.

Reena, who had never even learned to ride a bicycle—a skill deemed fundamental for every child according to a book she once read—faced the realization that she was ill-equipped for the task. Meanwhile, Bhushan, who was equally clueless, felt a wave of dread as he recognized that he was now the only viable candidate to pilot the flying tent. His heart pounded in his chest as he took a deep breath. "I take back what I said; I no longer think of you as a genius," Bhushan lamented, his anxiety palpable. "We're all destined to end up in the Witch's lair."

Reena cast a solemn look at Nindhi. "Even if we manage to regrow our limbs, surviving a fall from this height is still doubtful if Amma strikes us before her broom explodes," she remarked, her tone heavy with concern.

"If we were to fall, death would be certain; our regenerative abilities would be of no use," Nindhi stated, deftly manoeuvring the steering orb for another turn.

Upon hearing this, Bhushan's heart skipped a beat, and his fear surged to new heights.

The tent's shield withstood a relentless barrage of red comets after a brief respite of about fifteen seconds, indicating the witch's renewed vigour.

"Very well, let's proceed," Reena declared with resolve. Nindhi, for the first time, cast a concerned look toward Reena, observing how her once vibrant skin seemed to tighten and wither under the strain of Amma's persistent assault against the shield. "No, we can't," Bhushan countered, his dread of plummeting from their precarious height mounting. Meeting Bhushan's gaze, Reena declared with steely resolve, "Better tighten your hat, Bhushan. If we don't act now, imminent death awaits us. With the witch's relentless assault intensifying, we have no other choice, Bhushan."

Immediate action was taken to execute the current plan. Bhushan was summoned from the cannon wand to assume control of the steering orb. Nervousness gripped him as Nindhi directed him on how to manoeuvre the tent. Symbols glowed a vibrant purple as Bhushan donned the brown gloves. With trembling hands, he placed them on the steering orb and began to operate it. To his surprise, the controls proved less daunting than he had anticipated. As he settled into the pilot seat, his fear gradually subsided.

Nindhi took his position in the tent's corner, declaring, "Your lead, Reena; I'm at your command." Reena nodded in acknowledgement, ready to engage Amma in conversation. "Bhushan, reduce the tent's speed," she instructed. The tent's speed diminished, and Nindhi swiftly set to work. He inscribed a circle on the wooden floor, adorned with intricate witchcraft symbols. As he placed his palm on the circle, he locked eyes with Reena, nodding in silent agreement.

The tent decelerated and came to a standstill amidst the swirling, ominous clouds, its shield wavering under the ceaseless assault from the witch. Despite Amma's recognition of the tent's halted state, her barrage showed no signs of abating. With fear etched across her face, Reena turned to Nindhi, acutely aware of the urgent need to neutralize Amma's relentless attacks for their plan to succeed.

Reena felt a hand on her shoulder and, turning her head, saw Nindhi standing beside her, holding a vial of crimson potion. He had retrieved it from the tent's magical storage.

"Drink," Nindhi urged.

Reena eyed him warily, the crimson potion glinting in the dim light.

"Drink this," Nindhi instructed, his voice steady, "and you will gain the power to communicate and hear from afar."

Reena, her energy nearly spent, hesitated momentarily at the brink of exhaustion before she mustered the last of her resolve and drank the crimson potion. As the liquid touched her lips, Nindhi held the bottle firmly, ensuring no drop was wasted. The moment she swallowed, a torrent of sound flooded her senses; the relentless clamour of the red comets bombarding the shield resonated with a deafening intensity. Despite the overwhelming noise threatening to unseat her focus, Reena fought to maintain her concentration, determined to see their plan through.

"Reena, speak up," Nindhi urged urgently. "Engage Amma."

"Amma, can you hear me?" Reena's voice echoed through the air, distorted yet clear, as if travelling through a long corridor. The moment Amma heard Reena's voice, she halted her relentless bombardment.

"I hear you," Amma responded coldly, her voice tinged with a bitter edge. As her sanity waned, her resolve to annihilate them intensified. "Perhaps these pests will surrender and return to the castle with me," she thought, her determination sharpening.

"Amma, could you please draw closer?" Reena requested.

"I believe your voice is perfectly audible from your current position," Amma responded with a cold, steely tone.

"We wish to negotiate," Reena pressed on, her tone calm but laden with fatigue. "We are beleaguered from the relentless chase, and our resolve is waning."

Amma stood in silence for a moment, her eyes gleaming and, figure a dark silhouette against the tempestuous sky. Reena watched her intently from within the tent, sensing that the witch had perceived the subtle shift in their circumstances and had chosen to pause, her vigilance unwavering.

"Where is Bhushan?" Amma inquired, her gaze sweeping across the empty cannon wand from behind the half-closed curtain of the main entry, her eyes tinged with a mix of curiosity and suspicion.

Reena started to whisper to Nindhi, but he swiftly intervened, pressing a firm hand over her mouth to silence her.

"Stay silent, or she'll hear you," Nindhi cautioned, his voice urgent. "Only say the required words. Focus on luring her closer to the tent." With that, he released his grip from Reena's mouth, allowing her to speak as he returned to his place on the inscribed circle.

"Bhushan is gravely injured, Amma," Reena conveyed with a trembling voice, "he isn't healing. Please, we need your help to save him."

Nindhi signalled his approval with a thumbs up, bolstering Reena's confidence. She took a deep breath, determined to draw Amma closer.

"Amma, please aid him. He's not even thirteen yet," Reena implored, her voice tinged with desperation. Bhushan listened to Reena's words but paid them little heed, struggling to maintain his focus on the tent's controls. His hands trembled slightly, yet he remained steadfast, knowing their survival depended on his concentration.

Amma listened intently to Reena, her suspicions aroused by the situation. Concealing her wand hand behind her back, she began to twirl it, weaving intricate incantations. Her sharp eyes, glimmering with mistrust, scrutinized the tent, searching for any hint of subterfuge. Rooted to her spot, she showed no inclination to advance, her demeanour cold and calculating.

"Amma, please!" Reena's cries crescendoed, her voice laden with desperation as she implored for assistance once more. The raw intensity of her plea reverberated through the air, striking a poignant contrast to the chilling silence emanating from the witch.

After an extended ritual of swirling her wand and reciting a complex incantation, a bat-like shadowy entity emerged, its wings flapping silently as it took flight.

"Amma, we beseech your aid," Reena entreated.

"Very well," Amma conceded swiftly, "I shall guide you all home afterward."

With measured steps, the witch approached the tent, her eyes fixed on the menacing, bat-like spectre that hovered ominously near the tent.

The entity descended to the base of the tent, alighting upon the shield before transmuting into a dark, crackling energy. Slowly, the once delicate pink shield began to shift into this foreboding shadowy hue. Reena felt her hands quivering, initially attributing the tremors to the strain of maintaining the shield. Yet, soon thereafter, tendrils of dark lightning surged from her hands, snaking through her veins and penetrating her skull. The once-protective barrier around the tent dissipated in response. A searing cry erupted from Reena's throat, its resonance piercing the air with such force that even Amma instinctively shielded her ears. Reena crumpled onto the wooden floor of the tent and the sole defence mechanism of the tent was rendered null and void.

Nindhi rushed to Reena's side, scooping her into his arms and desperately trying to revive her, but she remained unresponsive. Frustration boiled within him as he glared at Bhushan for his lapse in attending to the crystal orb. As Nindhi turned to reprimand Bhushan, a thunderous explosion shattered the silence, jolting everyone within the tent. Nindhi was thrown to the ground but quickly scrambled to his feet. Peering through the door, he saw Amma's relentless bombardment continuing unabated.

"Advance!" Nindhi roared, his voice cutting through the chaos.

Bhushan, gripped by panic, fumbled as he tried to move forward. His elbow collided with the steering orb, causing the tent to jerk violently backwards and lurch towards Amma.

"Full speed ahead, Devil's Eye! FORWARD, FORWARD, FORWARD!" Nindhi's desperate cries pierced the chaos, His frantic voice echoed through the tumultuous air as he threw himself in front of Reena, trying to shield her from the relentless barrage of red comets.

The tent's sturdy framework groaned under the relentless assault from Amma, casting doubt on its ability to endure much longer. An ominous dread filled the air within the tent, a palpable tension that Amma noted as the tent inched back toward her. Unmoved by the escalating chaos, Amma remained steadfast, her demeanour calm as she ceased her attack and awaited the tent's approach with calculated patience. She stood ready to ensnare them at the perfect moment and escort them back to their destination. Meanwhile, within the tent, Nindhi wrestled with the mounting turmoil, striving to regain control of the dire situation. Forsaking his efforts to revive Bhushan, Nindhi lunged for the cannon wand, determined to confront the witch. Yet, as he seized the wand's handle, it began to slip, its integrity compromised by the previous relentless onslaught.

Swiftly leaping from the cannon wand's seat at a crucial moment spared his life as the wand lurched and tumbled out of the tent. As he lay on the tent's surface, he glimpsed Amma's menacing visage, her eyes gleaming with malevolent satisfaction and her smile contorted into a sinister grin. Rising swiftly, he dashed toward Bhushan to wrest control of the steering orb. Yet, his gaze was drawn to Reena, her body drifting lifelessly toward the door.

Leaping into action, he grasped Reena's hand as she dangled precariously from the tent's edge like a pendulum. Glancing at the witch, he observed her twisted smile growing even more sinister.

"What in the world are you doing, Bhushan?" Nindhi roared, his voice laden with frustration and urgency.

The front of the tent was rising, creating a steep, slope-like angle as it moved backwards through the air. Bhushan, overcome with panic, had lost control of the tent's compass. Amma savoured the unfolding tragedy with a vicious glee in her eyes. With the tent now just a few feet away, Amma poised her wand for action. As the tent stabilized in mid-air, its surface levelling out, Nindhi laboured to pull Reena back inside. Despite the struggle, his forearm throbbed with pain. Desperation set in as he fought to drag Reena to the safer confines of the tent.

The witch watched with anticipation as the tent drew closer, envisioning her triumphant return home with four of her meat-providing captives. Greed swelled within her with each passing moment. Things were spiralling out of control for Nindhi. "Is this the end?" he thought, panting heavily on the wooden surface, his strength waning as the weight of despair bore down on him.

He gazed at the moon, shrouded behind the clouds, through the window, savoring the ominous sight. Turning to Bhushan, who had abandoned the steering orb in panic, and then to Lily, nestled in slumber within the wooden tendrils, he contemplated their uncertain fate. The atmosphere grew heavier, filled with dread and the looming sense of impending doom. Cradling Reena in the corner, his gaze traced the threads of their predicament until abruptly, he noticed the spell circle on the floor ignite with a brilliant crimson light.

Amma hovered inches from the tent, her menacing form casting an eerie shadow as she edged closer to the door. Nindhi, battling against mounting anxiety, fought to reach the glowing circle on the floor. His hand trembled uncontrollably as it made contact. Just as he prepared to utter the spell, a shadowy figure at the threshold caught his eye—a witch with a sinister grin, poised to breach the tent and seal their fate.

Locking eyes with Amma, Nindhi thundered, "Khaṇḍayati!"

Amma's visage vanished from the tent's doorway, as though yanked away by an overwhelming force. Her broom disintegrated into shards, the calamity catching her utterly off guard. Nindhi raced to the entrance, watching as the witch plummeted from a daunting height before vanishing from view. "Farewell Witch," he murmured.

CHAPTER-28

Soft Winds of Change

With a sudden jolt, Reena awoke, her breath coming in quick, shallow gasps as she took in her surroundings. The lingering effects of unconsciousness left a sense of disquiet, pressing heavily upon her chest. Turning her gaze to the left, she saw Bhushan staring at her, a smile spreading across his face. "You're finally awake," he murmured, his voice laden with relief.

Reena swiftly turned her head to the right and found Nindhi seated beside her, his face adorned with a warm, relieved smile. With a gentle tug on her shoulders, he assisted her in settling back onto the surface. "Feeling good?" he inquired, his hand tenderly brushing against her cheek. Reena took a moment to collect herself, her head still reeling from the recent events. With a sudden nudge of panic, she seized Nindhi's hand and exclaimed, "Where are we? Did Amma imprison us?"

"Ouch," Nindhi winced, his voice strained.

But he quickly composed himself, his grip on Reena's shoulders tender yet firm, his voice brimming with triumphant relief. "We did it; the witch is dead," he exclaimed.

Reena's thoughts were shrouded in confusion, struggling to grasp the reality of Amma's demise. She turned to Bhushan and saw a jubilant smile mirrored on his face, reaffirming Nindhi's proclamation.

"We did it, Reena!" Bhushan exclaimed with bursting enthusiasm as Reena turned her gaze towards him. "Nindhi blew up her broom, and the witch crashed into the woods." Reena absorbed Bhushan's words, but the reality of it all was formidable to grasp. Her gaze then shifted to Lily, who slept soundly, free from the wooden tendrils that once bound her.

"I need to remove her tendrils too in order to repair the tent," Nindhi explained, his voice tinged with urgency. "Amma caused significant damage. I haven't been able to fix everything, but it should be enough to get us to our destination."

"Is she still asleep?" inquired Reena.

"It appears so," confirmed Nindhi.

Nindhi studied Reena with a hint of curiosity, recognizing the hesitance in her eyes to fully accept the witch's demise. Given the witch's formidable power and the peril she had posed, it was understandable that coming to terms with her defeat might be a struggle. "Reena, I know it's hard to grasp, but indeed, we succeeded. Hours have elapsed without a trace of her pursuit. We saw her fall, and since then, we've kept a watchful eye. It's time to accept that we've outwitted her; she no longer poses a threat."

"What happened to me?" Reena queried.

"You were unconscious," Nindhi explained. "The magic she wielded was unfamiliar to me, but I have a hunch it may be derived from the Tome of Krutagshni."

"The tome of what?" questioned Reena.

"Krutagshni? I don't recall encountering that one," Reena mused. "It wasn't in Amma's library, or perhaps she kept it hidden. Yet, I've come across it in another text. It's an arcane art linked to the devil, so profoundly dark that those who studied it often met their end. The book itself was reputed to be lethal to its readers."

Reena's heart raced at the mention of the book, and she swiftly redirected the conversation.

"Did you witness her demise?" Reena inquired. "Do you believe she could have survived such a monumental fall?"

"I'm uncertain, but it's indeed hard to fathom," Nindhi replied, his fingers thoughtfully tracing his chin.

"No witch could endure such a fall; their magic wands alone cannot confer flight without their brooms," he elaborated. Despite his reassurances, Reena remained ever watchful, her senses finely attuned to any signs of imminent danger.

Unexpectedly, Bhushan interjected, addressing Reena with trepidation. "Reena, while you were unconscious, Nindhi confided in me. Was... was she planning to imprison us... me and Lily, behind that pink door? I mean, consume us... our limbs indefinitely. Is that what she intended?"

Reena's expression darkened. "Yes."

"So, we were never truly siblings, were we? We were merely the ones she intended to capture?" Bhushan questioned.

"Yes," Reena confirmed softly, her gaze lingering on Bhushan as she noted the profound sadness etched across his features. It was evident how deeply the revelation that Lily and Reena were not his true siblings had affected him.

"But we can still live together as if we were true siblings, just as we did under Amma's roof," Reena reassured, her smile a beacon of solace.

Bhushan gazed at Reena, his face a canvas of awe and emotion. A single tear traced a glistening path down his cheek, an unspoken testament to the depth of his feelings, despite his attempts to keep his emotions in check.

"I don't think we should continue referring to her as Amma," Nindhi interjected with a note of finality. "She was nothing more than a witch." His words were met with nods of consensus from all present.

Turning towards the tent window, Reena gazed out at the passing landscape, its beauty taking her whiff away. She inhaled deeply, catching a tantalizing aroma that drifted through the air. Closing her eyes, she savoured the moment, relishing the gentle breeze as it softly brushed against her face. Her body was enveloped in a sensation of vibrant aliveness, a profound feeling she had never before experienced. The moonlight cast an enchanting glow over the verdant trees and meandering streams below as they soared high above the jungle, their beauty illuminated in the soft, silvery light. Though the mountains were shrouded in the shadowy veil of the darkened sky, their towering silhouettes lent an air of mystery to the celestial canvas. The clouds, drifting alongside the tent, gave the impression of a grand escort guiding them toward destiny, yet the tent outpaced even the swiftest of clouds.

Bhushan, witnessing Reena immersed in the splendour of the scenery, was inspired to join in her reverie. He moved to the opposite window, leaning out to embrace the invigorating touch of the crisp breeze as it brushed against his face. He parted his lips, welcoming the brisk breeze to dance upon the delicate surfaces within his mouth, sending tingles of cool sensation throughout, a newfound sense of liberation washing over him with an unprecedented sense of freedom.

Nindhi nestled in the corner, his eyes steadfastly fixed on Reena. He pretended to immerse himself in the pages of a book, yet his true focus remained on Reena, peeking at her through the book's cover. The solace he found in her enjoyment by the window eclipsed the beauty of the world outside; her presence rendered the external scenery pale by comparison.

He had never known such serenity before; the warmth of her smile and the glimmer of amusement in her eyes made him momentarily forget all the trials he had faced. In her presence, she seemed to embody the idealized figure he had only glimpsed in films and read about in novels.

His desire to explore the world and its myriad wonders was undeniable, yet it was the profound yearning to meet a certain girl that captivated his heart. This longing was imbued with an unmistakable uniqueness, a sensation that set it apart from any other. When he contemplated the essence of love, it felt as though he were suspended in mid-air, untethered by a broom. Gazing upon Reena, he was enveloped once more in that sublime, weightless sensation, as if he were drifting through an enchanting dream.

(cough, cough... cough)

The focus of everyone's attention abruptly shifted to Bhushan, who was struggling to catch his breath, gasping as though he had swallowed a breath of air wrong. Reena and Nindhi's laughter bubbled uncontrollably, their amusement unabated by Bhushan's visible irritation. After several moments of futile coughing, Bhushan's frustration was palpable. With a huff, he turned back to the window, resuming his silent vigil over the passing landscape.

As time wore on, Reena's anxiety gradually ebbed away. The haunting spectre of Amma no longer loomed over her thoughts, leaving her with a tentative sense of peace. Perhaps, she mused, the witch had indeed been vanquished. Turning to Nindhi, she requested a reduction in the tent's speed, hoping to immerse herself more deeply in the tranquil beauty of the landscape. With a nod, Nindhi obliged, easing the pace. Reena's gaze drifted to the vast, glowing moon visible through the window, its ethereal light casting a serene glow over the night sky.

The moon bathed the sky in its silvery luminescence, painting it in hues of deep blue. Against this celestial canvas, birds flitted like ephemeral shadows, their forms silhouetted against the moon's radiant glow. As they glided past the luminous orb, Reena saw them as kindred spirits, voyaging alongside her in their shared odyssey. "I wish this moment could stretch into eternity," she mused quietly. After a few minutes, she turned to the window and continued, "I wonder what the world beyond is truly like and what kind of people dwell within it. Is it as wondrous and diverse as the realms we have explored within the pages of our books?"

Nindhi glanced at Reena and said, "I hope wherever we end up is a place where we can live in peace and happiness. And let's hope there are no more witches lurking about... I've had my fill of losing limbs." He chuckled at his own quip, but his laughter did little to lift the mood of the others. Nindhi's laughter faltered as he quickly recognized his mistake. Blushing with embarrassment, he retreated behind the pages of his book, hoping to hide his discomfort. The humour of his words seemed misplaced against the backdrop of their recent trials. Reena, her thoughts momentarily haunted by the grim image of Nindhi's near demise, turned abruptly towards him. Reena's voice was tinged with a mix of concern and curiosity as she asked, "With the witch vanquished and no one pursuing us, I need to know how you survived after she severed your head." Her question captured the attention of everyone in the tent who was awake, their expressions shifting to one of intense interest.

CHAPTER-29

Shimmering Shanties

Reena's probing questions ignited a flicker of suspicion within Bhushan. Could this be yet another of the Witch's devious machinations? Having witnessed a day brimming with unforeseen magical encounters, Bhushan found himself unable to dismiss the unsettling thought that Nindhi might be a clandestine agent of Amma. His fists clenched, poised to lash out at Nindhi at the slightest provocation. Yet, as his gaze flickered toward Reena, who exhibited no trace of alarm, Bhushan hesitated. The impulse to confront Nindhi simmered, but he chose instead to bide his time, awaiting Nindhi's response.

Nindhi, leaning against the rough wooden wall of the tent, adjusted his posture, settling into a cross-legged position. The timeworn, brown-covered book he had been holding was now closed and placed beside him. His eyes moved from Reena to Bhushan, lingering for a moment before he offered a calming smile. "Let's chalk it up to fate," he remarked, his voice laced with a hint of uncertainty. "The specifics of how I survived are hazy. When Amma severed my head, I think I slipped into unconsciousness, probably from blood loss. Everything after that is a muddled blur. When my eyes finally opened... I found myself surrounded by sand as if I'd been plunged into a pit of mud. Even when I tried to speak, my mouth filled with gritty sand, choking my words before they could form. It soon dawned on me with horrifying clarity that my head had been severed from my body. At first, an overwhelming terror seized me, but I gradually steeled my nerves. With cautious determination, I attempted to move my hand, and to my astonishment, I realized I retained full command over my body despite the ghastly separation. Laboriously, I clawed through the clinging muck, and after what felt like an eternity, my fingers finally brushed against the contours of my own severed head. Aligning my head back onto my body, I was astonished as it began to heal with an eerie swiftness, the wound sealing itself within mere minutes. Yet, for days thereafter, I was plagued by relentless fits of coughing, expelling remnants of earth, unable to rid myself of the gritty taste of mud that clung stubbornly to my mouth and throat."

"But how did you survive? Both you and Amma have stated that the only way to kill a Mugas adept is by severing the brain from the body—decapitation, in essence. So, how are you still alive?" Reena interjected, her voice tinged with a mix of bewilderment and urgency.

Listening intently, Nindhi's eyes sparkled with a hint of excitement as he replied, "I was as astonished as you might imagine. However, after delving into some research, I uncovered that a Mugas adept endowed with healing abilities has a survival window of seventy-two hours even after decapitation. Essentially, I managed to emerge from the very ground where Amma had buried me. As I endeavoured to escape toward the tree, I saw the witch emerge from it, her presence a grim reminder of our perilous situation."

"Once she entered the house, I approached the tree with utmost caution, conducting a thorough investigation. Despite Amma's apparent intent to destroy the tree, she had not yet done so. I cast a longing glance back at the tent, wishing it were fully prepared for flight. But alas, it was not, and the thought of abandoning you, Reena, was unbearable. Therefore, I collected all the essential books, parchments, plants, seeds, and artifacts, hastily retreating to the rear of the house. There, I returned to my grave and concealed myself, commencing the construction of an underground workshop. Once it was completed, I resumed the arduous task of assembling the tent."

"I comprehend the torment you endured confined within that pink door room, yet I was powerless at that juncture. My focus was entirely on constructing the flying tent. I painstakingly assembled and forged materials, accounting for every conceivable threat to its stability. Subsequently, I augmented the tent with intricate piloting enchantments and fortified it with supplementary wood, shields, and other protective spells."

"I also laboured to create magical instruments and potions I considered vital for our journey. At times, I discreetly acquired plant ingredients from the witch's concealed garden. Each day was devoted to our escape from this grim predicament, Reena. I immersed myself in my studies, losing all sense of time... Days slipped away as I devoted myself to perfecting the tent, ensuring it could shelter you, your siblings, and myself. I also devised almost twenty five different strategies for confronting the witch, meticulously preparing for every conceivable eventuality. It was for this reason that I bewitched the broom. I deeply regret the delay, Reena; the process took longer than anticipated, but it was imperative. Without such meticulous preparation, our chances of escape would have been perilously slim."

Reena gazed at Nindhi with a blend of curiosity and heartfelt gratitude. Without a moment's hesitation, she leaped from her seat and embraced him tightly, tears shimmering in her peacock-like eyes. "This tranquillity, Nindhi, is all due to you," she whispered, her voice trembling with emotion.

As Reena's head lifted from Nindhi's shoulder, she turned towards him and placed a tender kiss on his cheek. A wave of warmth surged through Nindhi, causing his cheeks to flush a delicate shade of pink. The sensation sent shivers down his crest, a peculiar yet comforting restlessness that jolted his heart. "So this is what it feels like to be kissed by a girl," he mused, savouring the blend of warmth and exhilaration.

"I'm hungry," Bhushan's cry broke the moment, echoing from the corner of the tent.

As Lily stirred from her slumber, the collective greeting of "Good morning, Lily" resonated through the tent, drawing everyone's gaze toward her. She shifted gracefully, nestling onto Reena's lap. To their surprise, her eyes remained dry, unburdened by tears of sorrow for Amma. Meanwhile, from the tent's enchanted compartment, Nindhi retrieved a sack brimming with Mugas. He portioned the contents into bowls and distributed them among the group. Despite their hard-won freedom, none were eager to partake in the Mugas, but with no other provisions in sight, they had little choice but to accept the offering.

They endured the bleakest Mugas of their lives, the green morsels marred by scraps of the brown sack's fabric. Despite the unappetizing fare, the taste of freedom proved far sweeter than any delicacy. Each bite was a tangible reminder of their liberation from the witch's malevolent lair. Noting the diminishing fuel levels in the hourglass displayed on the tent's control box, Nindhi poured another barrel of Mugas into the engine, hoping this would sustain them until they reached the nearest village.

Reena, with a hint of curiosity in her voice, asked, "So, it truly operates on Mugas? The engine?"

"Indeed."

"And what about the Astral crystal?" She pressed further.

"It proved challenging to craft, perhaps impossible through magical means alone, so I devised an alternative method," Nindhi explained with a smile.

After their meal was completed, the group retired for the night, their bodies seeking solace in slumber. Yet, Nindhi remained awake, his eyes fixed intently on Reena. A burgeoning affection stirred within him, whirling through his thoughts like a storm of tender dreams.

Gradually, he adjusted the tent's velocity, his hands deftly managing the controls. Hours of travel passed, and soon, the distant shimmer of lights emerged from the heart of the forest, guiding their way forward.

"Rise and shine, everyone! Wake up!" Nindhi's voice reverberated through the tent with relentless urgency, rousing each of them from their slumber. Curiosity flared in their eyes as they stirred, drawn by his fervent summons. As they gathered around, they turned their gaze to the window at Nindhi's insistence, eager to uncover the cause of his excitement.

The siblings rushed to the windows, their necks craned in eager anticipation. Their eyes widened in awe as they gazed below, where a constellation of shimmering lights bathed the landscape in a magical glow. The quaint, charming houses scattered across the scenery seemed to sparkle with an inviting allure, painting a picture of serene enchantment.

It seemed to be a tribal village nestled within the heart of the dense jungle, Nindhi mused, though he remained uncertain of their disposition. Memories of movies depicting tribal communities as hostile and cannibalistic—reminiscent of his own mother's fears—lingered in his mind, casting a shadow of apprehension over their impending arrival. Suddenly, his attention was captured by a colossal, illuminated edifice that resembled a temple. His heart raced as he beheld tribal figures performing sacrifices within its hallowed interior.

As the group peered out of the window, Lily's voice rang out with innocent eagerness, "I wanna shee too!" Reena gently clasped Lily's hand and led her to the window. The little girl's eyes sparkled with delight as she exclaimed, "Nu hombe!" Reena's lips curled into a warm smile at Lily's enthusiasm, though she chose not to correct the child's playful mispronunciation. "We could make this our home for the rest of our lives," Reena declared, her voice brimming with hope and excitement.

CHAPTER-30

Hunter

Their spirits soared at the sight of the dazzling lights below. The night sky seemed to shimmer even more vividly above the village, and the distant cadence of drums filled the air with a rhythmic allure. However, amidst their collective enthusiasm, Nindhi's mood remained sombre and contemplative, the steady thrum of the drums triggered a wave of apprehension in him. After their extensive journey, he had anticipated encountering a more conventional village beyond the forest's edge, not a tribal enclave. Shaking off his unease, Nindhi turned his focus to the crystal orb. With a few deft gestures, he conjured ethereal wisps of cloud that danced within the orb's depths. Intrigued, the three siblings gathered around, their curiosity piqued by the captivating spectacle.

"What are you doing?" inquired Reena, casting a curious gaze at Nindhi.

Nindhi, focusing intently on the orb, elucidated, "I'm attempting to get a clearer view of the village. Tribal societies are seldom depicted as friendly; they're frequently likened to cannibals, akin to Amma. I'm merely trying to discern what sort of people we might be dealing with."

"Very well, proceed with your assessment," Reena encouraged. "Nevertheless, I have a favourable premonition about this village."

Nindhi, maintaining his silence, kept his gaze steady on the crystal orb. Gradually, as the mists within began to part, the village was laid bare before him. His initial suspicion about it being a tribal settlement was confirmed. Beneath the mesmerizing canopy of the night sky, the entire village seemed to be alive with activity, its vibrant energy adding to the enchantment of the scene.

The air brimmed with an aura of festivity and joy, infusing every corner with its infectious spirit. Egg-shaped mud dwellings, adorned with reed and dry grass roofs, radiated warmth from small pitchers embellished with cheerful faces, each cradling a flickering flame that danced merrily within. The dusky inhabitants emerged from their abodes, accompanied by their families, each bearing baskets brimming with fruits and grains. A child, his face aglow with an exuberant smile, scurried along with a large basket perched precariously atop his head. Upon reaching his destination, he tipped the contents of his basket into a towering bonfire, joining others who similarly unburdened their baskets into the flames.

The villagers danced in a lively swirl around the colossal bonfire. Men, adorned with silver chest plates emblazoned with a lion emblem, led the circle, while the women, draped in vibrant yellow garments akin to sarees, added a splash of colour to the spectacle. Nindhi marvelled at the sight, finding the attire of these tribal people—so vividly different from the hostile, primitive images portrayed in films—both surprising and intriguing.

All the women donned majestic crowns, meticulously crafted from stacked pitchers, each embellished with intricate paintings. At the pinnacle of these crowns, a pitcher alight with fire cast a warm, flickering glow over the scene. A sea of spectators encircled the bonfire, their gazes fixed on the dancers as they moved rhythmically around the towering blaze. Perched atop the roaring fire was a tall effigy, constructed from cloth, sticks, and reeds. Its painted eye, almost dried and lifeless, gazed out with an unsettling stare. The villagers, dressed in vibrant traditional garb of yellow and indigo, then began to dance in harmonious rhythm around the blazing figure as well, their movements synchronized with the pulsating drum beats.

"What's unfolding over there?" Bhushan exclaimed, his eyes widening as he pointed towards a child in the crystal orb. The child, adorned with a feathered crown, was dashing across the scene, clutching something tightly in his hand.

Nindhi made sweeping gestures around the orb, altering the view. The scene shifted to reveal children gathered around smaller bonfires, including the boy with the feathered crown. They were skewering something over the flames. As the food began to redden, one of the children wrapped it in a large leaf, took a bite, and his face lit up with evident joy.

They observed a towering statue, crafted from edible material, depicting a robust deity-like figure. It stood unclothed save for leaves draped around its lower half. The statue's lion-like face, flowing hair, and beard were striking. An unusual emblem etched on its chest caught Nindhi's eye. He read it aloud: "Munda."

The statue, towering to rival Amma's castle, loomed majestically. Several villagers, perched atop it, chiselled away at its surface, causing its shoulders to become uneven. The chiselled soft fragments were wrapped in large leaves and distributed among the festival-goers, who eagerly received the offerings. Once the pieces were received, the villagers carried them to the bonfire, where they skewered the food on sticks, roasting it before consumption—a ritual imbued with deep cultural significance. The siblings, captivated by the vibrant scene, felt themselves caught up in the festive excitement.

Bhushan's eyes widened at the sight of the colossal food sculpture, a hunger igniting within him. "Let's land there!" he exclaimed eagerly.

"No, it's too risky," Nindhi interjected.

"Why?" Bhushan queried, his enthusiasm dimming.

"If these individuals are anything like Amma, it could spell disaster for us," Nindhi cautioned.

"But what if they're not? What if they're friendly, and we find safety among them?" Reena countered, her voice laced with hope.

Before Nindhi could respond, Reena's voice rang out once more. "You're undervaluing them, just as I once did with Amma. You're repeating my mistake. Look, the fuel is running low,' she said, pointing to the dwindling green hourglass, a stark indicator of their remaining fuel. "If we don't find another village soon, we're done. And I refuse to die now, not after escaping the worst nightmare of my life."

Nindhi was momentarily rendered speechless, his mouth opening and closing as he struggled to find the right words. Finally, he said, "Alright, but we'll need to scout them out before making any approach."

"Agreed," the siblings chorused in unison, their voices resonating with determination.

Nindhi adjusted the course and directed the tent towards the forest's fringe, choosing to descend into an open clearing. He indicated the treeless expanse, a circular patch encircling a small lake that glimmered under the moonlight.

He instructed everyone to settle onto the cushions and then engaged one of the levers. The tent began its gradual descent, hovering just a few feet above the ground. Without warning, a burst of scarlet light erupted, engulfing the tent in a searing blaze. With a thunderous crash, the tent hurtled to the earth, its beams and supports splintering into the air, cloaked in flames. A portion of the blazing wing plunged into the lake, its fiery rage subdued as it vanished beneath the surface.

The four azure orbs rolled away from the inferno, coming to rest at a safe distance. With a resounding pop, they deflated and reverted to their original form as blue cushions. Breathing heavily, Reena crawled onto the velvety grass and collapsed, finding solace in the cool touch of the earth beneath her. She took deep breaths, savouring the fresh air after the stifling confinement of the globe.

Fortunately, Nindhi had managed to secure his seat on a pillow just in time. Though they all sustained minor injuries—scratches, burns, and bruises—their wounds healed almost instantly, thanks to the protective magic woven into the tent.

"What just happened?" Reena asked as she rose from the grass. When no one responded immediately, she turned her gaze to Nindhi, who stood with his eyes fixed skyward. Bhushan, too, was engrossed in the heavens above. Following their lead, Reena directed her attention skyward, her heart racing at the sight of an ominous silhouette against the darkened sky. Terror gripped her as she beheld a monstrous avian creature, its grotesque wings resembling twisted tree branches. The creature cast a scarlet hue across the heavens, its presence both chilling and formidable. "Run!" she bellowed, her voice piercing the air as she dashed in the opposite direction. To her astonishment, her call fell on deaf ears; no one moved. Turning to look back, she saw her companions frozen in place, ensnared by the same spell of dread. She came to a halt, her eyes locked on the dark silhouette as it slowly dissolved into a shroud of black smoke. From its previous vantage point, a crimson streak shot across the sky, plummeting toward the earth with a fiery blaze. Upon striking the ground, a reverberating thud resonated through the air, followed by the emergence of a thick, swirling haze. Within this mist, a figure began to take shape—a humanoid form moving with deliberate and purposeful steps toward them.

As the figure advanced, it grew ever larger, its immense stature casting a formidable shadow over them, like a titan rising from the depths of legend. Nindhi's heart skipped a beat, his breath catching in his throat as the impossible reality of the figure before him settled in—a sight too surreal, too terrifying to comprehend.

"It's the Witch!" Nindhi's voice cut through the air, thick with panic, as he urged everyone to flee. The sheer terror of the realization struck them like a cold blade—Amma, the malevolent force they had escaped, had survived the tremendous fall. Hearts pounding, they scrambled to their feet, dread coursing through their veins as they sprinted away from the advancing horror.

Casting a fleeting glance over her shoulder, Reena's heart sank as she saw Lily had fallen behind. Panic surged within her, but so did a fierce determination. She wheeled around, sprinting back to her sister, her hand outstretched to grasp Lily's. Just as their fingers touched, Reena's eyes were drawn skyward to a terrifying spectacle—a scarlet streak, like a malevolent comet, arcing from the ground and hurtling directly toward them, its fiery path set on a collision course.

With a desperate flick of her wrist, Reena conjured a shimmering pink sphere around Lily, sending her sister rolling swiftly toward the safety of the forest. Her heart pounded as she prepared to shield herself, but before she could summon her magic, a pair of spider-like claws, cold and unyielding, clamped onto her arm. In an instant, she was yanked from her feet, slammed against the unforgiving earth, the breath torn from her lungs as the claws pinned her down with a ruthless grip. The force of the impact sent a violent tremor through her body, as though every bone within her had been shattered at once. The reverberation surged from her head to her toes. Her arms, twisted at unnatural angles, were crushed in multiple places, each fracture a searing point of pain that threatened to overwhelm her senses.

Reena's scream of agony tore through the night as tears cascaded down her cheeks, mingling with the dirt and blood. Her vision, clouded by pain and fear, slowly sharpened, revealing the ghastly visage hovering above her. A face, deathly pale, stared down at her, its skin marred by a twisted honeycomb pattern that seemed to pulsate with a life of its own. A gruesome, slimy tongue resembling an octopus tentacle hung grotesquely from her gaping mouth, her razor-sharp teeth flexed, ready to rend flesh, clicked within the maw and snake-like tailed hairs swayed in the air, with her multiple red, yellow, and green eyes were locked on Reena, gleaming with cruel intelligence. In the dim, flickering yellow light of the burning tent beside them, the full horror of Amma's face, the most terrifying sight in the darkness was revealed.

Reena, her vision blurred by tears, glanced up at the witch towering above her. The creature's claw-like feet dug painfully into her arms, pinning her to the ground with an unyielding grip. But it was the witch's eyes that filled Reena with a deeper, more paralyzing fear. Those multiple eyes, glinting in the dim light, were utterly devoid of warmth or life—cold, empty voids where once might have dwelled some semblance of humanity. Now, they were nothing but soulless orbs, reflecting only the abyss of cruelty that lay within. It was as though Amma had plunged into the depths of madness, her mind a shattered labyrinth of twisted desires. The witch's desire to capture children, which had driven her actions before, now seemed devoid of any life or purpose.

With a cold, merciless grip, one of Amma's spider-like claws constricted around Reena's neck, cutting off her breath. The witch's twisted wand pressed against Reena's temple. The antennas of a zombie-like butterfly protruding from the wand pierced Reena's skin, sending a sharp, searing pain through her skull. Amma's voice, a terrifying cacophony akin to the screeching of a sword dragged against metal, cut through the air with venomous disdain. "You think a mere human like you can kill me?" she spat, her words dripping with malice. "You're nothing but a pitiful piece of rancid meat."

Reena writhed in desperation, her frantic attempts to wrench herself free from the witch's iron grip proving futile, as her breath hitched and sputtered, the very air of life being squeezed from her throat against the cold, unyielding ground.

"DIE!" The witch thundered.

With a swift motion, the witch brandished her wand through the air, leaving a crimson trail in its wake. Bhushan and Nindhi watched in helpless horror, their hearts pounding as they sprinted toward Reena, only to realize with sinking dread that they were too far to reach her in time.

The witch's rage boiled over, her once-latent craving for power now twisted into an insatiable thirst for blood. Any vestige of restraint or compassion had evaporated, replaced by a relentless drive to impose her will upon the world. No longer interested in keeping her captives as mere means, her eyes blazed with a singular, murderous intent. This was no longer about power but about pride—an unforgivable insult to her authority that mere children had dared to defy her. Now, her only aim was to snuff out Reena's life, and she knew exactly how to obliterate one who possessed the gift of Mugas.

She wielded the wand with precision, her chant growing fervent as the scarlet glow intensified, bathing the scene in a fiery hue. Just as she was poised to deliver the fatal strike to Reena's temple, a sharp, swift object shot through the air, piercing her hand with a resounding bang. The force of the impact caused her wand to slip from her grasp, clattering to the ground.

Amma inspected her hand closely, her gaze narrowing as she noticed a small, gleaming object lodged within the wound. As her flesh began to mend itself, the fragment of metal was expelled from the gash. Before she could fully recover, another projectile, swift as lightning, shot through the air, striking one of the red eyes on her forehead with deadly precision.

Amma emitted a metallic shriek, her voice echoing with a chilling resonance as she beheld the two figures emerging before her. Clad in khaki uniforms and sturdy helmets, the hunters from the nearby village stood resolute, their rifles aimed with grim determination. Despite their attire, which starkly contrasted with the tribal villagers, it was evident that these hunters had arrived from that direction. Likely guests in the village, they might have been tracking game when they intercepted the monstrous creature's assault on the child.

"Release the child, you fiend!" The hunter's command reverberated with righteous fury. The witch, momentarily taken aback by the harsh appellation, glanced at her hands with a dawning realization. A jolt of terror gripped her as she comprehended that her unrestrained fury had grotesquely warped her into a monstrous abomination—a transformation she had been insidiously unaware of until this grim moment.

Bhushan and Nindhi paused at a prudent distance, their eyes fixed on the unfolding drama. Nindhi, driven by a sudden surge of urgency, plunged his hand into his pouch, frantically rummaging for any object that might assist in freeing Reena. His heart sank as he discovered, much to his dismay, that he possessed nothing of immediate utility.

Amma, having risen from her kneeling position where she had subdued Reena, relinquished her crushing grip on the girl's battered arms. The witch, now turning her menacing attention toward the two hunters, advanced with purposeful strides. The hunter, witnessing Amma's wound miraculously healed before his eyes, staggered back in terror. In a frantic bid for survival, he emptied his rifle in a desperate flurry of gunfire, but the witch, impervious to his assault, remained undeterred.

The hunter, visibly rattled by the macabre spectacle he had just witnessed, fumbled with his ammunition, his hands quaking with apprehension. As he finally managed to reload his weapon and dared to glance up, his eyes widened in disbelief. Before him stood a vision of ethereal beauty: a radiant woman in a flowing white gown, her breast heaving, cradling a bouquet of sunflowers in her delicate hands.

The hunter's eyes, now glowing with an eerie scarlet light, were locked in a trance of fervent desire. He stood rooted in place, utterly captivated by the enchanting figure of the woman in the flowing white gown, her approach, adorned with sunflowers, casting a spell of mesmerizing allure over him. The hunter's weapon fell from his fingers as he began to drift towards her, each step light and dreamlike. As they closed the distance, the air between them became charged with their shared breaths. The witch seized the moment, drawing him into her embrace. Their tender lips met in a profound and passionate kiss, a union of desperate longing and enchantment.

Nindhi and Bhushan edged closer to Reena, their movements careful and deliberate as they sought to help her. She was sprawled on the ground, her face pressed against the earth. Just as Nindhi bent down to rouse her, a sharp, guttural scream—marked by a subtle lisp—pierced the air, startling them both.

Nindhi's gaze fixated on the horrific tableau before him: the hunter writhing on the ground, his hands clutching his mouth as a torrent of blood gushed forth like a tap left open, his legs flailing in sheer agony. Above him loomed the witch, her razor-sharp fangs sunk into his tongue, gnawing with a grotesque hunger. The ghastly scene sent a shiver of dread down Nindhi's spine.

Nindhi turned to Bhushan, who was on the verge of a terrified scream, his face contorted in horror. Acting swiftly, Nindhi clamped his hands over Bhushan's mouth, stifling any sound. They both fell to the ground, the urgency in Nindhi's whisper barely audible as he implored Bhushan to remain silent.

Nindhi slowly withdrew his hands from Bhushan's mouth. As they both rose, they watched in stunned silence. The witch, now consumed by her grotesque hunger, continued to feast on the remains of the hunter, while the other hunter, shrieking in terror, fled into the distance. In an ominous display of brutality, the witch wrenched the hunter's head from his body, sending the helmet skidding across the ground with a resonant thud near Nindhi. Like a feral creature, she tore into the flesh and began to feast.

Nindhi and Bhushan were gripped by a profound sorrow for the brave hunter, whose noble attempt to save them had led to his tragic end. As the witch's feral hunger consumed her, Nindhi seized the moment to act. He gently roused Reena, helping her to her feet. Reena, still shaken but resolute, pointed Bhushan toward Lily's location. Without a moment's hesitation, Bhushan sprinted in that direction.

Reena battled against the overwhelming grief, her resolve unwavering even in the face of such despair. With Nindhi's steady support, she limped forward, her eyes darting for a place of refuge. As they progressed, her fractured arms began to mend, though the pain was still fresh. Amid their hurried retreat, Nindhi's sharp eyes caught sight of a slender object clutched between Reena's teeth—the very wand of Amma.

A surge of awe and hope gripped Nindhi as he realized that without her wand, Amma would be rendered powerless, unable to cast her malevolent spells. However, a crunching sound echoed through the air, indicating to Nindhi that he had stepped on a branch. The sharp snap of a broken branch resonated through the air, instantly drawing Amma's attention toward the sound.

They watched in horrified fascination as Amma's neck twisted unnaturally, reminiscent of an owl's eerie flexibility. Her mouth was crammed with chunks of raw liver, its blood mingling grotesquely with that of the slain hunter. Her face was marred by a disturbing splatter of crimson, while her eyes, cold and unfeeling, bore a chilling intensity. With an expressionless visage, she fixed Reena and Nindhi with a chilling stare. After swallowing the whole liver, her voice of a sword scraping against metal, cut through the air. "Prepare to meet your end, KITTENS," she intoned.

CHAPTER-31

Wolves

Up ahead, Reena and Nindhi beheld the witch in a state of unbridled fury, her presence both wild and menacing. Her hair began to writhe and transform into dark, sinuous tentacles. With tremendous force, these appendages lashed out towards them. Just as the tentacles were about to make contact, They both vanished into thin air. The witch stood momentarily stunned, her eyes narrowing as she contemplated the sudden disappearance of her quarry. The realization struck her like a bolt—her wand's magic had spirited them away. Forsaking her feast, Amma dashed into the jungle with relentless speed, determined to recapture them.

"Shall we play a game of hide and seek, my little ones?" the witch taunted, her voice dripping with malice as blood dripped from her fangs. With a cruel grin, she wrapped her tentacles around a nearby tree, the air sizzling with the acidic smoke from their touch. "Even if you've stolen my wand," she hissed, her eyes gleaming with menace, "you cannot escape me." With a violent heave, she uprooted the tree and cast it aside, her rage manifesting in every movement.

Nindhi watched from his concealed position behind the towering tree as Amma plunged into the forest, her presence a menacing force.

"She's coming our way... What's our strategy, Reena?" Nindhi whispered. Reena crouched beside him, scrutinizing the wand with a newfound determination now that her arms had completely healed. "We hold her wand; the power to vanquish her lies within our grasp... All that remains is to seize the opportune moment," Reena declared, her eyes still locked on the wand as her fingers traced the eerie contours of the zombie-like butterfly.

"No," Nindhi countered softly, "we can't, it might not work on her. Have you ever wielded the martyrdom spell before?"

"No, but I've studied the mantras," Reena insisted, her voice filled with determination. "We managed to cast the spook spell and apparated into the forest. I believe I can cast the martyrdom spell. I'm confident we can annihilate her!"

"No, Reena, it's far too perilous. There's a real risk you won't be able to defend yourself this time. And if you're caught, I'm uncertain if I can assist you. The witch's behaviour has shifted; she's become far more dangerous than before," he cautioned. As he spoke, a thunderous crash echoed through the forest. Nindhi peeked around the edge of the tree trunk and saw Amma drawing closer, mere feet away. When he turned back to Reena to suggest a new hiding spot, he was met with an empty space—she had vanished.

Moving with utmost stealth, Nindhi relocated his position, each step deliberate and noiseless as he avoided any branches underfoot. The witch soon unearthed his previous hiding place, but he remained concealed in his new sanctuary. Hidden behind a massive boulder, Nindhi scanned the forest intently, his eyes searching for Reena. He soon caught sight of her, huddled behind a robust tree. Her grip on the wand was resolute, and she stood poised on the balls of her feet, bracing herself to confront the witch.

Nindhi watched in mounting alarm as Reena teetered on the brink of a perilous choice. He tried to offer a whispered warning, but his words were swallowed by the rustling leaves. Undeterred, Reena stealthily pursued Amma, waiting for the perfect moment to act. At last, she found a strategic position and took cover behind a nearby tree.

Reena stole a glance at Amma, who was scanning the area with a fierce intensity. She shut her eyes momentarily, clutching the wand tightly as her heart pounded with trepidation. Gathering her resolve, she aimed the wand towards Amma. But as she prepared to recite the mantra, the witch had already dissipated. As Reena wrestled with the mystery of Amma's sudden disappearance, a clawed hand unexpectedly clamped around her neck, lifting her off the ground. Her legs hung motionless, swaying like withered vines, while her face flushed a deep crimson from the suffocating pressure. The wand slipped from her fingers, falling with a clatter to the forest floor below.

With a sudden and savage force, the witch flung Reena through the air, propelling her like a deadly projectile. Reena crashed into some trees, each collision uprooting and shattering them with explosive force. Finally, she hurtled from the forest's edge and plummeted to the ground, landing with a sickening thud and lying motionless amidst the debris.

Amma, having cast Reena away, bent to retrieve her wand, but it eluded her grasp. After a desperate search yielded no results, realization dawned upon her. She unleashed a deafening roar, a metallic screech that reverberated through the forest, before surging towards Reena with unbridled fury.

As Reena's eyes fluttered open, she was met with a horrifying scene. A severed head lay beside her, its face marred with bite marks and gaping chunks missing. Nearby, a dismembered body, its limbs conspicuously absent, was the grim banquet of a ravenous pack of wolves. One of the wolves locked its burning yellow eyes onto Reena and approached with menacing intent. It sniffed at her before lunging, its sharp fangs sinking into her leg and shaking with ferocity. However, a sudden burst of pink light erupted, sending the wolf hurtling away and causing the remaining pack to scatter in terror.

Reena's grip on the wand faltered again and the wand slipped from her grasp, her hands quaking as she clutched her head in torment. With a final, strained effort, she untwisted her neck twice, her cry of anguish echoing through the forest as the healing began. The intense pain left her dizzy and disoriented, and she collapsed once more. As she caught sight of the smouldering remains of their tent, recognition dawned, and she collapsed onto the ground, her vision fading. Every bone in her body seemed shattered or fractured, and though some of the severe injuries were beginning to mend, she remained immobilized, utterly drained of strength.

Suddenly, a metallic roar shattered the silence. Reena turned her head weakly towards the sound, her vision hazy and her eyes half-closed, to see the Witch charging towards her with terrifying speed.

"You wretched little pest!" The witch roared, her voice dripping with venom. "You dared to cast a pilfer spell on my wand... I've had enough of you, you insignificant scoundrel."

Reena saw Amma storming towards her and tried to grasp her wand on the ground, but her hand remained lifeless, unresponsive to her desperate efforts. Her body, still grappling with the aftermath of healing, left her vulnerable and defenceless against the approaching storm. Reena struggled to move her hand, finally managing to clutch the wand despite her weakened state. She raised it shakily towards the advancing witch and began to murmur the martyrdom spell. Yet, it was too late; the witch loomed above her, her spider-like claw gripping the wand's front as Reena lay helpless on the ground.

The witch wrenched the wand from Reena's grasp, determined to seize it before she could finish the fatal incantation. Sensing the imminent loss, Reena mustered her remaining strength and yanked her hand downward. A burst of scarlet light erupted, sending a plume of silver smoke spiralling into the air. The witch staggered back, disoriented, her head whirling from the sudden shock. Brandishing the wand with unrestrained fury, the witch's rage surged uncontrollably. Her clawed hand gripped the front half of the wand, its end adorned with the ghastly image of a zombie-like butterfly. The realization struck her with dread: the other half lay clutched by Reena, who was sprawled on the ground several feet away. The witch's terror and fury converged as she saw her magical wand snapped in two.

CHAPTER-32

Warriors

The witch ascended from the earth, her fists clenched with an iron grip. The relentless string of defeats at the hands of mere children had driven her to the very rim of delirium. With her wand shattered, the realization dawned upon her that her capacity to wield magic with its full potency was now grievously diminished. It was the wand of her choosing, forged through the torment of seventeen wandmakers to create the most powerful instrument of magic in existence—now utterly obliterated. The witch lunged at Reena, who was frantically trying to crawl away. Reena's terror deepened as she felt the crushing weight of the witch descend upon her, claws sinking mercilessly into her shoulders.

"I've had enough of you, you sleazy little brat," snarled the witch, her massive fist crashing into Reena's jaw with a bone-shattering force.

"You little pests..." she seethed, landing another crushing blow to Reena's jaw. "I'll make sure..."—*crash*—"you pay for this,"—*crash*—"you vile vermin."

The ground was spattered with blood as the witch relentlessly pummelling Reena. Her jaw felt as if it were being shattered like shards of glass in a sack, her cheek swollen and bruised to a deep purple, yet the witch showed no mercy, raining down blow after brutal blow, her fists unrelenting. Amma unleashed a blood-curdling scream, her metallic voice slicing through the air, as she sank her fangs deep into Reena's neck. Despite the searing pain, Reena could not utter a sound; her shattered jaw and swollen face left her muffled, trapped in agonizing silence. In a frantic attempt to defend herself, Reena drove the broken half of the wand into the witch's ear. The witch convulsed in pain, yet her grip on Reena's neck remained ironclad. With a savage twist, she ripped out a chunk of flesh and spat it out with disdain.

Reena writhed in silent torment, her screams reduced to faint whispers by the unbearable pain. "Say your final farewell," the witch hissed, her jaw unnaturally distending as her teeth elongated into deadly spikes. As she lunged to sever Reena's head, a sudden, piercing pain shot through the witch's neck, as though something had driven an inch deep into her flesh. She tried to twist her neck, but another strike landed. Turning her head, she saw Nindhi standing resolute, brandishing a machete high. Stunned, the witch's attempt to speak was cut short as the machete descended, striking her neck twice more. Her head was severed from her body, tumbling to the ground and rolling away.

The severed head rolled several times before coming to a stop, returning to Amma's human form. Nindhi hurried to the head, giving it a forceful kick that sent it skittering a few more feet away. He then turned to Reena, grabbing her shoulders and pulling her from beneath the witch's enormous, lifeless form. Reena struggled to rise, eventually collapsing back to the ground as her body, though healing, left her disoriented. As her blurred vision gradually sharpened, she saw Nindhi, consumed by fury, hacking at Amma's lifeless body with the machete. His blows severed one of her arms before he finally returned to Reena's side and sat down beside her.

"Loathsome witch!!" Nindhi spat out, his breaths ragged and heavy.

"Thank you," Reena said, "she almost took my head off."

"I can't believe she survived such a fall," Nindhi gasped.

"She's a witch, a spawn of the devil... utterly unpredictable," Reena remarked, her voice laden with exhaustion.

Her gaze fell upon the machete in Nindhi's hand, and she inquired, "Where did you find that?"

Nindhi cast a fleeting glance at Reena and motioned toward the lifeless hunter's body. "I procured it from there," he said, "It was in his possession."

He rose, tossing the machete aside, away from them, and then turned to Reena, offering his hand. She accepted it with a smile, pulling herself to her feet. "Shall we make our way to the village?" he proposed. "I suspect Bhushan and Lily may have reached there by now." Together, they ventured towards the village from the depths of the woods.

Both of them made their way towards the village, Reena's body having healed enough to walk, though she still felt the persistent aches of her ordeal. They had scarcely taken a few steps when the sound of rustling leaves and snapping branches reached their ears. Startled, they exchanged astonished glances before turning to investigate the source of the noise.

The headless body remained upright on the ground, its severed arm clutched in one of its spider-like hands. With unnerving dexterity, it reattached the arm to the gaping wound from which it had been chopped. Miraculously, the arm healed as though it had never been severed. Amma's monstrous form surged forward, her renewed strength propelling her with terrifying speed. Reena and Nindhi, their hearts pounding in terror, dashed towards the village, their flight a frantic scramble to escape the relentless pursuit. As Reena sprinted down the path, she caught sight of the witch's head, still writhing and rolling toward the direction of its reassembling body. With a swift, decisive move, she grabbed the head by its tangled hair. Recalling Nindhi's warning about the seventy-two-hour window for healing, Reena's instincts drove her to act swiftly. She quickly fashioned three tight knots in the witch's hair, securing it to prevent any further manipulation by the witch's tentacles.

They raced through the forest with the witch relentlessly pursuing them. "Return my head, you vile wretch!" the disembodied head screeched, its voice echoing through the trees. Reena's attention was riveted on the source of the shriek. With a swift motion, Nindhi stepped in and, wielding his machete, cleaved through the witch's tongue, silencing her enraged demands. "She won't be uttering another word," Nindhi assured with grim satisfaction. Reena's gaze fell upon the dark machete in his hand, the very same weapon he had discarded earlier after decapitating the witch. "He must have recovered it on the way," she surmised.

They cast a wary glance over their shoulders, watching as the headless body tore through the forest with relentless fury. Their desperate sprint carried them through the dense foliage until, at last, they burst into the tribal village—unintentionally ushering an unwelcome intruder into their midst. As they entered the village, they marvelled at the exquisite egg-shaped houses, each adorned with cyan-coloured wooden doors and windows that gleamed more vividly than any scene glimpsed through a crystal orb. In their frantic state, they sought refuge behind one of these charming abodes, their hearts pounding with a mix of awe and terror. Before long, the headless body of the witch stormed into the village, its unnatural senses quickly zeroing in on Nindhi and Reena's hiding place. Gripped by panic, they bolted in a different direction, their desperate flight a frantic attempt to escape the witch's relentless pursuit.

The air was heavy with cries of terror and the frantic rhythm of fleeing footsteps as panic swept through the village. Reena and Nindhi observed the chaotic scene: villagers scattering in every direction, their fear almost tangible. Amidst the turmoil, a band of men charged forward, brandishing an array of spears, clubs, and axes. Nindhi quietly followed the group, keeping a safe distance as they confronted the formidable, headless figure amidst the charming, egg-shaped houses of the village. Rejoining Reena, he gripped her hand firmly as they veered off in a different direction. The scene around them was a tableau of raw fear: women clinging to their children, both hurrying desperately to find sanctuary. However, their attention was suddenly drawn to a group of men, armed with bows and arrows, who nimbly traversed the rooftops. Leaping from one house to another, they executed their desperate bid for defence with practiced agility.

Nindhi and Reena took refuge in an abandoned dwelling, where they discovered a makeshift bed crafted from stacked reeds and a rudimentary stone table. With urgency, Nindhi secured the door, fastening it with a latch fashioned from intricately engraved stones, the he tossed the witch's head onto the table and, with a determined effort, plunged his machete from one temple to the other in a bid to end her reign of terror. However, to their dismay, the witch remained unaffected. Her laughter reverberated with a sinister resonance, her grin a disquieting mockery of their efforts. As she made repeated, futile attempts to bite them, their alertness kept them out of her reach. It became increasingly clear that the witch's healing abilities were far beyond Reena's powers, an ominous sign of her formidable strength.

Unable to vanquish the witch, they exchanged uneasy glances, their apprehension mirrored in each other's eyes.

"I drove the blade in as deeply as I could," Nindhi confessed, his voice laden with distress. "Yet she's still alive."

"It appears that killing the brain only works for those with the Mugas ability," Reena reasoned.

"Well, I think..." Reena trailed off, her words faltering as an unsettling, familiar murmur reached her ears. She glanced at the witch's head on the table before darting outside the house. Nindhi called her name thrice, but she instructed him to stay with the head. Emerging into the chaos, Reena saw several limbless tribal warriors being hastily carried to safety by others. The street was drenched in a macabre river of blood. From her concealed vantage point behind a nearby house, Reena's hands pressed against her lips and her eyes glistened with tears. She moved with great caution toward the source of the chaos, driven by grim curiosity. As she approached, the unfolding scene revealed a tableau of terror: more injured tribal warriors, dismembered and agonized, were being carried through the blood-soaked streets, their plight a stark testament to the nightmarish reality of their situation. Two severed heads were hurled through the air, colliding with the wall of a nearby house with sickening thuds. Reena's gaze followed the trajectory, and she saw the headless witch, now brandishing a black sword, mercilessly cleaving through the brave warriors who had ventured to challenge her. The once-celebratory ambience had descended into a nightmare of blood and chaos.

CHAPTER-33

Gunny Needle

The headless witch assumed a more composed stance, her form looming over the battlefield where every tribal warrior lay vanquished, their bodies strewn about like forsaken marionettes—some mutilated, others lifeless. As she poised to continue her pursuit of the fleeing children, a powerful arrow suddenly struck her from behind, piercing through her spine and embedding itself deep within her abdomen. With a brutal jolt, she was violently yanked backwards, crashing hard against the unforgiving earth. Reena, her heart pounding, cautiously advanced to investigate, taking cover amidst the clustered huts. A discordant symphony of music and war cries assaulted her senses as she witnessed a procession of tribal warriors marching forward. Two of them sprang forward, brandishing their keen axes, which bit deeply into the witch's forearms but failed to cleave them entirely. However, the impact was enough to weaken her grip, causing her sword to slip from her grasp.

The other tribesmen surged forth, hurling a storm of spears and arrows from the shadows of the rooftops. The witch, helpless and exposed, was bombarded with an unyielding onslaught, her form savagely torn apart by the unrelenting assault. The magnitude of the devastation would have claimed the life of any mere mortal, yet she endured. Amidst the chaos, the witch rose defiantly, wrenching the massive, anchor-like arrow from her back. Defying the bounds of mortality, each arrow was expelled from her flesh, and every wound healed with uncanny swiftness. As if guided by some invisible magnetism, her sword leapt into her grasp, and with a single, sweeping arc, she severed the ranks of her assailants, painting the ground with a vivid trail of crimson. As she prepared for another decisive blow, an arrow struck true, embedding itself in her chest, fired from a tribal archer stationed atop one of the egg-shaped dwellings. In a fluid, decisive motion, her sword sliced through the air, unleashing a torrent of dark energy. Turning the warrior into an eerie shroud of black smoke.

The surviving archers stood transfixed, their eyes widening in horror as their comrades evaporated into a swirling haze of darkness. Shifting her focus, the witch levelled her katana at the remaining foes, sending forth jagged bolts of shadowy energy. Each bolt struck with precision, dissipating its target in a shroud of wisps of blackness. Overcome with terror, the remaining archers scattered, fleeing in every direction as panic seized them.

As the headless witch reduced her foes to clouds of black smoke, a massive arrow suddenly drove through her arm, forcing her to drop her ebony blade with a resonant clang. Whirling to confront the source of this new threat, she locked eyes with the solitary archer who had not fled—an imposing figure clad in a fearsome lion's mask, its gaze unyielding and fierce. With sinewy arms pulling the taut string of his war bow, the archer's aim remained steadfast as he released another immense arrow. The projectile flew true, striking the headless witch with a sickening thud. The arrow impaled her chest, driving her back with a jarring force and pinning her firmly against the sturdy structure behind her. However, the sheer weight of the witch's body proved overwhelming for the fragile walls, which disintegrated into dust under the immense force. A thick cloud of gritty debris surged outward, momentarily shrouding the witch from sight.

Leaping from rooftop to rooftop, he swiftly closed the gap between himself and the witch, only to be confronted by a sudden barrage. A stream of inky darkness surged toward him with terrifying speed. In a frantic, desperate motion, he narrowly sidestepped its lethal trajectory, though not without suffering the aftermath. The searing beam grazed his forearm, leaving a deep, raw wound that immediately welled with crimson. Tendrils of black smoke curled from the gash, and he grimaced in pain, his lower face, visible from under a lion mask and his intense gaze, remained locked on the evil entity before him.

Amidst the relentless barrage of dark energy, he moved with agility, deftly weaving through the malevolent onslaught. Seizing a fleeting moment of opportunity, he loosed a pair of arrows from his war bow with unerring precision. The shafts cut through the air, striking the witch's obsidian blade and pinning it securely against the wall of a nearby dwelling.

Reena watched in rapt amazement, witnessing a battle against the witch unlike anything she had ever seen. The headless monstrosity shifted its focus, turning toward the spot where its dark sword was pinned.

Unable to summon her sword with magic, the headless witch approached the pinned weapon, intent on reclaiming it. As she reached out, a blazing arrow struck the void of her neck, where her head should have been, igniting her body in a fierce conflagration. The warrior, clad in the guise of a lion, watched from a distance as the witch writhed in the torment of the flames. As he cautiously drew nearer to inspect, the witch's spider-like claws, suddenly, ensnared him.

Reena observed the tumultuous scene, then hurried back to her refuge, her heart weighed down by the sorrow of the villagers' tragic fate. Yet, amid the despair, the valour of the lion-masked warrior captivated her, even as he now found himself trapped in the clutches of the headless witch. As she fled, a projectile hurtled toward her, landing with an unpalatable thud—it was the head of the lion-masked warrior. Reena inhaled sharply in shock, but her feet did not falter in their desperate flight. She dashed into her refuge and swiftly closed the door behind her, sealing herself away from the chaos outside. With tears shimmering in her eyes, Reena approached Nindhi.

"When did she regenerate her tongue?" Reena inquired, hastily wiping away her tears with her sleeve.

"I don't know," Nindhi responded, his voice tinged with concern.

"She... she's slaughtering the entire village. The dark blade... it's been summoned," Reena stammered, her breaths coming in ragged gasps.

Nindhi seized the witch's severed tongue lying on the table and raised his machete to strike again, but Reena swiftly grasped his arm. "We can't keep doing this; she'll just regenerate it," Reena asserted. "Do you truly believe she can wield her magic without chanting?"

"Chanting spells, whether whispered or shouted, is essential; simply thinking them won't suffice. However, if the witch possesses the ability to cast spells through mere thought, it's a moot point now," Nindhi explained, his grip tightening around the sinuous tongue. "Her wand is lost, and her sword has already been summoned; there's nothing left for her to wield. Without her wand, she's powerless when it comes to charms; she wasn't born a witch, save for her monstrous abilities. We must sever her tongue, or she could pose an even greater threat."

As Nindhi prepared to sever the tongue, Reena halted his motion. Her gaze was drawn to a faint glimmer in the corner, something that stirred a sense of familiarity within her. Approaching, she uncovered several bags woven from coarse brown twine. Grasping the luminous object, she realized it resembled her own needle, though much larger. Returning to Nindhi, she brandished the sturdy implement, its eye threaded with a thick strand of brown cord.

"It's known as a gunny needle," Nindhi remarked, his tone laced with curiosity. "What do you intend to do with it?"

"I'm going to stitch her tongue to her face," Reena declared as she approached the severed head and began her grim task. The witch's head thrashed in an attempt to evade her, but Nindhi held it firmly in place. When Reena finished, the tongue was secured, resembling a serpent coiled from cheek to forehead.

Seizing the machete from Nindhi, Reena drove the blade into the witch's eyes, blinding her, and then punctured her ears, stuffing them with ragged shreds of fabric. With a length of cloth torn from a dress found within the house, she fashioned a blindfold, wrapping it securely around the witch's eyes and ears, effectively muffling her senses.

"We must take action to stop her," Reena declared to Nindhi. Understanding her strategy against the witch, Nindhi nodded in approval. Her strategy aimed to sever the witch's control over her own body, a clever attempt to render her powerless. "Let's depart and find a solution to this atrocity," Nindhi proposed earnestly.

They both emerged from the house, scanning the chaos for any sign of the witch. They observed villagers, torches gripped tightly in their hands, charging toward the headless figure, hurling flaming torches and arrows in her direction. The witch trembled, teetering on the brink of collapse. Seemingly severed from her head, the witch groped in the darkness, unable to discern her surroundings. The method of blinding and muffling her senses had proven effective; her attacks against the tribal warriors lacked precision, each strike as erratic as that of someone flailing helplessly in the dark. Though assailed by flaming arrows and torches, the witch remained impervious to their effects. The chaotic scene before her triggered a haunting flashback; Reena's mind raced back to a chilling memory of Nindhi lying lifeless and headless on the ground, while Amma stood unscathed amid the flames of the Phoenix spell bomb.

Nindhi advanced a few paces and noticed the villagers igniting their torches with a peculiar liquid. Intrigued, he observed as they doused their torches in the vibrant substance before rushing to aid their comrades. Drawn to the source, he discovered a tall pitcher filled with a striking purple fluid, clearly designed to fuel the flames. He then spotted an isolated house perched higher than the others—the only hut made of gravel, yet seemingly abandoned, the lone structure in that area. Sprinting toward it, he quickly surveyed its layout: a single door flanked by two front windows and one at the rear. A plan crystallized in Nindhi's mind, and he grinned, confident in his newfound strategy to finally end the witch's reign. He dashed back to the site of the purple liquid and called for Reena, who quickly joined him.

"I've devised a foolproof method to eliminate the witch, and this time, we shall prevail," Nindhi declared with resolute certainty. Reena pondered what strategy he might have concocted. Just then, a familiar voice called out their names. They both turned to see Bhushan approaching. Relief washed over Reena as she greeted him, "Bhushan, it's such a relief to see you unharmed. I've been so worried. Where is Lily?"

"She's safe, you needn't worry. The villagers have taken her in, showing great hospitality by providing for us since our arrival," Bhushan explained. "They urged me to take refuge with them, but my concern for you led me here, and at last, I've found you," Bhushan replied. "Your arrival couldn't have been more timely, Bhushan," Nindhi responded. "I believe you can assist me with something crucial." He added with a strategic tone, "I've crafted a strategy that will ensure the witch's definitive downfall."

CHAPTER-34

The Stone Dwelling

They huddled in a circle, arms draped over each other's shoulders, murmuring in discussion. After a moment, they dropped their arms and returned to their positions. "It won't work, Nindhi. You don't understand how she withstood the spell bomb before," Reena argued.

"Yes, it will. We have to take our chances, Reena. I've explained how we can make it work, how we can defeat her," Nindhi replied, his tone firm as he rummaged through his pouch in search of something.

"But what if we fail? We placed so much hope in the Phoenix spell bomb, and you know how that turned out," she said, her gaze locked on Nindhi. "Are you even listening!?"

Nindhi listened to Reena, his expression unyielding. He then drew a pair of white gloves from his pouch and stated resolutely, "Just as you said, Reena, we're out of options… it's do or die." His gaze locked onto hers. A heavy silence enveloped Reena as self-doubt crept in, tinting her thoughts with cowardice. Perhaps the horrors she had witnessed were sowing fear in her heart, or maybe she was simply exhausted from the relentless struggle against this undying witch. The cause was uncertain, but anxiety quietly seeped into her heart, leaving her to wonder if she was merely overthinking. Her eyes shifted from the headless witch wreaking havoc in the distance to Nindhi, who was now handing a pair of white gloves to Bhushan.

"What if we destroy only the head? Perhaps the body will perish," Reena proposed, brandishing the witch's head in her hand.

"It's a possibility, but I'm uncertain. If by any chance she survives, we won't have another chance to eliminate her completely, and she will continue to ravage the village," he replied, his face etched with concern.

"I'm prepared," Bhushan declared. Both Nindhi and Reena turned toward him as he examined his long white gloves. Nindhi then retrieved a spherical glass jar from his pouch, resembling the phoenix spell bomb but filled with a viscous substance instead of liquid—a purple, gelatinous material with two button-like eyes. He handed the jar to Bhushan, instructing him to follow. Together, they set off, advancing toward the witch, leaving Reena behind. In stealth, they moved forward, concealed and silent. Despite the witch's dulled senses, they chose to proceed with caution. As they neared the witch, they took refuge behind the crumbling ruins of a house and peered out, observing her as she presided over the devastation of the villagers.

"Do you understand your task?" Nindhi whispered. Bhushan nodded in affirmation.

"Alright, good luck, my friend. Rejoin us once you've completed your task," Nindhi said, giving him a reassuring clap on the back before setting off.

Gazing at the glass jar, Bhushan watched as the gelatinous creature twisted and writhed, struggling to escape. "Alright, just aim for the exposed area on her back," he muttered to himself. Then, silently, he moved forward, weaving between shattered homes and blood-soaked walls, careful to remain hidden from the witch and shielded from the horrifying spectacle unfolding before him. The witch's senses were now dulled and the chaotic whirl of severed limbs in the air began to subside. Yet Bhushan's heart raced even faster. He steeled himself for the task ahead, driven by the knowledge that his actions could save the remaining villagers.

He navigated past several houses until he found an optimal position for his attack. As he opened the jar lid, a label affixed to it caught his eye—"Pey-Nigalanki." Carefully, he turned the jar over, letting the creature inside slide onto his hand like a living fluff of mugas. Grasping the slippery creature proved difficult as it writhed in an attempt to escape. Nonetheless, Bhushan tightened his fist around it and launched it at the exposed area of the blood-drenched white gown on the witch's back, striking his target with precision. As the creature made contact and adhered to her bare skin, the witch, sensing the assault, swung her sword wildly, cutting down another tribal warrior unfortunate enough to be in her path. Bhushan closed his eyes as he witnessed the poor man being halved in front of him due to his actions, feeling the weight of despair settle in. Yet, there was nothing he could do. He hurried back to Nindhi, confirming the completion of his task. Nindhi exchanged a knowing glance with Reena, signalling that it was now her turn to act.

Reena dashed ahead, leaving Nindhi and Bhushan behind. As she approached the witch, she positioned herself directly in front of the disoriented creature, not far from the giant statue. With a firm grip, Reena yanked off the blindfold and swiftly removed the fabric stuffed in the witch's ears. As the witch regained her senses, she scanned her surroundings, noticing her body embroiled in a fierce struggle with a group of villagers.

"CATCH ME IF YOU CAN!" Reena bellowed into the witch's ear, effectively capturing her attention. The headless body, poised to strike down another tribal warrior, whirled toward her. It beheld Reena, arm raised, gripping the witch's head by its tangled hair. The head swung like a pendulum, its octopus-like tongue grotesquely sewn to its face.

The villagers' focus shifted from the witch to the young girl clutching the grotesque head, their assaults coming to a halt as curiosity sparked about her identity. Fearless, Reena radiated courage, her demeanour not just brave but almost luminescent, casting her in the light of a saviour. As the headless witch surged toward her, Reena called out to the onlookers, "Help the injured!" before dashing away, the witch's head firmly grasped in her hands. She deftly drew the monstrous foe away from the villagers. The headless body pursued Reena relentlessly, smashing through the giant statue in its path, its spider-like claws tightly gripping the katana. The witch's head, dangling from Reena's grasp, emitted guttural growls of fury. Faithfully following the route Nindhi had outlined, Reena led the monstrous figure on a wild chase.

She discerned an unsettling frailty in the witch, a realization that filled her with dread, for she knew this battle should not be so easily won. As she sprinted, a sudden and intense sensation—both scorching and chilling—seared through her arm. Overwhelmed by the sharp pain, she crumpled to the ground. Struggling to her feet, Reena reached out with her right arm for support, only to be struck by the horrifying realization that it had been severed. Blood flowed profusely, and tendrils of black smoke curled ominously from the wound. Wincing in unbearable agony, she managed to pull herself upright. As her gaze shifted, she saw the witch hurtling towards her with unrelenting fury. Reena's eyes widened as her gaze fell upon the severed hand lying on the ground, now dissolving into tendrils of black smoke. Through the haze of shock, she caught sight of the witch's head tumbling toward its body. With a burst of desperate resolve, she lunged, grasping the head by its knotted hair with her remaining hand, striving to subdue it. Yet, the head convulsed violently in her grip, writhing with a malevolent force that defied her efforts.

As Reena grappled with the thrashing head, a looming shadow cast over her. Time seemed to slow as she witnessed the headless witch's hand, firmly gripping the hilt of a gleaming black blade, sweeping through the air in a deadly arc. The razor-sharp edge, mere inches from her vulnerable neck, cut through the silence with a menacing hiss. A slashing sound resonated through the air, followed by the wet splatter of blood on the earth. The sword clattered to the ground. Reena cautiously opened her eyes, only to witness the witch's head emitting a piercing lisp howl, its mouth gaping in a horrific scream. The witch's hands lay severed, blood gushing profusely from the stumps of her arms.

Reena's gaze shifted to Nindhi, who stood panting, his grip firm on the bloodstained machete. His chest heaved with exertion, each breath a testament to the fierce battle they had just endured.

"Run," He urged, his eyes meeting Reena's.

With the witch's head firmly secured in her grasp, Reena bolted away.

Meanwhile, Nindhi and the headless Daemonara circled one another like gladiators in the arena, each waiting for the perfect moment to strike. With a sudden burst of energy, Nindhi charged towards Amma, aiming to deliver a decisive blow. However, a kick—swift and sharp as a dagger—landed squarely in his gut. The force propelled him like a tempest, hurling him through the air before he crashed into nearby houses, the impact reverberating through the ruins. The witch reattached her severed hands, her rage palpable as she attempted to summon her katana. But it eluded her, seemingly vanished into thin air. After several futile attempts, her malevolent attention shifted towards Reena, who had successfully created a significant distance between them. Fueled by an insatiable desire to reclaim her head, the witch surged forward, propelled by dark determination and relentless fury.

Bhushan arrived at the scene of Nindhi's crash, finding him ensnared within a chaotic heap of shattered rubble. As he approached, a sense of dread enveloped him; three thick, splintered wooden beams jutted cruelly from Nindhi's abdomen, their jagged edges glistening ominously in the moonlight. A look of horror swept across Bhushan's face at the gruesome sight, his heart pounding in response to the grim reality before him.

"Devil's eye, Nindhi!! What happened?" Bhushan asked, his voice laced with concern as he knelt beside his friend.

Nindhi's gaze met his, eyes half-lidded, revealing the agony etched into every line of his face. Blood trickled from his lips, pooling against the debris.

"Let me assist you," Bhushan urged, stepping forward to help, but Nindhi grasped his hand with a tremulous, frail grip. "No," he insisted, his voice barely above a whisper, laced with defiance.

"Have you stashed the sword?"

"Yes, I adhered strictly to your instructions. The katana has been moved beyond her reach; she is unable to summon it," Bhushan affirmed, his voice steady despite the chaos surrounding them.

"Good. Now, go aid Reena. I... I regret my failure to hold the witch at bay for long. You had so little time to hide the sword," Nindhi admitted, his voice thick with remorse.

"Do not be troubled. Fortune favoured us this time, though you had steeled yourself for death. Now, permit me to aid you, so that we may fulfil the final task," Bhushan implored.

"No, help Reena," Nindhi insisted, extending his hand toward Bhushan.

Bhushan held Nindhi's gaze for a moment, then, with deliberate care, took the Phoenix spell bomb from Nindhi's grasp, resolve hardening in his expression.

As Reena reached the stone hut, she pushed against the door, feeling its sticky dampness under her palms. The headless witch followed closely behind, crashing into the hut just as Reena slipped inside. Within the dim confines, the witch's gaze fell upon her severed head lying on the wooden floor. In a swift, horrifying motion, she grasped it, reattaching it to her neck. With a determined yank, she tore away the octopus-like tongue that had been grotesquely stitched to her face. The sudden sound of a glass jar shattering echoed through the space, seizing the witch's attention. In an instant, the hut was engulfed in roaring flames, the flickering light casting eerie shadows that danced along the walls, illuminating the witch's twisted visage with an ominous glow. Peering through the open window, the witch caught sight of a distant figure, their silhouette defined by a wide-brimmed cowboy hat, sprinting towards the village after igniting the house. A wave of realization washed over her—she had unwittingly stumbled into a meticulously crafted trap. The implications unfurled in her mind like a dark tapestry, the threads of her impending doom woven by those she had underestimated. Rage surged within her, fueling her desire for vengeance as she turned her attention back to the chaos unfolding around her.

The witch stood resolute, her unwavering confidence bolstered by the fireproof potion she consumed daily. Yet, the urgency to escape the engulfing flames became her primary focus. She lunged for the crashed door, but the bricks had expanded, sealing her in. The door and windows melded into the walls, leaving no openings, transforming the structure into a solid prison. Darkness enveloped her, thick and suffocating, the crackling of flames echoing like a cruel reminder of her impending doom.

"Trapped, are we?" a voice taunted from the shadows. As the flames licked their way inside, igniting the centre of the room, the source of the voice emerged into view, illuminated by the flickering yellow glow of the fire. Reena stood defiantly against the witch, her silhouette bold and unyielding.

"You're not going anywhere," Reena asserted firmly, her voice unwavering despite the crackling flames that threatened to consume them both. The Daemonara shot her a withering glare, eyes narrowing with contempt, but Reena stood her ground, refusing to back down.

"Do you truly believe you can hinder me, you mere mortal?" The witch's voice reverberated with a metallic shriek.

"Yes," Reena replied, unwavering.

With a sinister creak, the three knots of the witch's hair unfurled, resembling twisted, shadowy branches eager to escape their confinement. With a powerful surge, they shattered the roof of the house, sending debris flying in all directions. As stones, boulders, and splintered wood crashed down around them, Reena remained steadfast, displaying an unwavering resolve in the face of impending doom. Meanwhile, the witch leapt in a desperate bid to escape the inferno engulfing the house, her tendrils coiled around a robust tree branch, arching high above the dwelling, supporting her. However, her efforts were thwarted as something seized her leg, halting her mid-air ascent. Glancing downward, the witch beheld a hand with sinewy fingers wrapped tightly around her leg—the hand belonged to Reena. Covered in flames, Reena struggled to maintain her grip on the witch with her only hand; she knew she couldn't afford to release her. The heat scorched her skin, yet her determination burned brighter than the flames engulfing them. The witch writhed in fury, her face twisted in rage, but Reena's resolve only strengthened. Meanwhile, the flames intensified, casting an ominous orange glow that enveloped the floor and walls of the hut, illuminating the shadows that danced around them. As the fire consumed everything in its path, including the surrounding boulders and stones, the witch's gaze darted around, a mixture of fear and rage evident in her eyes. Desperation clawed at her as she recognized the peril she faced. With a swift, vicious kick, she aimed for Reena's face, her claw-like foot striking with unrelenting force. Reena's head snapped back, pain radiating through her skull, but she refused to relinquish her grip. Torn flesh bled, mixing with the smoke that choked the air around them. Gritting her teeth, she fought against the agony, her determination surging like the flames that enveloped them.

The flames consumed Reena, their blistering heat scorching her skin and igniting her dress. Despite the excruciating pain, she screamed, her gaze fiercely fixed on the witch. While Reena writhed in agony, the witch remained untouched, save for her white gown, which too had caught fire. Reena's eyes caught sight of the witch's tendrils entwined around a sturdy tree branch arching over the house.

"It's useless, I can't be burnt," declared the witch.

Despite her faltering grip, Reena clenched her jaw and reinforced her hold, resolute in her refusal to surrender. She was unwavering in her determination to keep the witch confined, no matter the excruciating pain surging through her body.

Suddenly, a jolt of energy surged through Reena's right arm, a blend of agony and unexpected exhilaration. In a matter of moments, she beheld the miraculous spectacle of her severed limb regenerating with astonishing rapidity. The witch's jaw fell open in disbelief as she watched Reena's arm reform before her very eyes. With a surge of newfound vigour, Reena grasped the witch's foot with her freshly regenerated hand and pulled with all her might. The witch tumbled to the ground, creating a deep indentation in the wooden floor upon impact.

Rising defiantly from the cavity, the witch's eyes blazed with fury. "Do you truly think this feeble fire can extinguish me, you insignificant, bitch? I am an indomitable sorceress who has roamed this earth for a millennium. Countless souls have attempted to vanquish me, and all have failed. And now you, pathetic insect, dare to confront me armed with good-for-nothing flames?"

Reena stood in unwavering silence, her resolve as steadfast as ever. Suddenly, the sound of a pebble clattering to the ground behind the witch shattered the tense quiet. Startled, the witch spun around, her gaze locking onto the oddly shaped stone. A chilling realization crept over her, recognition dawning as she grasped its significance. Her eyes flicked back to Reena, who now wore a knowing, confident smile. "Yes! It's Pey-Nigalanki," Reena proclaimed, her voice slicing through the witch's spiralling thoughts. "The creature that drains the essence of potions. Your fireproof elixir is no longer shielding you. You're vulnerable now, stripped of your immunity to flames." A wave of dread washed over the witch, chilling her to the bone. Panic set in, and all she craved was a swift escape from the inferno that now threatened to consume her.

With the swiftness of a tempest, Reena surged forward, her arms encircling the witch's waist in an unyielding embrace. The witch, lost in frantic thoughts of escape, was taken by surprise. She writhed and twisted, trying to wrest herself from Reena's grasp, but to no avail. The witch hadn't anticipated the formidable strength that Reena now wielded, a force that even she couldn't overpower. The witch's sharp fingers dug into Reena's neck in a desperate bid to sever her head, but each strike grew weaker, her hands trembling with an unfamiliar fragility. To Reena's surprise, she felt no pain from the witch's frantic assault. Instead, she raised her eyes, locking onto the witch's gaze. For the first time, fear flickered in the witch's eyes as the flames encroached upon her, their searing heat now penetrating her once invincible senses. Reena's smile widened as she declared, "This day will be remembered for all eternity when an ageless, invincible Daemonara met her end at the hands of mere children." The witch, now completely engulfed in flames, heard every word. In mere moments, she felt the searing heat scorch her once-untouchable body. Together, Reena and the witch succumbed to the inferno. "BURN, WITCH!" Reena's final words echoed, sealing their fate within the consuming flames.

Bhushan stood outside at a distance with Nindhi, who was still recovering, his arm draped around Bhushan's shoulder. They waited anxiously for Reena to join them as planned, but she never emerged. As the grim reality settled in, Nindhi's legs gave way beneath him, and he sank to his knees, tears welling in his eyes, his heart heavy with the weight of her sacrifice. Though his soul refused to accept it, he understood deep down that Reena was gone, her final words lingering in the air like a haunting echo. Desperately, he clung to the hope that she might somehow emerge unscathed. Turning his gaze, he saw Bhushan weeping, his eyes locked on the smouldering ruins of the hut, now reduced to ash and rubble. They stood together in silence, wordlessly acknowledging the inevitable as they watched the orange blaze consume the last remnants of the hut, which crumbled into ashes and were carried away by the wind. "Reena is dead," the thought reverberated in their minds, a solemn acceptance settling over them like a heavy shroud.

Abruptly, a crackling noise shattered the silence, drawing their focus towards its source. Emerging from the smouldering remains of the charred hut was a grotesque figure, its body fully burned and exuding an ominous presence. The figure's appearance was as repulsive as the witch's own ghastly visage. Slowly, the scorched form advanced towards Nindhi and Bhushan. With each step, the figure began to regain a semblance of life, mending itself as it advanced. To their shock, the ominous shape transformed into Reena. Her newfound healing ability left Nindhi awestruck, yet at that moment, her survival overshadowed everything else. They rushed towards her, enveloping her in a tight embrace, relief flooding their hearts as they held her close, grateful for her return from the brink of despair. Though she emerged from the ruins bare, her survival eclipsed any sense of awkwardness. Nindhi quickly offered his kurta, wrapping it around her as they shared a heartfelt embrace, tears of joy streaming down their faces. With the witch vanquished, they stood together, ready to embrace the dawn of a new chapter in their lives, filled with hope and resilience.

CHAPTER-35

Home Sweet Home

Two years had passed. The soothing rhythm of the waves played a lullaby in the environment, while a soft breeze danced with the scent of salt and sand. Sitting on the sun-warmed shore, Nindhi and Reena relished the juicy sweetness of watermelon. In these two years, it had become their cherished ritual to meet by the sea and lose themselves in conversation.

"There's something different about them," Reena mused, taking another bite. "Almost as if they've absorbed the sea breeze."

"I believe they're the same as always," Nindhi replied, taking a bite of his slice.

"Curious, it's as if a few scoops of sweetness have been siphoned away, replaced by a delicate touch of salt," Reena remarked, letting the seeds slip onto the blush-tinted sand.

Nindhi chuckled and took a bite of his slice. "Or perhaps... your jibes are so sweet they leave these watermelons paling in comparison," he teased, a playful glint in his eyes as he mocked Reena.

"I spoke in earnest," Reena replied.

"I understand. If it's a cake you desire, I can whip one up for you as well," said Nindhi.

"You know I can't indulge; ever since that nightmare, cakes have lost their allure for me."

There was a serene lull in the conversation as they relished the watermelons. With each succulent bite, Reena was transported back to memories of envisioning this very moment—sitting on the sun-kissed beach, delighting in the sweet juiciness of the watermelons. It appeared as though her dream had come to fruition. Enveloped in her reverie, she was suddenly roused by a voice nearby. Turning her head, Reena beheld a tribal woman approaching, bearing coconuts as a thoughtful gift.

"I shall take this," Nindhi declared, rising to his feet and striding towards the woman bearing coconuts. He accepted the cluster from her, exchanging a warm smile before engaging in conversation. The woman radiated vitality and gratitude, her words flowing effortlessly in her native tongue. Suddenly, she exclaimed, "Munda!" locking eyes with Reena before departing with a beaming smile.

Reena redirected her gaze to the picturesque scene before her: seagulls gliding gracefully overhead, tribal fishermen deftly casting their nets in the shimmering waters. The rhythmic sound of a knife striking against coconut husk resonated through the air. Soon, a hand reached out to her, presenting a coconut adorned with a bamboo straw, an inviting gesture that promised refreshment. With heartfelt gratitude, Reena accepted the coconut, cradling it gently in both hands before taking a sip. The invigorating flavour cascaded across her palate, prompting her to close her eyes and savour the moment, a blissful smile gracing her lips as she revelled in the sheer delight of the experience.

Nindhi gazed at Reena, captivated by the delicate blush that graced her cheeks. A serene aura enveloped her, drawing him in with its quiet charm. His feelings for her had blossomed into a profound love, yet he wrestled with the courage to voice them. A letter he had penned lay dormant in his pocket, the words yearning to escape but remaining unspoken.

"I remember," Reena reflected, "when you share how envisioning what you desire can manifest it into reality. I truly understand it now; I believe it wholeheartedly." Nindhi listened in silence, offering a gentle smile as he savoured the refreshing coconut drink. While he appeared calm on the surface, a tempest brewed within him, determined that today would be the day he would finally hand Reena the letter he had kept hidden away.

As the silence stretched on, Nindhi hesitated before intending to beckon her.

"Do you think 'Munda' would serve as an apt title for the novel?" Reena inquired, her face aglow with eagerness.

"No, not particularly. How far along are you with your novel?" Nindhi's question lingered in the air, momentarily overshadowing his unvoiced thoughts.

"More than half is complete, though I'm not entirely satisfied. I may need to revisit some sections for editing. Additionally, I intend to venture into the city next week to procure more books, along with sheets and inks for my illustrations," Reena elaborated.

"Illustrations for the novel?" Nindhi asked.

"Yes"

"Please reconsider. Incorporating illustrations may hinder the reader's imagination and compromise the essence of your novel," he implored, his concern palpable in his earnest tone.

"I beg to differ. I've already created some illustrations, and they were well-received by Bhushan," she retorted, her conviction unwavering.

"That's beside the point. Personally, I prefer to read without illustrations; they tend to clash with my imagination," Nindhi articulated, his tone reflective.

"I'm still determined to include them. I have a fondness for illustrations, and many classic novels feature them," Reena asserted.

"Fair enough," Nindhi conceded, breaking the silence after Reena's stubborn remarks. "If you wish to travel swiftly, my broom will grant you the advantage of an early return."

Finishing the last of her coconut, Reena rose and tossed it into the water. Turning to Nindhi, she expressed, "I prefer travelling by boat. I relish the journey, and I don't plan to return for a week." A smile danced on her lips as she added, "Would you care to join me on this adventure?"

Nindhi was taken aback, his eyes widening and his jaw nearly dropping. Excitement surged within him as he sprang to his feet and enthusiastically agreed. His hand instinctively delved into his pocket, and he stepped closer to Reena, their breaths nearly mingling in the warm sea air. Just as he was about to retrieve the letter from his pocket to present it to her, a sudden crash shattered the moment. The sound of shattering glass reverberated through the air, swiftly followed by urgent shouts emanating from the house.

"Devil's eye, they're at it again!" Reena exclaimed, urgency lacing her voice as she sprinted toward the house, leaving Nindhi standing there, the letter clutched in his hand, the words still unspoken and the moment lost to chaos.

Reena dashed toward the two unpainted wooden houses, one belonging to Nindhi and the other to herself and her siblings. The siblings' house stood out, adorned with a large pink board proclaiming "Home Sweet Home." Although the houses weren't quite as Reena had envisioned, they were steadily evolving into the dream she had nurtured in her mind. As she approached the house, Bhushan's voice escalated, accompanied by faint cries that resembled Lily's. Upon stepping inside, Reena discovered Bhushan scolding Lily, his expression a mixture of frustration and concern. The atmosphere was charged, and Reena felt an immediate urge to intervene and understand what had transpired.

"Oh, it's you. Look, she's marred my painting once more," Bhushan lamented, lifting his landscapes for Reena to behold.

As Reena scrutinized the painting, Nindhi arrived, his gaze drawn to the whimsical stickman rendered in vibrant red strokes.

"Lily, what possessed you to deface his paintings?" Reena inquired.

"All I yearn for is to create art like him," Lily lamented through her tears.

"Your skills don't match the effort, so cease your attempts at drawing," Bhushan reprimanded.

"Take it easy on her, Bhushan," Reena interjected.

"Oh, I doubt you'll be lenient with her once you see this," Bhushan remarked, turning away as he began to sift through Reena's books and sheets.

"Hey, that stuff is mine, don't..." Reena started, but her words faltered as she caught sight of Bhushan clutching an inky illustration of a house. It was one of her sketches intended for the illustrations in her novel.

"Will you go easy on her now?" asked Bhushan.

Reena felt a swell of disappointment and anger at the sight of the witty, distorted strokes of red paint marring her illustrations, yet she chose to remain silent. Instead, she approached Lily, gently taking her hand. "It's alright," she reassured Bhushan. "She will improve, and we must exercise patience with her. After all, she is still just a child." With that, Reena led Lily outside, where tears streamed down the little girl's cheeks, before shutting the door softly behind them.

"Take it easy on her!?" Bhushan yelled, his frustration palpable in his voice. He turned to Nindhi, exasperated. "Like she's ever gone easy on me for anything!" With a huff, he snatched his colours, brushes, and canvas, storming out of the house while venting his grievances about what he felt was Reena's unfair treatment towards him.

Nindhi found himself alone in the room, grappling once more with the disappointment of not having delivered his love letter to Reena. He sank into a wooden chair, his gaze drifting over the paintings that adorned the walls. Some were meticulously framed, while others lay unbound, each imbued with an enchantment. He approached the nearest wall and scrutinized one of Bhushan's paintings, easily identifiable by his distinctive signature. Although he had hoped to see a portrait of Reena alongside it, none adorned the wall. While Bhushan's skills were visibly improving with each stroke, Reena—relatively new to illustration—displayed an innate talent, her artwork blossoming with remarkable swiftness. Nindhi marvelled at how effortlessly she captured the emotion, each brushstroke revealing a deeper essence that resonated with him profoundly.

He recalled the stack from which Bhushan had retrieved Reena's painting and approached it, sifting through the pile of sheets. Among them, he discovered drawings depicting sun-kissed beaches, lush forests, and vibrant tribal scenes. Some remained incomplete, hints of potential shimmering beneath the surface, while others radiated remarkable beauty, capturing the soul of life and culture. Most of the drawings depicted scenes from their surroundings, capturing the essence of their shared experiences. Each illustration illustrated moments of joy and camaraderie spent together, immortalizing their laughter and adventures. While the drawings weren't flawless, the distinct attire of each sibling and Nindhi lent them an unmistakable identity, making the characters leap to life on the page. Nindhi couldn't help but smile as he traced the outlines of almost familiar faces, feeling the warmth of cherished memories radiate from the artwork.

Suddenly, inspiration struck Nindhi like a bolt from the blue—an idea to slip the letter between the stack of Reena's paintings. With a surge of urgency, he withdrew the letter from his pocket, his heart racing as he tucked it beneath the pile and settled nearby. Yet, a nagging unease lingered within him, his brow damp with perspiration, and his fingers tapping anxiously against his knees. Despite his initial action, his hand instinctively dove back into the stack, retrieving the letter once more. Hastily, he unfolded it, his heart racing as he began to peruse its heartfelt contents.

My Dearest Reena,

From the very instant our paths intertwined, even in my most vulnerable state, an enigmatic serenity cocooned me, as if your gaze alone had the power to soothe my soul. Our first shared glance, the lyrical timbre of your voice as it echoed within me, even the fire in your fiercest looks, eclipsed the allure of any mythical paradise. There was an ineffable essence to you, something otherworldly that captivated my heart beyond reason.

As time wove its intricate tapestry, I gradually came to understand its essence. In traditional love stories, love blossoms without any reason and rhyme, and I was often rebuked for my skepticism towards such phenomena. Yet, I've come to see how wrong I was. Love defies almost every logic. It is a force that is profoundly felt long before it can ever be truly grasped. Perhaps that's why it's called "love" — because it transcends understanding and can only be truly felt. I'm unsure if mere words can capture the depth of my emotions for you, but I've witnessed flowers bloom in the wake of your laughter, seen the air itself pirouette around your golden skin as you bask on the shore, and beheld birds and fishes serenading your beauty, while the sun bathes you in a light that makes you radiate like an angel from a fairy tale.

In truth, my words fail to capture the essence of your soul, and I fear nothing ever will. I confess, I may never fully comprehend you, and perhaps time shared will reveal more of your mysteries. Yet, there is a quiet voice within me that reassures—understanding you completely is not necessary. The mystery of living alongside you is the adventure I yearn for, for all the days of my life.

I cannot foresee whether your response will be affirmative or otherwise, but should rejection be my fate today, I vow to return tomorrow, and the day after, steadfast in my pursuit until I hear a "yes" from your gentle lips or until your heart finds solace elsewhere. Just as with friendship, love too is a two-way street. As your devoted admirer, my deepest wish is to see you bask in happiness, whether it be by my side or in the embrace of another.

Nindhi

After Nindhi finished reading the letter, a profound sense of satisfaction washed over his features. However, as he neared the conclusion, a subtle unease lingered, particularly concerning the way his name was inscribed at the end. In his pursuit of infusing the letter with an element of distinction or allure, Nindhi found himself lost in contemplation for a while. However, as inspiration eluded him, he chose to replace "Nindhi" with "Loving Nindhi," using the quill he had found beside the sheets and books. With the revised letter carefully tucked back among the pages, Nindhi believed his task was complete. Yet, something at the edge of his vision captured his attention, drawing him back to memories of the castle.

The vivid portrayal of the pink door captivated his gaze, igniting his curiosity and urging him to delve deeper. As he progressed to the next illustration, he encountered an intricate rendering of a ficus tree, followed by a depiction of a tent, and then a figure devoid of arms—

whom he instantly recognized as himself. He was engulfed by curiosity, particularly because Reena had never revealed any specifics about the nature of her novel. Whenever he inquired, she always insisted it would be a surprise for him. As he turned over two more drawings—a tent and a workshop—the subsequent scene took his breath away. The illustration portrayed a monstrous entity with a singular eye, clad in a suit, as it appeared to instruct a girl who bore an uncanny resemblance to Reena, distinguishable by her attire.

He grabbed the illustration, examining it with a blend of fascination, curiosity, and a touch of trepidation. As he scrutinized the painting of the one-eyed master, his attention was drawn to a sheet lying on the floor, mirroring those from Bhushan and Reena. Lifting the painting from the ground, he found it illustrated a colossal monster locked in a fierce battle with a child donning a cowboy hat. The vivid colours leapt from the canvas, and the initials in the corner confirmed it was a work by Bhushan. Reclining in the wooden chair, Nindhi carefully examined Bhushan's artwork, recognizing it as a vivid representation of his brother's recurring nightmare. In this dream, Bhushan often described a relentless struggle against a monstrous force, a creature that loomed over him, threatening to engulf both him and those he cherished.

Nindhi couldn't suppress a chuckle at the sight of Bhushan's vividly depicted battles on canvas. Each stroke of the brush captured the absurdity of the tales Bhushan spun, tales that always brought him amusement whenever Bhushan regaled him with tales. Yet, as his gaze returned to Reena's intricate inked illustration, a peculiar detail seized his attention, igniting a creeping sense of unease within him. A rush of panic coursed through Nindhi as he swiftly slipped out of the house, clutching both paintings tightly in his hand, folded for secrecy, as he hurried toward his own dwelling.

"Hey, Nindhi!" The voice sliced through the air, halting Nindhi's steps mid-stride. Horror etched itself across his features as his eyes widened in disbelief. He had not anticipated crossing paths with this individual in such a precarious situation. With a conscious effort, he steadied his expression and turned to confront the source of the voice.

He spotted Reena calling out to him from a distance, perched on the beach alongside Lily, both deeply engrossed in crafting an elaborate sandcastle. Swiftly, he tucked the folded paintings behind his back and returned their wave. Reena paused momentarily, a warm smile spreading across her face as she beckoned him to join their playful endeavour. Glancing from Reena to Lily, he noted the radiant joy illuminating Lily's face as she frolicked with Reena by the shore. A playful smirk crossed Nindhi's lips as he addressed Reena, saying, "Another time, Reena. I've got something pressing to handle." With that, he pivoted and strode swiftly towards home, disregarding any response from her. Once inside, he promptly secured the door behind him, a sense of urgency coursing through him.

Hurrying to his bedroom, he fastened each painting to the sides of a small, square curtain that hung on the wall, reminiscent of a modest window. The artwork on the left portrayed the one-eyed master from Reena's vision, a figure exuding an enigmatic allure, while the piece on the right illustrated the formidable one-eyed monster from Bhushan's recurring nightmare, its presence looming ominously. He raised his trembling, sweaty hand, casting anxious glances between the painting of the one-eyed master and the one-eyed monster. As the realization struck him that both artworks depicted the same visage, his fear intensified. With a tight grip, he yanked the curtain away in a swift motion, revealing a small mirror mounted on the wall, barely reaching Nindhi's chest. Yet, the mirror itself wasn't what was terrifying. Nindhi's reflection was not his familiar visage; instead, it bore a single eye and a grotesque countenance, mirroring the figure from both

Reena's and Bhushan's paintings. It was the face of the one-eyed entity, unmistakably identical in all three portrayals. At first, shock overcame him, and tears welled in his eyes as he stared at the horrifying reflection. Yet, in an unsettling twist, a smile crept across his lips—a smile that sent chills down his spine, a smile that deeply unnerved him.

Acknowledgments

If you find yourself at this page, it signifies your completion of my novel. I extend my heartfelt gratitude for embarking on this literary journey with me; your engagement is truly cherished. I wish for you to have found fulfilment in the narrative that unfolded here. Should the conclusion leave you in contemplation, remember: *The essence resides in the voyage itself rather than the destination. Ultimately, we are all left with the echoes of our experiences—those precious **Letters** etched in the fabric of our memories.*

Before this novel, my literary endeavours were confined to a webcomic titled *Zaminpur*, which is still unfolding. This whimsical adventure follows a group of children as they navigate the quirky incidents that unfold in their city. Now, I present to you my second narrative: *Amma Meiga*. The journey of writing this book was full of ups and downs, as this is my first venture into authorship. In every chapter of life, friends play a pivotal role. I once read somewhere, **"Always be grateful for the people who read your story,"** and I am profoundly thankful for the many individuals who read my manuscript before it reached publication and offered their invaluable assistance. Here are the names of some remarkable people who helped me achieve this dream.

Soorej, Vipul, Samia, Chhaya, Janvi, Paridhi, Ranya, Mohini, Anureet, Shubham, Noelia, Navjot Singh Arora, Zoe, Aastha, Aditya

You can connect with me on Instagram at @addalhotra or via email at addalhotra2000@gmail.com.

Step into "Zaminpur Tales," where a family embraces the quirks of their new home. Amidst weird and goofy daily life, the city brims with unexpected oddities and villains. But unity, technology, and clever minds prove their extraordinary tools in this whimsical adventure.

Accessible on Webtoon and Blocktoons

www.ingramcontent.com/pod-product-compliance
Lightning Source LLC
LaVergne TN
LVHW041905070526
838199LV00051BA/2510